SCENE QUEEN

THE COURT BOOK TWO

SPECIAL EDITION

CHARLIE NOVAK

May there always be sunshine men with terrible taste in music!

Love,
Charlie

Copyright © Charlie Novak 2024

Cover by Natasha Snow

Cover photography by Wander Aguiar

Editing by Jennifer Smith

Formatting by Pumpkin Author Services

All rights reserved. Charlie Novak asserts the moral right to be identified as the author of this work.

This novel is entirely a work of fiction. Names, characters, places, and incidents are the products of the author's imagination or are used fictitiously. Any resemblance to actual events, locales, organizations or persons, living or dead, is entirely coincidental.

A NOTE FROM THE AUTHOR

Many drag performers use different pronouns in and out of drag, depending on their style of drag and their personal gender identity, and the performers in this book do the same.

To help you get to know them, here's a list of *Scene Queen*'s drag stars and their pronouns in and out of drag.

Eva Nessence, drag queen: she/her in drag, he/him out of it.
Bubblegum Galaxy, drag queen: she/her in drag, he/him out of it.
Bitch Fit, drag queen: she/her in drag, he/him out of it.
Scary Kate, drag queen: she/her in drag, he/him out of it.
Slashley, drag queen: she/her in drag, he/him out of it.
Legs Luthor, drag queen: she/her in drag, he/they out of it.
Moxxie Toxxic, drag king: they/them in and out of drag.
Violet Bucket, drag queen: she/her in drag, he/him out of it.
Peachy Keen, drag queen: she/her in drag, he/him out of it.

Incubussy, drag king: he/him in drag, she/her out of it.

Like many artists, musicians, writers, and performers, you'll also find many of the drag artists in this novel are referred to by their drag name, or a variation, while out of drag as well as in it.

For my D&DVania Crew: Rosie, Stuart, Blair, James, Beth, Mia, and Jess.

Here's to fighting more monsters and seducing more villains.

I fucking love all of you.

CHAPTER ONE

Eva Nessence

IF THEY EVER PUT ME on trial for murder, the temptation to burst into a rendition of 'The Cell Block Tango' from *Chicago* would be impossible to resist.

Because that bastard who lived next door had had it coming from the moment he moved in six months ago.

And never more so than today.

It'd been nearly eight in the morning before I'd finally managed to throw myself into bed after my twelve-hour night shift, and while eight years in the ambulance service meant I was vaguely used to them, it didn't mean I liked them. Especially when they were like last night—stressful and emotionally draining. I might have gotten into this job to help people and I knew a lot of the situations we got called out to were emotional, but that didn't mean I appreciated people giving me shit because we hadn't appeared in the blink of an eye or because they didn't think I was doing my job properly.

The only thing that had gotten me through the last three hours, especially when shit had kicked off with some drunk students trying to climb over a wall and collecting, between them, a broken arm, a broken ankle, two concussions, a dislocated shoulder, and a metal spike embedded in their calf, had been the thought that I would have ten glorious days off before my shifts kicked in again.

Because trying to explain to an absolutely wasted nineteen-year-old that he needed to not pull the rusty bit of metal out of his leg had been like trying to explain nuclear physics to a corgi. Except the corgi would probably have been less fucking belligerent about it.

How half these students managed to make it through their degrees and become functional adults was a secret known only to the powers that be. And even then I thought any powers that were spent half their time laughing their fucking heads off.

I'd finally crawled home, dumped my uniform in the washing basket, and collapsed into bed with the plan of sleeping until at least mid-afternoon. But the Welsh bastard I had the misfortune of living next to had other ideas.

I wasn't sure what woke me first—the guitars, the drums, or the thumping techno bass, but none of them were appreciated. My body tried to fight the disturbance for as long as possible, desperately hoping it could convince my brain to ignore it and go back to sleep. I'd never been a light sleeper—I'd once slept through an entire thrash metal set at Download Festival—but not even the dead could've slept through the horrific techno-metal mashup currently pouring through my bedroom walls.

I groaned and pulled a pillow over my head in a basic effort to muffle the noise but the result was little more than fuck all. My hand shot out, reaching around for my phone, clinging to the hope that if I kept my eyes shut, then I could fall asleep again at any second. Even though I already knew it was too late.

I was awake and nothing was going to change that.

Fuck the bastard next door. And fuck whichever bastard decided to fuse thrash metal and techno together in some unholy mix of the loudest parts of both genres.

The clock on my phone said it was barely past ten in the morning, meaning I'd had two hours' sleep if I was lucky. And I was not spending my first day off like a zombie—I'd done enough of that in my early twenties working relief shifts with back-to-back nights for days on end and emergency call-ins on my supposed days off.

Those years were probably why nothing with caffeine did anything for me.

With a series of muttered grumbles that probably made me sound like an irritated cat, I rolled myself into a sitting position and stared with half-open eyes at my bedroom wall. I could hammer on it and shout at the bastard through the old brickwork in the hope he heard me, but there was a good chance he'd just ignore me or pretend he couldn't hear anything. With how loud the music was, he might not even have to pretend. I doubted even hitting the wall with a mallet would get his attention.

God, why the fuck couldn't he wear headphones like everyone else?

"Fuck you, you fucking bastard," I said to myself in a low, rough voice as I heaved myself to my feet and began searching for some clothes. Given the state of my underwear drawer, I really needed to do some washing. Commando it was.

I grabbed a pair of grey joggers that were semi-decent and an old Download hoodie that had once been black but was now more of a faded dark grey. The lettering on the back listing the line-up had started to peel and flake as well, and I knew I should probably stop wearing it if I wanted to keep it, but it was so comfy and perfectly worn in. And I'd rather wring the life out of it and enjoy wearing it than have it sit in a drawer, rotting away, where I'd forget it was even there. After all, what was the point of having it if I wasn't going to get any use out of it?

I didn't bother with a T-shirt or socks, just trudged downstairs barefoot and shoved my feet into a well-worn pair of Vans I pulled out of the small, overcrowded understairs cupboard. I kept meaning to clear it out, but it was another thing I'd put on my "list of things to do one day when I have some free time" that I'd never got around to. I doubted I ever would.

With my life, free time wasn't a thing that existed. Unless I counted the ten minutes I got on the toilet in the mornings or the occasional half an hour I could scrape together for a bath. But even then I was usually looking at social media to get ideas for routines, outfits, and content.

Mixing a drag career with one as a paramedic was a

chaotic concoction that usually led to far too many late nights, sore feet, an aching body, and a casual dislike of much of the general public.

But I wouldn't give up drag for anything.

Not even a good night's sleep.

The music was louder downstairs, which suggested the bastard was playing it in either his kitchen or living room. Grabbing my keys out of the drawer I'd thrown them in, I unlocked my front door and yanked it open, the heavy old wood refusing to budge at first. Cursing it, I slammed it behind me and blinked in the bright April sunlight.

Our street was quiet, apart from the bastard's music, with hardly any cars parked on the pavement in front of the two lines of small terraced houses. Technically, I could have stood in my doorway and banged on his door since ours were so close, but that would have made it easier for him to ignore me and pretend I wasn't there. By leaving my house and standing directly in front of his door, there would be no escape for him.

Unless he slammed the door in my face, of course, in which case my only options to get either revenge or his attention would be bordering on illegal. And as much as I'd love to egg his windows or his car, I also really wanted to keep my jobs. Plural.

Although Phil, who ran one of the drag clubs I was a regular at, would probably think it was hilarious. And I knew at least four of the kings and queens there would back me up, but since they were all what could only be described as chaos goblins, I didn't think I should be looking for their approval on this. Several of them already knew about the bastard anyway and their suggestions about what I should do to him, or with him, were pure filth.

They were the only reason I knew he was Welsh and most likely named Rhys, because during a night at mine in January, Eli, also known as the miscreant Bitch Fit, whose hearing shouldn't be as good as it was after years of standing in front of speakers, had heard him through the dining room wall talking excitedly with someone.

I'd done my best to ignore it, but that had only further encouraged Eli and Rory, the bouncing Bubblegum Galaxy who was acting as Eli's gleeful sidekick.

The pair of them were incorrigible and it was times like that I strongly debated why they were my best friends.

Thinking about them and their would-be delighted reactions to this situation wasn't helping. I took a deep breath in the hope of instilling some calm into the searing, exhausted rage bubbling in my chest and then knocked sharply on the door. There was a button for a doorbell too, which looked fairly new, so I pressed that as well for good measure.

Time seemed to slow to a crawl, but eventually I heard the music stop and the sound of footsteps walking towards me. I steeled myself, preparing to use my best calm but firm voice—the one I'd developed to deal with people displaying any signs of anger or aggression—but when the door swung open, all my thoughts seemed to vanish in a puff of smoke.

Because in the six months the bastard had lived next door, I'd never actually gotten a proper, close-up look at him.

Fuck. Me. Sideways.

He had tousled dark hair and full, pierced lips wearing a casual smile, with warm green-brown eyes that roamed over me in an interested way. There was a bar through his eyebrow and more piercings in his ears, and his pale skin was covered in a myriad of tattoos which threatened to hypnotise me. He was wearing a vest top that highlighted his muscular arms and toned torso, the fabric clinging to his skin and making it very clear his nipples were pierced, and a pair of loose black joggers sitting low on his hips. There was a sliver of skin visible between the waistband of his joggers and the bottom of his vest top like it had either ridden up or been artfully arranged that way. All I knew was that I could see the hint of a tattooed wing, which sent my imagination into overdrive as it tried to work out what was there.

Looking that casually sexy should be fucking illegal.

"Hey," he said in a deep, lilting voice that sent a shiver over my skin. No. Bad body. Just because it had been a while since I'd gotten any sort of action, that didn't mean I needed to dissolve into a pile of goo in front of the first man who smiled at me. Especially not when I was mad at him. "Can I help you?"

"Hey," I said as I tried not to smile at him. I refused to use his name too. That might encourage further conversation about how I knew who he was since we hadn't exchanged words until this point. "I'm Evan. I live next door and two hours ago I came off a twelve-hour shift."

"Ooft, sorry to hear that. That sounds killer."

"Yes, well, it wouldn't be quite as bad if I could get some sleep." I glared at him pointedly, hoping he'd get the gist. When he just stared back, I sighed. "Your music. It's too bloody loud. Turn it down." And then, knowing I needed to be vaguely polite, I said through gritted teeth, "Please."

"Not a fan of Mashed Up Monsters? Anything you'd like me to play instead?" He grinned impishly like the whole thing was vaguely amusing.

"Nothing."

"Aww, come on now, it's not that bad."

"It is at the volumes you play it," I said. "Can't you at least wear headphones?"

"I suppose." There was a gleam in his eyes that screamed trouble and it made my cock twitch in my joggers. And fuck, now was not the time for that. "If you're having trouble sleeping, I'd be happy to help tire you out."

I stared at him. Was this bastard actually flirting with me? Did he think that one smirk and a casual suggestion was all he needed to get me naked?

If it was anyone but him, I'd have said yes in a heartbeat. I'd probably have said yes to him too if the situation had been different—if he hadn't disturbed my sleep and annoyed the fuck out of me for the last six months. But my attraction was weighed down by anger and exhaustion, and I wasn't going to let him think one pretty smile was all he needed to get away with being an utter bastard.

"I don't need help," I said, my words coming out in a low growl. "I'm already exhausted as fuck. I just can't sleep because you've never heard of a volume control, so turn your bloody music down."

He was still grinning as he shrugged. "All right, I suppose I can do that. And you did ask nicely."

"Thank you."

"You're welcome," he said sweetly, like he was doing me a fucking favour.

I turned away and reached for my keys to let myself back into my house when he added, "By the way, my name's Rhys. And the offer still stands… if you ever want tiring out, you know where to find me."

Then he shut the door, leaving me open-mouthed and speechless on the pavement.

CHAPTER TWO

Rhys

I probably shouldn't have found it so fun to tease Evan, but it wasn't every day a gorgeous man I hadn't fucked turned up at my door looking so delicious I wanted to swallow him whole.

I did feel slightly guilty for waking him up because I genuinely hadn't realised how loud the music was. I'd just desperately needed something to cover up the sound of the silence, and playing music was the only thing that worked. Even after eighteen months of living on my own, I still wasn't used to it, although with having spent twenty-nine years living with my twin brother before that, maybe it was to be expected. After all, Ianto and I had spent our entire lives almost attached at the hip until he'd found his true love just over two years ago and everything had changed.

I didn't begrudge my little brother his happiness because he and Ben were perfect together, and it wasn't like

I never saw him since I still spent several evenings a week at his house and we worked and trained together, but I couldn't deny things had changed when Ianto had moved in with Ben. I'd never tell him I was struggling, because I didn't want him to worry, but the fact was I'd been desperately lonely since the day he'd left and nothing I did made me feel better.

The only thing that helped was listening to music. It drowned out my brain and for a bit I could forget there was only me in the house.

Maybe I needed to look at getting a pet or something. It was a little pathetic that I, a thirty-year-old man, couldn't spend time by myself without wanting to climb the walls. At least a pet would give me someone to talk to—though probably not a dog since I worked so much and spent all my spare time doing sport, and it wouldn't be fair to leave it alone so much. Maybe a cat, although I didn't know much about them. I'd never had any pets, although our aunty Linda and uncle Gavin had had a cat when we were growing up, and Connor, my pole dance instructor, and his husband, Patrick, had an enormous ginger cat named President Whiskers. If I remembered, I'd ask Connor tomorrow night and see if he had any advice.

I stood in my small living room listening for a moment and smiling to myself as I heard the muffled sounds of Evan stomping upstairs. These little terraced houses weren't big, although I knew a couple on our side of the road had extensions or small conservatories on the back to add some additional space, and from the work I'd seen going on one house, a couple of doors down was getting a loft conversion. An amused feeling flickered into life in my chest as I wondered if Evan's bedroom shared a wall with mine. Since our front doors were so close, I assumed our houses were mirrors of each other, but it would depend on whether he preferred the front or back room upstairs.

I was going to assume the front since it didn't get the morning sunshine and would be better if he was coming off night shifts.

Not that I was going to do anything with that information. I wasn't that much of an asshole.

Slowly, I wandered through into the little kitchen-dining room at the back of my house and rooted around in my backpack for my earbuds. I glanced at the time on my phone as I connected the earbuds and opened my Spotify—it wasn't quite half ten, which meant I had an hour and a half before I started work and I needed to finish making my lunch and have a shower since I'd been too lazy to have one straight after my run this morning.

I'd already started on lunch prep, so I finished that off before heading upstairs to take a nice, leisurely shower. The earbuds were vaguely waterproof as long as I didn't stick my head under the water, and they'd given me a rather lovely idea. I stripped off my clothes and left them on the floor in my bedroom before wandering through to my tiny bathroom, leaning over the bath to turn the shower on. While it heated, I scrolled through my phone to find what I wanted.

I subscribed to a couple different MyFans because I was a man of varied taste when it came to porn, and while there was plenty of free porn all across the internet, sometimes having what you wanted on tap was so much better than spending ages trying to find it. Especially because the MyFans videos didn't cut off at the good bits.

The number of times I'd been so close, desperately trying to wait for the performers to come, and then the video had cut off and told me to go pay for it had been fucking infuriating. So I'd decided to skip the frustration and get what I wanted, when I wanted it. Because I was all for being edged by the right man, but not by Pornhub.

I spent a few minutes narrowing it down to three of my favourites, humming to myself as I debated between them. One was audio porn that would give me delicious descriptions and instructions along with the most gorgeous moans and wet, slapping sounds, and the other two were favourite videos. The first had the stunning silver fox, Wolf, a ridiculously flexible, dark-haired twink, a shower, a sofa, and *the* most perfect cum shot of all time. The other was a gang bang with Wolf, four other tops, and an adorable blond in the middle, and could only be described as both utterly filthy and adorably sweet, which were two concepts you wouldn't usually put together. Especially not with a gang bang.

I'd watched both videos dozens of times and imagined myself as the adorable blond at least half of those. I'd had a couple of threesomes before, but I'd never gotten to be in the middle getting utterly pounded and taken apart. Apparently tattoos, piercings, and muscles automatically screamed top, and while I liked topping it wasn't what I wanted every time. Sometimes there was nothing I loved more than being filled with cock.

The fact I didn't have hours settled the debate—I needed something fast and dirty so I had time to get washed, dressed, and make sure I left the house in time to get to the gym. Gang bang it was.

I started the video and tapped the screen to move it a couple of minutes in, past all the sweet but unimportant start to when dicks were properly involved. A shiver ran across my skin as filthy sounds flooded my ears, my cock already achingly hard and desperate for attention. I gave it a casual stroke before making sure my earbuds were in properly, adjusting the volume on my phone so I could hear everything over the flow of the water.

My cock throbbed as a long, needy moan echoed through the earbuds followed by low words that said, "Open wide, sweetheart." I huffed out a little moan, my mouth falling slightly open as I imagined someone saying them to me.

The water was hot against my skin as I climbed into the bath, the pressure just hard enough to work into all the tension along the top of my shoulders as I stepped under the spray. My fingers were wet as I grasped my shaft again, stroking it slowly as sloppy, muffled moans and deep grunts of satisfaction flooded my senses.

"Fuck, you're so tight," one of the tops said as another added, "Fuck yeah, open his tight hole up for us."

I closed my eyes, imagining being on my knees and utterly surrounded, their hands roaming over my skin and sliding inside my mouth and my ass. Sometimes, when I was alone, I'd ride one dildo and suck another just to get some sense of what it would be like to be utterly and totally filled.

I always came quickly that way.

One day I wanted to get one of those fucking machines. I'd been looking at them for years but had never plucked up the courage to buy one in case Ianto found it, and although we didn't really have boundaries, there were some things I didn't want him to know.

Maybe now I lived alone I'd finally get one.

I jerked my cock harder, revelling in the stream of filth pouring from my earbuds. My heart pounded and my body burned because, fuck, I'd needed this. In my fantasy, I looked up at the men in front of me, but instead of seeing the sexy tops from the video, I imagined only one man.

Evan.

My body jolted and a gasp slipped from my lips, echoing off the tiles so loudly I could hear it over the porn. Fucking hell, I'd only seen the man close up once and he was already making an appearance. I wasn't sure if that said more about him or me. He was gorgeous, though, with that rumpled look and those piercing blue eyes that were trying so hard to be annoyed at me, even while he was checking me out. Then there were his full lips that had been pulled down at the side, but all I'd wondered was what he'd look like if he smiled or if his expression was always one of permanent annoyance.

I wished he'd taken me up on my offer just so I could see what he looked like when he was relaxed. Not that I'd expected him to, because while his eyes had definitely been interested, his mouth had been *this* close to telling me to go fuck myself.

Which was what had happened anyway, so he hadn't exactly been wrong.

My hand flew over my cock as I imagined him here with me, telling me to touch myself… to make myself come for him. The wet sounds of the gang bang and the heated, filthy words and deep groans added to the fantasy as I imagined Evan jerking off as he watched me before pinning me against the wall and spreading my legs. His fingers would slide between my ass cheeks to open up my hole before shoving his cock deep inside me, pounding me deliciously hard until I painted the tiles with my cum.

"Oh fuck!" I groaned, my hand flying out to hit the wall and steady myself as my orgasm hit me like a ton of bricks. My legs trembled as my cock pulsed in my hand, shooting cum across the tiles and down the side of the bath. My chest heaved, my head tipping forward and just as it did, I remembered the bloody earbuds.

"Shit, no! Come here… you… fuck…" Chasing my earbud across the floor of the bath and trying not to let it get soaked or covered in cum definitely wasn't the ending I'd planned for my quick shower wank, but it was the one I got and by the time I'd retrieved it and stopped the other one from going flying, the last vestiges of my orgasm had well and truly faded.

Which felt like a bit of a fucking waste. What was the point in having an orgasm if you weren't going to savour it?

I put my earbuds on the windowsill next to my phone

and hit pause on the video, leaving droplets of water across the screen. Grabbing my shower gel, I began to rinse myself off, trying very hard not to look too closely at what I'd been fantasising about. And not the gang bang part.

I'd literally only spoken to Evan once, even though Ianto had been trying to get me to introduce myself since I'd moved in. Even from a distance I'd thought he was cute, but now… God, I was properly fucked.

There were only two options now really.

Either I totally ignored him, did my best to be a good neighbour, and never thought about him again—which sounded boring as fuck if I was honest—or I could gently keep prodding him in the hope I got to see more of him. And if I played my cards right, I might eventually get him to take me up on my offer.

I grinned to myself as I lathered soap across my chest. If there was one thing I'd always been good at, it was being just the right amount of annoying.

CHAPTER THREE

Eva Nessence

"Has anyone seen my tweezers? And my lashes. I could've sworn I put them in here," said Bubblegum as she began emptying half her make-up bag over the counter in our dressing room, scattering brushes, sponges, pencils, and palettes across the already cluttered surface.

I glanced across at her from my seat at the end, pausing for two seconds with my eyeliner held in mid-air. I needed utter concentration not to fuck it up, and Bubblegum throwing things around was not going to help.

"When did you have them last?" I asked, casting my eyes across the chaos. I'd be hard-pressed to see anything in that mess, let alone something as small as a pair of tweezers. Sharing a room with Bubblegum Galaxy and Bitch Fit was like sharing a cupboard with two small tropical storms who continuously left carnage in their wake without batting an eyelash.

Once or twice when I was really frustrated, I'd debated shoving all their shit in rubbish bags for the pair to sort, but since I loved both of them, I usually settled for a pointed comment or three.

"Wednesday," Bubblegum said. She tipped the now empty make-up bag upside down and shook it and then huffed in frustration. "Fuck, I really thought I put them back."

"Don't you have spares?"

"Tweezers, maybe. Lashes…" Her words trailed off as a look of realisation dawned on her face. "Fuck! I bet they're on my dressing table! I took my lashes off at home on Wednesday and I bet I forgot to put them back. I usually…" She shook her head, a playful little smile curling the corner of her lips. "I got distracted and forgot."

"Let me guess," Bitch said from the corner where she'd been rooting around in a rack of clothes. "Your sexy-as-fuck rugby player came and did deliciously filthy things to you while you were getting out of drag and you forgot to put things away?"

"Maybe…"

"That's a yes then," Bitch said with a gleeful smile. "It's written all over your face."

"Come on, don't tell me you wouldn't get distracted by Tristan if he walked into your dressing room naked?" asked Bubblegum.

"Oh, I absolutely would, Sparkles. Tristan is utterly delicious. But we're not talking about me."

"We could," I said. "Especially because you've been looking for something to wear for nearly twenty minutes and are still in your underwear. I suppose you could go on stage like that—it would be a novelty at least."

"Ha-fucking-ha." Bitch stuck her tongue out at me and smirked before pulling a pink and black plaid skirt off a hanger. "Are you jealous, my little gothic bestie? Do we need to find someone sexy to come and sweep you off your feet for the night? Not to be rude, but when was the last time you got laid?"

"None of your business," I said, turning back to the mirror. I clearly wasn't going to get any peace, so I'd have to suck it up and do my eyeliner under duress. Maybe if I concentrated hard enough, I'd be able to drown out this conversation long enough that Bitch and Sparkles would get bored and start talking about something else.

"Definitely not for a while then," Bitch said. "Sparkles, do you have any friends we can set Eva up with? What about any of West's teammates? There's got to be at least one or two of them who'd be interested in our lovely friend here."

"Hmm, maybe... I don't know about the team, but Moxxie said their cousin is single and he's cute. They posted a photo with him on Instagram." Bubblegum grabbed her phone off the counter, ignoring the rest of the mess she'd created, and began to tap the screen. "What sort of people are you into? Do you have a type? If it's been that long, I'm guessing you're not a Grindr person, which is fine but—"

"Sparkles, I love you but if you finish that sentence, I will not lend you my tweezers or give you my spare lashes," I said in a muttered voice as I attempted to even out my eyeliner. It wasn't perfect but it would do as long as nobody looked too closely. Luckily The Court was a place where you painted for the back row, so it wasn't as if we were in front of high-definition cameras.

"My lips are sealed," Bubblegum said, locking her phone and putting it back on the counter. "But my offer still stands if you change your mind."

"God, Sparkles, you're so easily bought," Bitch said as she walked up to us pulling a crop top on and adjusting her breast plate.

"I am, but I'll do pretty much anything for some lashes right now. So, unless you have something to offer, I'm sticking to my silence."

Bitch laughed. "Not unless you want the old lashes I've worn like, twenty times."

"Twenty times? How?"

"Sheer fucking stubbornness," Bitch said. "And I'm cheap. Why fork out for expensive ones when the cheap Superdrug ones work just as well?" She grinned and began searching through the chaos for her lipstick. "Besides, it's all part of my *aesthetic*."

"Ah yes, something that should have been thrown into the rubbish years ago," I said with a smirk as I reached for my own lashes and pulled out the spare pair in the bottom of my make-up bag. "Here you are, Bubbles. You don't need to give them back either."

"Aww, thanks, babe. I'll get you another pair."

"It's fine." I gently picked up one of the lashes with my tweezers and started applying glue. "Just keep them in your bag so you've always got a spare pair."

"Done!"

I smiled to myself, pleased I'd managed to distract them. I knew their intentions were good, but I didn't need them to put my love life under a microscope. Even if I'd wanted to find someone, my life couldn't support a relationship. I had a stressful full-time job, a second job that was virtually a full-time job in its own right, and…

My phone vibrated frantically on the counter in front of me as the third stressful part of my life called. Not that I'd ever say that out loud—it wasn't as if the situation could be helped.

"Hey, what's up?" I asked as I answered, holding the phone just enough away from my ear so I didn't cover the screen in foundation. I could have put the call on speaker, but I tried really hard to keep my personal life private and I didn't want Bubblegum or Bitch listening in even if I knew they wouldn't judge.

"Hey," said Kirsty, my older sister and one of my best friends. "I know you're working tonight but I have a massive favour to ask you."

"Sure, ask away."

"I just got a call from work and they've got a shift going on pick and pack in the morning, but it's a five o'clock start and I was wondering if—"

"Yeah, no worries," I said, knowing what she was going to ask before she even finished asking. Kirsty worked every shift she could at her local Tesco Extra, picking up extra hours as often as possible. I didn't blame her because being a single mum to two kids was tough, especially with the way costs had skyrocketed and the fact her ex-husband was a deadbeat piece of shit. Babysitting Grace and Milo wasn't always sunshine and roses, but it wasn't like Kirsty had any other options for childcare and I didn't intend to make her life any harder than it already was when I could help out.

Kirsty had always looked out for me when we'd been growing up—she'd practically raised me even though she was only five years older, and now it was my turn to help her. It was the least I could do to repay her. Besides, it wasn't like she just dumped her kids on me without warning and took off partying.

"Are you sure? I know it's Saturday tomorrow and I'm sure you have plans."

"If by plans you mean sitting on my sofa and watching whatever I can find on Netflix before my show tomorrow, then yes, I have plans. I'll come over after the show tonight. I should be there about midnight but don't stay up."

She chuckled and then yawned loudly. "At this rate I'll be in bed by eight. Do you want dinner left out?"

"No, I'll be fine." I'd get something on the drive back to Nottingham from Lincoln, which was about an hour. There were drag bars in Nottingham I worked at sometimes, but I'd gotten onto The Court's roster well before any others and now I'd never consider leaving. It was my home, my family, and I loved it.

Even if it was a pain to haul my exhausted ass up and down between the two several times a week and it cost me a fucking fortune in petrol.

It was a good thing I made good money from being a paramedic because drag wasn't exactly cheap either. Especially since Eva's gothic aesthetic oozed dark, bold glamour, unlike Bitch's appearance, which seemed to have been inspired by emo teens and the local rubbish tip.

Getting something to eat from McDonald's on my way home would save Kirsty some money too. I knew she wouldn't think anything of feeding me, but I was conscious of the way every penny stacked up.

"Are you sure?" she asked.

"I'm sure. I'll see you later."

"See you later," she said. "And if I somehow manage to sneak out without waking you up tomorrow morning, my shift finishes at one, so I'll see you after. And if you need to take them back to yours, then do. I'll leave Grace's car seat inside."

"We'll probably just sit on the sofa and watch Disney movies." I glanced to my left, realising Bubblegum and Bitch were very obviously trying not to listen and doing a terrible job. Seriously, neither of them should ever consider an acting career unless they wanted to fail spectacularly in five seconds.

"Okay, you're a star," Kirsty said and I couldn't miss the relief in her voice. "I really appreciate this, Evan. Seriously, you're a lifesaver."

"It's nothing," I said. "I'll see you later. I need to put my eyelashes on."

"Good luck! I love you."

"Love you too." I hung up and put my phone down before turning back to my lashes. The glue had dried before I'd managed to put the first one on. I sighed and picked up the tiny bottle and started carefully daubing more along the lash line.

"Everything okay?" Bitch asked, far too casually for it to be casual. She was fishing but in the least subtle way possible. Then again, nothing Bitch did was subtle, either in or out of drag, and I couldn't hold that against her. It did make for some interesting stories.

"Yeah, fine," I said as I finally managed to put my left lashes in place. "That was my sister."

"I didn't know you had a sister," Bubblegum said. The disbelief was plain in her voice and even out of the corner of my eye I could see her staring at me. "Since when have you had a sister?"

"Since I was born."

"Seriously, I've known you for…" Sparkles thought for a second, counting something on her fingers. "Three years now and not once have you mentioned having a sister! What other secrets are you hiding?"

"Plenty." I grinned as I reached for the other lashes. "That's why my wigs are so big—they're full of secrets."

Bitch snorted. "Alright, Miss Wieners. Wait, if you're Gretchen, does that make me Regina? Because Sparkles is clearly our adorable Karen."

"What are you talking about?" Bubblegum asked, looking between the two of us in confusion. Although whether it was real or fake, I wasn't sure. Bubblegum could be sneaky when she wanted, and she loved teasing Bitch.

"Oh my God! Sparkles, please tell me you've seen *Mean Girls*? Please tell me I'm not that old."

"When did it come out?"

"I don't know," Bitch said with a wave of her hand. "Two thousand and something. Four maybe? Five?"

Bubblegum snorted. "Then probably not. I'd have been, like, three or four."

"Jesus fucking Christ. I'm so fucking old." Bitch groaned and I laughed. "Right, that's it. We need a movie night. We're going to make you watch every classic noughties teen movie, and there will be a quiz at the end. I'll host. Eva, you and Moxxie can bring snacks. One of the others can bring the drinks."

"Wait, why am I involved in this?" I asked with one eye closed as I tried to let my lashes set.

"Because, darling, Bubblegum here is seriously lacking in her education and I'm not losing my pop culture references because she's too young to quote *Mean Girls* or *Bring It On*."

"You do realise *Bring It On* is older than her?"

"Oh, do fuck off, babe," Bitch said, blowing me a kiss. "Or I'll start bringing up your love life again."

CHAPTER FOUR

Rhys

THERE WAS no reason for me to be hanging around in my living room watching out of the window to see when Evan came home, but here I was doing it anyway.

I'd seen him leave last night with a large backpack, but I'd not heard him come home and his car wasn't parked outside either. I hoped he was all right.

The problem was I didn't know him well enough to know if this was a common occurrence or if it was just a one-off. Until we'd spoken the other day, I hadn't really paid that much attention to him, but now I'd seen him up close and decided I wanted to annoy him into fucking me, I'd found myself heavily invested in his movements. Which, granted, sounded a little fucking creepy but it wasn't as if I was stalking him or bugging his house. I was just keeping a vague ear on him.

At first, I'd thought he was at work since he'd

mentioned doing night shifts, but it was Saturday afternoon now and no night shift I knew lasted that long. I supposed he could have come and gone again in the time I'd been out that morning since I'd had classes to teach at the gym followed by some personal training clients, but given how grumpy Evan had been about losing sleep, I didn't think he was the type to give up his rest to do something else.

I was pretty sure he didn't have a boyfriend, especially given the way he'd looked at me, but maybe he'd found a hook-up and decided to crash with them. After all, sometimes all night wasn't quite enough to get it out of your system.

There were other reasons too, like some sort of family event or weekend away, but my mind kept drifting back towards the sex idea. I didn't want to admit I was jealous, but since Evan knew he had someone willing next door, I didn't know why he'd want to go and find someone else. It sounded egoistic, but I'd seen the way his eyes had lingered on my tattoos and run down my body, which was pretty fucking banging if you asked me.

No, he was definitely interested. He just didn't want to admit it.

All I had to do was find a way to make him.

A car pulled up outside, bumping onto the pavement and parking in front of our doors, and I turned my head to glance out the window to see who it was. A smirk slid onto my lips as I saw Evan's head emerging from the driver's side, his tousled brown hair looking like someone had run their hands through it numerous times and a tired air about him. He was still wearing the same clothes I'd seen him leaving in last night and I couldn't resist looking at the way his jeans hugged his ass as he bent over to grab his backpack off the front seat.

As he stood up and reached for his keys, I threw myself off the sofa and bolted for the front door—my feet moving before my brain had processed what I was doing. I got the feeling this wasn't going to end well, but at the same time, I couldn't stop myself.

I'd always thought my brother was the nosy one because Ianto always had to know everything, but right now, it was hard to pretend I wasn't being nosy myself. Whatever Evan did had nothing to do with me, but here I was, pulling my front door open and sticking my head out as he stepped onto the pavement.

"You're alive then," I said with a wry smile. Evan paused mid-stride and turned to me with those piercing blue eyes of his, raising an eyebrow like he couldn't believe what I'd said.

"I am," he said coolly. "Are you stalking me now as well as disturbing my peace?"

"I wouldn't say stalking. More just keeping an eye on you to make sure you don't vanish off the face of the earth."

"And if I did?"

"Well, at least I'd be able to tell the police when I last saw you."

Evan snorted. It looked like he was trying very hard to fight back a smile. My own grin widened and I mentally ticked off another point in the column under my name. If it was me versus him, I was winning. Spectacularly, I might add. "Am I supposed to thank you for your generosity?"

"You could do," I said. "I take payment in cash or bank transfer, although I'm not opposed to more alternative methods of payment."

"Careful," he said in a low voice that sent shivers running down my spine. "Anyone would think you were flirting with me."

"And if I was? Would that be a bad thing?" There was a pause and from the stunned expression on Evan's face, he hadn't been expecting me to just come out and say it. But in my experience, being direct was usually the best way of getting what I wanted.

"Y-ye… N-no… I…" He scowled. I grinned.

"You like the idea of me flirting with you."

"I didn't say that."

"Didn't you?"

His scowl deepened and he turned back towards his front door, pulling his keys out of his pocket. "Why are you so annoying? And what the hell did I do to deserve this?"

I was running out of time, but that didn't worry me too much. The fact he'd deflected told me I'd got him on the back foot. Now all I had to do was stop him from running away from his feelings. "I wouldn't say annoying," I said, smirking at him and leaning against my doorframe, carefully adjusting my stance to show off as much of my body as possible. My T-shirt was riding up slightly, and I casually used one hand to gently tug the corner of it up and expose a little more skin. "Just determined."

"Determined to do what? Piss me off?" Evan asked, glowering at me.

"Maybe." I winked at him. "What's in the bag? Been

anywhere exciting? I'm going to assume you've been doing something fun since those are the clothes you went out in yesterday."

"So you are stalking me?"

"No, I just happened to see you leave. And that didn't answer my question."

"That's because it doesn't deserve an answer."

"Something secret then. That sounds fun."

He rolled his eyes and pursed his lips, his hand clenching around his keys, which jangled noisily. He looked like he was two seconds away from either punching me in the face or pushing me against the wall and kissing me. I just hoped it was the second.

That was the problem with being annoying—sometimes it was a fine line and could go from good to bad very quickly. Usually I got what I wanted, but I'd had to dodge the odd angry fist once or twice. Although on those occasions, copious amounts of alcohol had been involved, we'd been in the middle of clubs, and I'd been mostly winding people up for the fun of it.

Ianto had said I was being a dickhead, but there was something very satisfying about finding the straight wankers hitting on uninterested girls and putting their own moves on them. Funnily enough, they never really saw the hypocrisy in their situations, and none of them had seemed to understand my point.

"Not secret, private," Evan said through gritted teeth. "There's a difference."

"Will you tell me your secrets?"

"No."

"What about if I tell you mine?"

His piercing eyes roamed over me, and the expression that settled on his face was an unimpressed one. I'd have been hurt if I wasn't expecting it. "I can't imagine you'd have any interesting ones. You look pretty easy to read."

I put my hand on my heart dramatically. "That hurts, that does." I grinned. "Go on then, read me."

He sighed and folded his arms. "You clearly work out a lot, so you're definitely vain. You're good-looking and you know it, especially because you keep adjusting your T-shirt in the hope I'll get distracted by your tattoos, but you're also looking for validation, which explains why you desperately want me to notice. You keep annoying me, so you clearly want attention like some sort of needy puppy, and while I'm sure you'd be a good boy and back off if I told you no, you want me to actually say it because you need direction and order."

He took a step closer and I swallowed, heat fluttering under my skin. Evan smirked and lowered his voice. "I think you pretend to be brash and irritating, showing off like a teenage boy trying to impress someone, but deep down you're not cocky or confident. You're just a needy, desperate, spoilt brat who wants someone to notice them." He stepped even closer and I couldn't stop my breath from catching in my chest. My tongue darted out to wet my lower lip and my mouth hung open like I was suddenly trying to catch flies.

Evan reached out, his fingers cupping my chin as his thumb brushed my bottom lip, and fuck was I tempted to suck it. "Look at you," he continued, his words making the hairs on my arms stand up. "Trying to make a scene, all because you want me."

I made a very undignified noise and he chuckled darkly. Provoking him was one thing, but I hadn't expected him to get such a good read on me so quickly. Was I really that obvious?

Although it wasn't like I'd been trying to be subtle, so maybe I shouldn't have been surprised.

"See, you can't even deny it," Evan said, his bright eyes meeting mine. The intensity of his gaze threatened to swallow me whole and my knees almost buckled underneath me.

"I'm not going to," I said, forcing the words out before they got lost in my throat. I was so close to getting everything I'd dreamed of, but there was still a chance it would slip away. After all, he might decide the best way to deal with me was to leave me hanging, and I couldn't have that. "What are you going to do about it?"

His thumb stroked my bottom lip between my snakebite piercings, and the tiny part of the back of my brain that was still functioning noticed how careful he was. Like he didn't want to catch them and hurt me.

"I shouldn't do anything."

"You want to, though," I said and tried to smile.

"That would be just giving you what you want." He leant closer, his breath ghosting across my skin. His mouth was right there. I could've leant in and kissed him if his hand wasn't holding my head in place. "And I shouldn't reward bad behaviour."

"What about what *you* want?"

"I…" He looked deep in thought for a second, like the concept of doing something he wanted was alien to him. "That doesn't matter."

"Yeah, it does." I stared straight back into those beautiful eyes, searching for any fragment of hesitation. But all I saw was unbridled desire. One he seemed determined to pin down and chain in place. And I couldn't have that. "You want me," I said softly… teasingly… "I want you. What have you got to lose? Go on, you know you want to. Just one little taste. You never know, you might like it."

"Fuck, you're annoying," he said before slamming his mouth into mine.

CHAPTER FIVE

Eva Nessence

I shouldn't have kissed him.

I shouldn't still be kissing him.

But he was so fucking annoying and it was the only way I could think to make him shut up. At least, that was what I was going to keep telling myself. I wasn't going to consider admitting Rhys had been right, not even to myself. Because I didn't have the strength to resist, and I wanted him so fucking much it made my skin itch.

I was physically and mentally exhausted, still wearing yesterday's clothes, and I should have gone home to shower and sleep, but fuck, maybe it was time to do something indulgent for once. Give in to my desires instead of pretending they didn't exist because I never had time for them.

Rhys's lips were soft, the silver bars through his

snakebites hot and firm, and I wondered what other piercings he'd have for me to play with. I'd seen his nipple bars through his T-shirts, but did he have more than those?

He groaned and his hand tugged at the front of my jacket. "Come in," he said. "I don't think we should fuck in front of the street."

Shit, we were stood in his front doorway where anyone could see us. And while I loved an audience under the right circumstances, this wasn't one of them. I stepped forward, pushing him backwards into the house, my hand still on his jaw. I dropped my backpack from the other and then used it to slam the door shut behind us, leaving us totally alone.

A quick glance around confirmed our houses were mirrors, and like me, Rhys was using this room as a living room. His sofa was to my right, bright teal and ready and waiting for me to bend him over the back of it. The blind on the window was still up, but that was easy to fix.

Grabbing his T-shirt with my free hand, I spun him around and walked him backwards for a step or two until his legs hit the back of the sofa. I was still kissing him, nipping his bottom lip and claiming his mouth with my tongue, but I didn't know how to stop.

Rhys groaned, his fingers still clasping the front of my jacket. I'd expected more pushback from him, but he was so fucking pliable it made the simmering heat inside me start to boil. There was just something about having another man at my mercy that turned me on. Maybe it was because my life was so chaotic and I wanted one thing I had absolute control over, or maybe I was a bossy bitch who hated not getting his own way.

Whatever the reason, feeling Rhys melt as I shoved my knee between his thighs, trapping him between me and the back of the sofa, was heady as fuck.

"Stay there," I said with a low growl as I broke away to walk over to his window to lower the blind. It was easy enough to gently tug the cord and pull it into place. Rhys watched me with a wanton smile and smirking eyes. It was obvious he was getting everything he'd wanted, and while a small part of me wished I hadn't given in, the rest of me was determined to make sure he never forgot me.

If he wanted me, he was going to get me. All of me.

And if that ruined him…

I really could be a petty bitch.

As I looked at him, Rhys slowly pivoted and bent over the back of the sofa, sticking his butt out to show off how round and perfect it was. My cock throbbed with need, reminding me how fucking desperate I was. "Want to fuck me?" he asked casually. "My ass is really fucking tight."

I bit back a groan but from the way his smile widened, it was obvious my expression had betrayed me. "Do you have lube? Condoms? If you're that tight, I'm not fucking you dry."

"Not even if I want it to burn?"

"No." I'd occasionally do spit as lube, especially if it was with someone I'd fucked before. But not today.

"Spoilsport," he said playfully. "There's some in the front pocket of my bag. You never know when you'll need them." He pointed at a backpack on the floor tucked in beside the sofa and resting on a pair of expensive-looking black trainers that had bright rainbow detailing along the side of the soles. The brand logo was rainbow coloured too. It pulled me up short for a second because despite his flirting, I somehow hadn't expected Rhys to be the sort to flaunt his queerness like that.

"Nice, aren't they?" he asked and I realised he'd seen me looking at them. "My brother and I have matching ones—bought them as a little treat for our birthday this year."

"Yeah… they're cute."

"That's the problem with working in fitness; I go through trainers at a rate of knots. And I'm so sick of wearing boring ones."

"I can't imagine you being boring," I said as I reached for the bag, lifting it off the floor with one hand and using the other to open up the front pocket. Inside was a small bottle of lube that had definitely been used more than once and a travel pack of condoms. The box for those was new, so I assumed Rhys had recently restocked.

"I'm taking that as a compliment," he said. "Everyone needs a bit of fun in their life."

"I didn't say you were fun. I just said you weren't boring."

"Isn't that the same thing?"

"No," I said, putting the bag down and walking back to him. He looked so good bent over the sofa, ass in the air waiting to be played with. I reached over and set the lube and condoms on one of the sofa cushions so they wouldn't get lost or in the way, and then I grabbed the waistband of Rhys's jogging bottoms and yanked them down around his thighs.

"Fuck!" His surprised gasp melted into a moan as I grabbed one of his butt cheeks, squeezing the firm muscle. Rhys really did have a nice ass, and I couldn't wait to taste it. I dropped to my knees behind him, tugging his joggers down even further so he'd be able to spread his legs. The floor was cold, hard, and covered in a threadbare carpet which would kill me if I knelt on it for too long. But I was sure I'd find a way to distract myself from the pain.

"Mmm, this is nice," I said, squeezing his other butt cheek as I admired his thighs and the curve of his ass. His thighs were firm, defined muscle covered in dark hair and more tattoos, but his ink hadn't quite reached his behind. "Spread your legs for me and use your hands to show me that hole."

Rhys groaned as he shuffled his feet to widen his thighs, pushing his bottom out even further as he reached back and grasped his cheeks with both hands, pulling them apart to reveal the furled skin of his hole. It was dark pink and surrounded by dark hair that looked like it had been trimmed or shaved at some point recently. I'd been with guys in the past who'd waxed everything off, but I'd always been turned off by that. So what if hair sometimes got in my mouth while I ate them out? It wasn't anything to be embarrassed about, and I wasn't the kind of man to make a massive song and dance about it.

"Fucking gorgeous," I said as I slid my hand up the inside of his thigh. At this angle, I could see his balls and the shadow of his hard cock, but neither seemed to be pierced, at least from where I was sitting. I ran one finger teasingly over the back of his balls, making him gasp. I loved how noisy he was. Then again, given that he hadn't been able to keep his mouth shut, I hadn't expected him to be quiet.

"You're teasing now," he said, his voice slightly muffled from where his head was hanging over the back of the sofa.

"Oh honey, I haven't even started teasing you yet."

I leant forward and buried my head between his cheeks, flattening my tongue and running it across his hole. Rhys groaned, incoherent words escaping from his throat as I flicked my tongue over his sensitive, puckered skin. He tasted like musk and sweat but there was something else on his skin, like citrus, that somehow made me think of summer.

I laved my tongue over his hole again and again, licking his rim and softening the tight muscle. He cursed and pushed back onto my face, begging for me as I sucked and teased him, using every fucking trick in the book to eat his ass like it was my last meal. Saliva dripped down his skin as the wet, messy sounds of my work mingled with Rhys's desperate moans.

My fingers snaked between his legs to brush over his balls, rolling them between my fingers and tugging them gently—not enough to hurt, but enough to surprise him with the change in sensation.

"Holy fuck," he cried. His hips jerked as if he wasn't sure whether to press back against my mouth or thrust forward. "E-Evan…"

I smirked against his hole. I liked the way my name

sounded on his lips, especially spoken like that. He was practically begging already.

"Pass me the lube," I said, lifting my head enough that he'd be able to hear me. It meant I got to look at his wet hole too, the puckered skin pulsing. Even his ass was fucking desperate for me.

Rhys let go of his ass and reached onto the sofa, and I heard his fingers on the cushions as he grasped the bottle. I chuckled as he practically threw it at me, but I caught it easily and opened the lid, pouring some of the thick gel onto my fingers. Rhys watched me over his shoulder, and I winked at him as I slid two wet fingers down his crack to circle his waiting hole.

"Y-yes," he said. "More."

I grinned and pushed one finger inside him. "Such a needy hole," I said as I pumped my finger slowly in and out of him. His channel was hot and deliciously tight, and I couldn't wait to feel it squeezing my cock. "Look at you, so fucking desperate for it."

"Y-yeah… I fucking need it. I'm… shit, I'm so fucking horny I think I'm going to explode."

"Don't be dramatic," I said, playfully swatting his ass with my free hand before reaching between his legs to loosely grasp his cock. I jerked it slowly, my fingers barely wrapped around the hot skin as I pushed another finger inside his hole.

"You'd be fucking dramatic if you were me," Rhys said, thrusting his hips as he tried to chase my hand as if that would somehow get him more friction. "You're bloody killing me here."

"And I'll keep doing it if you keep whining." I let go of his cock completely to emphasise my point and Rhys whimpered.

"That's not fair."

"Did you expect me to play fairly?" I asked as I curled my fingers inside his hole and pumped them in and out, searching for that sweet spot to make him scream. "You're irritating, annoying, and desperate to get your own way. What reasons do I have to be nice?"

Rhys groaned again. "Because… fuck, I don't know. Because you're not a complete dick?"

I laughed, my words dripping with sarcasm as I said, "You know me so well."

Whatever retort Rhys was dreaming of throwing at me melted into a moan as my fingers rubbed over his prostate. My dick ached where it was still trapped in my jeans, and it was getting harder to ignore the pain in my knees from the floor. Next time I was dragging him upstairs to a fucking bed.

Not that there was going to be a next time.

This was a once and once only type of thing so I could get the burning irritation out of my system.

And no matter how fun playing with Rhys was, I didn't need anything else in my life. I could barely manage as it was.

Slowly, I pulled my fingers out of his ass and grasped the back of the sofa to use as leverage as I climbed to my feet, praying my legs hadn't gone numb and fallen asleep because toppling straight onto my face would not be a good look. And as talented as I was with concealer, I couldn't cover up a black eye if I smacked my head on the edge of the sofa.

I reached over the cushions and grabbed the box of condoms, pulling off the plastic wrapper and digging the top of the box open. I took one of the foil-wrapped condoms out, putting it between my lips so I had both hands free, threw the rest of the box back on the sofa, and reached for the button of my jeans.

Rhys watched me as I tugged my jeans down around my thighs, finally releasing my hard cock from the confines of its denim prison. "No underwear?" Rhys asked with a playful smile as I carefully ripped the condom wrapper open and began to roll it onto my shaft. I was so fucking turned on, with uncontrollable need and tension boiling under my skin. The desperation was almost making me angry.

"No," I said as I grabbed the lube, which I'd left in easy reach, and poured more onto my fingers. I didn't usually go commando, but I refused to re-wear dirty underwear and I hadn't had a spare pair in my bag since I hadn't been expecting to go to Kirsty's. Next time I repacked my backpack, I'd have to make sure I had a couple of pairs of socks, pants, and maybe a T-shirt in there, just in case.

"Sexy."

"Not sexy, just..." I didn't bother finishing that sentence. Rhys didn't need to know my personal shit. Instead I shuffled behind him, gripping his hip with one hand as I smeared lube on my cock. I lined my shaft up with his hole and pushed inside with one swift, firm motion, drinking in the deep groan echoing from Rhys's chest as I did.

Rhys's channel was hot and tight around my cock, squeezing me tightly and enveloping me in sensation. I put my other hand on his hip, gripping his body tightly until my knuckles almost turned white and pushing down the sudden, crushing desire in my chest as I forced myself to breathe. I wasn't going to come. Not yet.

"F-fuck—" Rhys started but I didn't let him finish. I pulled back until my cock was barely inside him and then slammed back in, cutting off whatever he was going to say and turning it into a strangled moan. Shifting my feet an inch wider, I began to fuck him hard and fast, thrusting deep into him with every snap of my hips.

I needed him to feel me, not just now but later… tomorrow… I needed him to wake up and remember me. To think about me all night and all day, knowing I'd done this to him, reminding him of just how much pleasure I'd given him.

I wanted to ruin him.

Rhys groaned and pushed back against me like he was trying to take me deeper somehow, even though my balls were already brushing against his ass. I could see him gripping the sofa cushions, his knuckles also white, and I smirked as I shifted again, aiming to drive my cock straight over his prostate.

I knew I'd hit my mark when he howled, his body jolting underneath me. He glanced at me over his shoulder, mouth slack and eyes soft with pleasure. He really did look pretty getting fucked.

My cock hammered into him over and over, and I knew I wouldn't be able to deny the inevitable for much longer.

I slid my hand around his body, reaching for his cock. Rhys gasped as I wrapped my fingers around his shaft, the soft skin so hot it threatened to burn my hand as I began to jerk him roughly, trying to match the pace with my thrusts. It was messy and uncoordinated, but from the sounds dripping from his lips, I didn't think Rhys cared.

Pretty, loud, and pliant. Three of my favourite things.

"Fuck," Rhys said with a gasp, his body tensing, and I knew he was close. "I… I'm gonna…"

"That's it," I said, growling out the words as I thrust hard into him. "Come on my fucking cock. Fucking come for me."

Rhys cried out, his channel squeezing impossibly tight around my cock as his own pumped thick streams of cum across my fingers. I stroked him through his orgasm, dragging him out to the point of oversensitivity as I continued to fuck him. I was so close to my own release, and I wasn't going to give it up.

"E-Evan," Rhys panted. His chest was heaving, his legs starting to tremble. It was a fucking heady realisation, knowing I'd done that to him, and it snapped the last threads of whatever was holding my orgasm back.

I groaned as I buried my cock deep inside him, shooting my release into the condom as pleasure ripped through me, stealing the breath from my lungs and turning my muscles to jelly. I couldn't remember the last time I'd had such an intense orgasm, and I was almost glad my mind had gone blank because I didn't want to think about how boring it made my life look.

I still had one hand on Rhys's cock, the other on his hip, holding him against me. I knew I had to release him and end this, but now it was over… I felt a pang of reluctance.

Rhys turned his head and looked over his shoulder, a satisfied smile on his face. "Maybe I should annoy you more often if that's the result," he said and sighed, stretching his back. "Worth it."

That was enough to send reality crashing down around me. I let go of Rhys's softening dick and pulled out of him, carefully tugging off the condom and tying it off before reaching for my jeans. My hand was covered in cum, and at least half of it was now on my clothes. Rhys was watching me, that smug smile still on his lips. "I don't suppose you might be up for another round later?"

"No," I said as I looked for somewhere to dump the condom. I didn't want to just leave it on the floor or the sofa. I wasn't that tasteless.

"Sure?"

"Yes." The words "once was enough" were sitting on my tongue, but I couldn't bring myself to say them. And that frightened me more than anything else. That should have been it. I should have been done.

But the need was still there, like an itch under my skin I didn't know how to shake.

Rhys grinned and straightened, joggers still around his knees. "Oh well, you can't blame me for trying." He held out his hand. "I'll put that in my bin."

"Er, thanks." I handed him the condom and looked

around for my bag, which was still on the floor by the door. I walked over to it, probably faster than was polite but I needed to get out of there before I lost control of my emotions. As I reached the door, I turned and looked at him. "I'll see you later."

If Rhys said anything in return, I didn't hear it over the sound of the door banging shut behind me.

CHAPTER SIX

Rhys

"Are you nearly ready or do I have to sit here for another twenty minutes watching you try on the same three T-shirts?" Ianto grinned at me from the middle of my bed where he was sat cross-legged with his phone resting on his knee. The two of us were going out together to see the goth rock band Carmilla, and for some reason I couldn't seem to settle on something to wear, which was ridiculous really because it wasn't like I was aiming to impress anyone.

But ever since Evan had bent me over my sofa on Saturday afternoon, it felt like my insides were tied in knots and I'd drunk nothing but caffeine. I'd even cut coffee out in the past two days to see if it made a difference, but no, my whole bloody body felt like it'd somehow been switched on to vibrate.

"Shut up, I've not been that bad," I said as I picked up a

black T-shirt off the floor and pulled it on. I'd probably put it on and taken it off at least twice already.

"Really? We were supposed to leave ten minutes ago. Every time I've tried to order an Uber, you keep telling me you're not ready."

"Fine, I'm ready now." I turned away from my wardrobe and Ianto raised an eyebrow at me. "What?"

"A black T-shirt? All this fucking fuss over a black T-shirt?"

"I couldn't decide between that and the red." Because neither of them stopped my skin from burning. But at this point, I couldn't blame my washing powder or my shower gel. It was all the fault of the gorgeous, snarky, secretive man who lived next door and had fucked my brains out before leaving with barely a thanks.

Did he know how long it'd taken me to scrub the cum out of the sofa? I'd been this close to having to rearrange the whole room so it didn't show.

Ianto shook his head and shuffled over to the edge of the bed. "Please tell me you're not going to try and pick someone up tonight? I thought you wanted it just to be the two of us."

"I do," I said. "Don't worry, the only man I'll be leaving with tonight is the one I'm blood-related to."

Ianto laughed and followed me downstairs where we both pulled on our shoes. I shoved my wallet and keys into my front pockets, and while Ianto finally ordered us an Uber, I scrolled through my phone to make sure I had the tickets on hand. I hated it when I finally got near the front of a queue at gigs and the people ahead of me weren't prepared, so everyone had to wait while they fumbled around trying to find everything. It was really bloody rude, in my opinion.

As we waited outside for the car, I resisted the urge to turn my head and peer into Evan's house. There was a light on in the top window, so he had to be home, and I wondered what his plans for the night were. Would he be off on another night shift? A mysterious night away? Or would he be spending it in bed? If he was doing that, would he—

No. That wasn't a rabbit hole I needed to go down.

Evan had made it very clear our fuck was a one-time-only deal, and it wouldn't do me any good to wish for more. Besides, it wasn't like I'd ever been a more kind of person. Relationships were for other people, like Ianto and Ben. I was just here for a good time.

The car pulled up in front of us, and I shoved all thoughts of Evan to the back of my mind as I climbed in. Tonight was about having fun with my twin brother, not plotting ways to get my sexy, sarcastic neighbour to fuck me again.

It didn't take long for Ianto and me to get to Rock City in the middle of Nottingham where the gig was being held. Rock City was a pretty legendary venue, and I'd spent many a long night there since we'd moved to the city thirteen years ago, both for concerts and nights out. My favourite memory was from a Halloween all-nighter when Ianto and I had found ourselves in the basement and the entire room of drunken revellers had sung 'Livin' On a

Prayer' and 'Bohemian Rhapsody' back to back and absolutely word perfect.

"Do you want to get anything?" Ianto said once we got inside, gesturing at the merch stand.

I frowned and peered a little closer, then whistled under my breath. "Bloody hell, that's expensive. Fifty-five quid for a hoodie, seriously?"

"We've paid more before," Ianto said, but he sounded just as put out as I felt.

"Yeah, but still." I did love the designs, though. Whoever did Carmilla's merch was really fucking talented. And I hadn't brought a hoodie with me because I'd been considering buying something here. I chuckled as a young couple slid past us and up to the counter. "God, I sound so fucking old, don't I?"

"You do. But I can't agree with you because that makes me old too. I don't think seventeen minutes is enough to claim an age difference."

I snorted. "Definitely not. If I'm going down, I'm taking you with me." I looked at the hoodies again, and then at my brother. I still hadn't told him about my hook-up with Evan and it was starting to weigh on me. We'd always told each other everything and Ianto was my best friend above anyone else. One of his exes had once described us as unhealthily codependent and while he'd been a twat, he hadn't been totally wrong. But after what we'd been through, I couldn't imagine not being close to my twin.

Even the idea of being apart from him made my heart physically hurt.

"Come on," I said, giving him a soft smile before stepping forward. "I want a hoodie. What about you?"

"You don't have to get me anything," he said, nudging me gently with his elbow. "I have money."

"I know, but I also know you and Ben are saving up for that holiday to Greece."

Ianto looked down at his shoes and smiled. "Yeah... I still can't believe he finally agreed to take two weeks off in the summer. Although... I think Aaron had something to do with it too. And Patrick." He chuckled. "I wouldn't be surprised if an intervention was staged."

I laughed with him. Ben ran a pub called The Pear Tree in a village outside Nottingham with his best friend Aaron and Aaron's husband, Josh. Aaron was a fiery asshole but it was clear he and Ben were close, almost as close as Ianto and me, and I knew they'd been through some shit without them saying it. Patrick was the mild-mannered Irish pastry chef who was obviously the quiet but resolute voice of reason behind everything.

From what Ben had said, Patrick was the *only* person Aaron would ever listen to, and the general consensus amongst the pub staff was that if Cthulhu ever made his earthly appearance, Patrick would have him mopping floors and peeling apples in two minutes flat.

"Good," I said. "You both need a break."

"Will you be okay without me?" Ianto asked. "We'll be gone for two weeks. I'll still message you every day, though. I can't imagine not talking to you."

"Who said I'm not coming with you? I'll be folding myself up into your suitcase. I've seen the place you're going and I'd quite like a swanky all-inclusive holiday. It's got those fancy pool cabanas too, the ones that look like a proper four-poster bed and everything. I'll just camp out there and eat my weight in calamari and ice cream. Oh, and I'll have some of those fancy cocktails too, the ones with the fruit and little umbrellas."

"Just don't try swimming afterwards," Ianto said with a grin. "I'm not fishing you out."

"No, you're to let a sexy Greek lifeguard save me."

"Got it, I'll just play damsel in distress."

"Perfect." I gestured at the merch in front of us. "Now can you tell me what you want so we can go get a drink?"

We ended up with matching hoodies that we both threw on before we headed into the darkly lit central room, which was already getting busy even though we'd made sure to get there nice and early so we could find a good spot to stand. We made our way to one of the bars around the edge of the room where Ianto insisted on buying us both drinks before weaving our way through the crowd to a good spot near the middle where we'd have a great view and be able to get involved with any bouncing around. Rock City wasn't huge, but we'd probably be able to get a little circle pit going in the middle.

"Can I ask you something?" Ianto asked as we sipped our drinks, trying not to get jostled by the growing crowd around us.

"Sure."

"Are you okay?"

His question caught me off guard and I didn't answer for a moment, which gave me away before I could even open my mouth. "Yes? But also no." I sighed and took a long swig of my rum and Coke. "You know I told you about the guy from next door?"

"Yeah, the sexy, uptight one who was complaining about your music and couldn't stop staring at you." Ianto's gaze narrowed and he smirked. "Did something happen?"

"Define something."

"Don't be a twat, you know exactly what I mean. Unless he punched you or something, in which case I'm going to be having words."

"No, there was no punching. Everything was *very* consensual."

Ianto stared at me, his mouth falling open. "Holy shit, Rhys, did you hook up with him? When? What happened?"

"Saturday afternoon," I said quietly. "And it's been throwing me off ever since."

"Why?"

"I don't know." I took another long sip, draining the rest of my cup. "He came home in the afternoon and I... well, he'd been out since the previous evening, so I stuck my head out the door to check he wasn't dead." Ianto snorted. "And we talked for a few minutes and then he told me I was annoying, kissed me, and then we fucked in the sitting room."

Ianto's face wrinkled up. "Oh God, did you fuck on your sofa? I was sitting on that this afternoon!"

"Not *on* it."

Ianto opened his mouth, then obviously thought better of it. He sipped his drink and then said, "So basically, you annoyed him into hooking up with you?"

"Pretty much."

"I don't think I've heard a more you way of finding a fuck buddy."

"Except he's not. He said it was only a one-time thing. And now..." I gestured at my chest. "Everything feels weird. Usually I don't care if things are a one and done, that works great for me—you know I'm not a boyfriend person—but he's so..." I growled in frustration because I literally didn't know how to put my feelings into words.

"Is it because he told you no?" Ianto asked. He was studying me with a thoughtful expression and playing with one of his snakebites, which he sometimes did when he was really thinking something through. I'd always told him off for it because I didn't want him to hurt himself, but now I wanted whatever wisdom he could drum up from the depths of his brain.

"I've been told no before."

"Have you?"

"Of course."

"Have you been told no when you really want something?"

"Yeah, obviously," I said.

Ianto sighed. "Look, it's very obvious from what you've said that you like annoying him. That it's fun."

"That's because it is."

"And that's my point," Ianto said, his voice full of exasperation. "I love you, Rhys, but you can be annoying as fuck when you want to be and you know it."

"I'm still waiting for you to make a point," I said as the crowd squeezed in around us. On stage, the technicians were finishing setting up for the opening act, which meant we didn't have long to finish this conversation before we were drowned out by the sound of heavy metal.

"You like annoying him, it's fun, and it's now gotten you what you want: sex. But you want to keep annoying him and fucking around with him because you're enjoying yourself, but he doesn't want to fuck you again *because* you're annoying him."

"I don't think it's just that," I said, not totally fond of my brother's accusation, although he wasn't far wrong. "I think he's got other reasons too. I don't know what they are, though, because he's so secretive."

"Of course he's not going to tell you if he hates you," Ianto said with an exaggerated eye roll.

"He doesn't hate me! I don't think he'd have fucked me if that was the case."

Ianto stared at me, clearly fighting back laughter. "What the fuck do you think hate sex is?"

"Okay, but it wasn't hate sex… it was more like 'you're annoying me, so I'm going to fuck you to shut you up' sex," I said. "And you can't say they're the same thing, because they're not."

"Fine." Ianto's amusement was written across his face, but the way he put his hand on my arm told a different story. Because while we'd always taken the piss out of each other, we'd always been there to help and support each other in any way we could. "But it still sounds like you're frustrated because you want more, even if that's just another round, and he's unlikely to give it to you. I guess you either have to find a way to talk to him again, or you'll have to live with it."

I frowned and bit my lip because I didn't fancy living with it, so I supposed that meant I'd have to annoy Evan into talking to me again. I just had to figure out how.

The lights dimmed and a roar went up from the audience as a guitar screeched and the opening act, a metal band named Krash Goblins, strolled onto the stage, the thundering of their drums drowning out my thoughts.

CHAPTER SEVEN

Eva Nessence

I HADN'T PLANNED on getting to Rock City as late as I did, but I'd gotten so engrossed in altering a couple of dresses I'd lost track of time and I'd barely had a minute to shove a toasted bagel down my throat before heading out the door. I'd been looking forward to seeing Carmilla for weeks and now I was on the verge of missing them.

Rock City was packed, as I'd expected, but I'd managed to squeeze into the crowd downstairs and when a group shuffled slightly, I found myself standing in a pretty good spot. The opening act were well into their set, the crashing drums and heavy guitars making the floor shake underneath me as the singer, a slender young man with long, fluffy black hair and heavy make-up, bounced around the small stage with undying energy as he screamed into the microphone.

I wasn't familiar with any of Krash Goblins's work, but

the singer's enthusiasm alone was enough to make me want to check them out.

They played another song before they headed offstage and the lights came up so the techs could start changing the stage over. The crowd around me began to drain towards the two bars on either side of the room but I stood where I was because I'd always been fascinated by tech changes. There was something amazing about a successful one, where everything moved like a well-oiled machine. Like so many things in life, it was one of those things that if it was done well, you barely noticed it, and if it was done badly, it stood out like a sore thumb.

I debated going to one of the bars, but the crowd around both was heaving and I didn't fancy spending the rest of the break waiting to get served and losing my spot. Instead, I looked around at the crowd because I'd always had a nosy streak. It was a pretty diverse group, although the number of teenagers and students in the crowd suddenly made me feel very old. I'd only turned twenty-nine in February, but I felt every year in that moment.

Maybe it was because my day job had sucked all the youth and energy out of me with endless night shifts and stress and left me a grumpy old man. I was even getting wrinkles around my eyes, which looked so good with the black bags underneath them that'd been a permanent fixture on my face since I'd left university.

My stomach lurched as my eyes caught on a familiar-looking figure. A couple of rows in front of me, chatting to a man who looked virtually identical to him, was Rhys. I knew it was him. There was something about his profile…

the sweep of his hair... the way the serpent tattoo sat on his neck, emerging out of the collar of the Carmilla hoodie he was wearing. He hadn't spotted me yet, which was good because I didn't want to talk to him. I'd been avoiding him all week, which I knew was childish but I didn't trust myself around him.

There was a very good chance I'd do something stupid if he spoke to me again, like ending up in his bed. And since I was back at work tomorrow night and I had to pick the kids up from school in the afternoon, I could do with not being knackered from staying up all night. Because if I hooked up with Rhys again, neither of us would get any sleep.

To distract myself, I pulled out my phone and started scrolling through Instagram, meticulously liking all my friends' photos even though I wasn't really looking at them. Lifting my phone, I took a quick shot of the stage and added it to my stories. I'd been aiming to get the whole set and banner in, but when Bubblegum messaged me two seconds later, that wasn't what she commented on.

> **Bubblegum Galaxy**
> Holy shit, babe, is that your neighbour?
> Are you there with him?

I frowned and opened up my stories to see what the fuck she was on about. And right there at the bottom of the screen, his head half turned towards the camera, was fucking Rhys. How the hell had Sparkles seen that? How the hell had she even recognised him? Was she looking at my pictures under a microscope? Or did she just have some sixth sense when it came to my dating life?

> **Eva Nessence**
> I'm not here with him. He's here with his brother.

> **Eva Nessence**
> And no, I'm not going to say hi.

> **Bubblegum Galaxy**
> Why not? He's cute! Are you there by yourself?

> **Eva Nessence**
> Yeah.

> **Bubblegum Galaxy**
> Then you have to go say hi!

The lights started to go down and the crowd around me began to cheer. I sighed with relief. Saved by the bell.

> **Eva Nessence**
> Maybe later. Show's just starting.

> **Bubblegum Galaxy**
> Have fun!! <3 <3 <3

I smiled to myself as I shoved my phone back into the front pocket of my jeans. Sparkles really was a sweetheart.

In front of me, Carmilla strolled on stage with a loud cry of "What's up, Nottingham!" and the room erupted. The lead singer, Mayday, was a tall, curvaceous woman with long dark hair, incredible gothic make-up with a red lip to die for, and an amazing selection of silver rings. She was wearing skin-tight red trousers, a black crop top with a fishnet shirt underneath, and black boots with heels that looked like a spinal column in burnished silver. It was fucking iconic and I needed a picture of her make-up so I could study it. My painting skills had gotten a hell of a lot better over the past few years, but Mayday's make-up was next level beautiful.

Behind her came the rest of the band: the drummer, Angel, in a tank top and loose trousers with more drumsticks shoved into his back pocket, his waist-length braids threaded with silver rings and his dark skin covered in tattoos; the lead guitarist, Twix, with his tie-dye cargo trousers and sequinned shirt, his dark hair carefully styled and sprayed with glitter; the second guitarist, Rebel, with his leather trousers and black T-shirt that had the words Protect Trans Kids emblazoned across the chest; and the bassist, Saint, who was Mayday's brother, in pinstripe suit trousers and a ruffled white shirt with the sleeves folded up to show off the leather cuffs around his wrists.

All of them were gorgeous as fuck and I couldn't take my eyes off them as they launched into their opening number. I'd been obsessed with Carmilla since I'd stumbled across them at Download Festival a couple of years ago.

I'd been working the weekend as a paramedic because it was a good way to experience the festival without forking out hundreds of quid. And while I hadn't gotten to see everything I would have if I'd been there on my own terms, mostly thanks to a heatwave, some fans deciding to wear boiler suits, and even more forgetting that water and sun cream were a thing, I'd gotten to see Carmilla when they opened the main stage on Saturday. The audience hadn't been enormous, but you'd have thought they were playing to a crowd of millions.

A smile stretched across my lips as I began to sing along, jumping up and down with the rest of the crowd. I could almost feel my batteries recharging, filling up my creative well and making my body thrum with energy. I'd needed this.

The band mixed older tracks with new, including their latest single I'd had on repeat all afternoon. A couple of times Mayday stopped to talk to the crowd as the band all took a quick break to throw back some water. She was funny and charismatic, like so many of the best lead singers, and told a quick story of the band getting lost in New York, which had led to them writing the next song. "And if you know it, you better be screaming. I wanna hear all of you, bitches!"

I knew which song it was going to be before they even played the opening note: 'Creature of Chaos'.

I loved their entire catalogue but that song was my obsession. One day I was going to put together the perfect lip-sync to it, and getting to watch Mayday sing it live was my fucking dream come true.

The crowd surged forward, everyone jumping up and down, hands in the air as chaotic energy pulsed through us. I was pushed forward, sliding through a gap in the crowd until I was stood less than three feet behind Rhys. My breath caught in my chest, but I didn't know if it was the press of the crowd, the adrenaline, or the sight of Rhys, arms in the air and a wild smile on his face. He turned to look at his brother, mouth open like he was going to say something.

Then the elbow of the man stood in front of him shot backwards and I watched Rhys's head jerk back in slow motion, blood spurting from his nose as he crumpled over. There was no sound, not with the speakers so close, but in my mind I heard the sickening crunch of bone.

My instincts kicked in and I moved without thinking.

"Out of my way," I snarled as I pushed my way towards him. His twin had pulled him to his feet, and even in the spiralling red light I saw the concern on his face. Rhys was clutching his nose as his brother looked around, and I knew he was looking for a way out. He must have seen me moving towards them because he frowned, but then Rhys turned and I watched his expression light up.

"Funny seeing you here," he said, letting go of his nose as I finally arrived next to him. There was blood running down his face and the bridge of his nose was already starting to swell, his eyes shining with tears.

"Causing trouble again," I said before turning to his brother, who was staring at us. The music was so loud I was almost shouting. "I'm Evan. I'm a paramedic. We need to get Rhys out of here so I can look at his nose."

"You haven't got a tissue, have you?" Rhys asked. "I paid nearly sixty quid for this hoodie and I don't want to ruin it."

"You're an idiot," I said, rolling my eyes before grabbing his wrist and starting to drag him out of the crowd. "Don't fucking touch it. You'll make it worse."

There would be first aiders somewhere in the crowd, probably by the stage with the security or at the side. Part of me was tempted to take Rhys to them and leave him there so he could annoy them instead, but the rest of me knew that wasn't an option. My training had kicked in, not to mention the damned protective instinct that had been my undoing since it had first emerged when I was eight.

I pulled Rhys towards the back of the crowd, growling at anyone in my path until they got out of my fucking way.

"We're not leaving, are we?" Rhys asked as we reached the back of the room. In front of me, I saw the bright lights of the entrance hall. That was where we needed to be. "It's only blood."

"We're going out here," I said, dragging him out past a couple of concerned security personnel, who I waved away. They'd probably go and fetch someone, but I wanted to check Rhys out before they arrived. "I think your nose is broken and I want to check."

"Broken?" asked a second voice with the same Welsh lilt as Rhys's but slightly lighter. I realised his twin had followed us out and was looking between the pair of us, waiting for an answer.

"Yes, broken." I pulled Rhys to a stop under one of the lights and positioned him in front of me. Typically, I didn't have any gloves with me.

"Does he need to go to hospital?"

"I'm not going to hospital," Rhys said.

"You don't get an opinion," I said as I gently grasped the edge of his jaw. "Lean forward. We need to stop your nosebleed. Can you pinch your nose or does that hurt?"

"I don't know. I—" He tilted forward and put his fingers on his nose, then yelped. "Fuck!"

"Still think it's not broken?" I asked. I wasn't usually this sarcastic with patients, but for him I'd make an exception. Except... his brother was still looking worried and goddammit. "It's going to be fine. It's not out of line, which is a good sign, and there's no cuts or open wounds. Do you have a headache? Any blurred or double vision?"

"No," Rhys said, trying to shake his head and stopping almost immediately. "It just hurts."

"It's going to. Any eye or neck pain?"

"No."

"Good. Do you have a stiff neck? And numbness or tingling in your arms?"

Rhys wiggled the fingers on his other hand. "No, all good."

"Good." He hadn't started vomiting either, and he also hadn't collapsed or passed out, and he didn't seem to have any difficulty speaking, which were all good signs as that ruled out a severe head injury, at least at this stage. I crouched down and looked at his nose, which looked like it was starting to stop bleeding. I really wished I had some wipes or tissues, anything to clean him up. It would let me check for any signs of cerebrospinal fluid, and while my gut instinct told me there wouldn't be any, I had to check because even the tiniest sign of it would mean Rhys needed to go to A&E immediately.

I pulled my phone out of my jeans and turned the torch on. "Close your eyes. I'm going to shine the torch on your face."

"Why?"

"Rhys, just do as you're told," his brother said and I chuckled.

"I like you," I said, shooting him a quick smile. "Is he always this annoying?"

"Sometimes," he said. "I'm Ianto by the way."

"Nice to meet you."

"Are you sure you don't need me to call anyone?"

"No," I said, looking back at Rhys. "I'm sure the first aider will be here any second, but it looks like it's only a minor break, so he should be able to go home." His nose was swollen and already starting to bruise, and by the look of it, the bruising was going to spread under his eyes as well. "You're just going to have a couple of spectacular black eyes."

"Shame it's not Halloween, really. I wouldn't need any make-up." Rhys grinned at me, but even I could see it was forced. He was in pain and trying to push through it.

I sighed. "Don't do that," I said quietly.

"Do what?"

"Pretend you're fine. You're not."

His lip twitched, the familiar mischief sparking in his eyes. "Aww, you do care."

"And now it's gone." I stood up to see Ianto still watching us. He was trying not to smile and I suddenly wondered if he knew what'd happened between us.

I decided I didn't care. Tonight didn't change anything.

I was only doing my job.

CHAPTER EIGHT

Rhys

"You don't need to fuss," I said as Evan opened my front door and gestured for me to go inside. "I'm not dying."

"I don't give a fuck. Get inside and sit down," Evan said as he followed me in and shut the door loudly. Under normal circumstances, I'd have been delighted to have him back in my house, but my nose was fucking throbbing and it was making my whole face ache. The first aider at Rock City had cleaned my face up and put an ice pack on it, but she'd agreed with Evan that I didn't need to go to hospital and she'd been happy to release me into his care.

Ianto had hovered worriedly during the whole thing, refusing to go back in and enjoy the rest of the concert despite me pointing out how much we'd been looking forward to it. I'd tried to argue he should go back in and then tell me about it, but he'd shot down all my points and in the end I'd had to give in—mostly because Evan had told me to stop talking.

I bloody hoped Carmilla came back on tour soon, or at least did a UK festival date, so I could see the rest of the set.

After all his hovering, I'd expected Ianto to come home with me, but when the Uber had arrived to take me back, he'd grinned and told me Evan would take good care of me and he'd call tomorrow. Bastard. If I didn't know any better, I'd say he was setting me up. In fact, he probably was, given everything I'd told him. Ianto was a bloody romantic at heart, and while I'd been very happy to watch him get swept off his feet, that didn't mean I wanted the same to happen to me.

Not that I could see Evan doing much of that. He didn't seem like the romantic type either.

"Sit," Evan said again, pointing at the sofa. I didn't have the energy to disagree with him. The pain was overriding my desire to be annoying. I'd had plenty of broken bones before, but I'd always managed to avoid my nose. I really hoped it wasn't going to need resetting. "Do you have any paracetamol? You probably need another ice pack too. Do you have any?"

"No," I said, resisting the urge to shake my head. "No ice packs. The paracetamol's in the kitchen. Second drawer down under the kettle."

"Stay there. I'll be back in a second." He shot me a glare before he stalked off through the house. I wasn't sure what he was expecting me to start doing—dancing around the living room? Head banging? Even the thought made me feel sick.

Fuck, I was supposed to be teaching in the morning. Was I allowed to do any exercise with a broken nose? It wouldn't be too bad if I could just walk around and help out rather than getting involved. I'd be able to find someone to help me demonstrate—there were enough regulars in my classes who could do that with their eyes closed.

I heard Evan rummaging around in the kitchen, but even craning my neck I couldn't see him. I thought I heard him open the freezer as well, but that didn't make any sense because I'd already told him I didn't have any ice packs.

"Here," Evan said as he walked back into the room. He was holding a glass of water in one hand and tucked under his arm was something wrapped in a tea towel. He handed that to me first as he said, "Frozen peas. They'll help with the swelling. Put them on your nose several times a day. Just make sure they're wrapped up."

"Gotta love a bag of frozen peas," I said. It made sense why he'd opened the freezer now and I couldn't believe I hadn't thought of it. "Miracle cure, they are."

"Use them a lot?"

"Not recently, but when I was younger." I took the glass of water he passed me along with two paracetamol. "Used to get into all sorts of scrapes and scraps."

"I can believe that," he said as he sat down on the other end of the sofa, watching me carefully. "I can't believe you've grown out of it, though."

"Hey, I could be a mature adult now."

"Are you?"

"No, why the fuck would I do that? Sounds boring to

me." I grinned as I took the painkillers and gently put the glass of water on the floor since the little table at the end of the sofa was at his end, not mine. "I'm responsible when I have to be, but you've got to have a little fun in life, otherwise what's the point?"

I lifted the peas and gently held them against my nose, hissing and wincing as they made contact with my skin. Even through the tea towel they were fucking freezing, and it stung worse than any wasp or jellyfish sting I'd endured.

"What do you count as fun?" Evan asked. He was leaning back into the corner of the sofa, one leg crossed over the other, those piercing eyes fixed on me and full of curiosity. It made my stomach twist, and I couldn't decide if it was a good or bad feeling. I wasn't even sure why he was still here, but I was glad he was. Being alone and injured would be the worst thing in the world. In the past, I'd always had Ianto to give me sympathy, and take the piss out of me too, but there'd always been someone with me.

And I didn't want to imagine going through it alone.

But I'd have to at some point. Because Evan wasn't going to stay forever. And Ianto didn't need me anymore.

"Probably not the same things you would," I said.

"How do you know?"

"Well, Ianto and I are training for our next Ironman," I said, watching as his face wrinkled in shock. It was a little hard to see from behind the tea towel, but the change in his expression was so dramatic I nearly burst out laughing.

"Those are the ridiculous triathlons, aren't they? Where you have to run a marathon and swim... I don't know, like thirty miles or some shit." He looked horrified at the very idea of it.

"Actually, the swimming is the shortest part, only two point four miles. The bike ride is a hundred and twelve miles, and then you finish with a marathon. Ianto and I have done three of them now, two at Tenby in Wales, which is great but hilly as fuck, and then one in Bolton. I keep trying to persuade Ianto to sign up to one in Europe, get a nice little holiday out of it, but I've not managed so far. Mind you, I never thought I'd get him doing more than one the amount he whined about doing the first, but as soon as we finished he asked about signing up for the following year."

"I still can't believe you'd sign up for one in the first place." He pulled a face and shuddered dramatically. "It sounds like torture to me."

"It gets a bit painful towards the end, but it's not horrible."

"That's because you're running on adrenaline and would happily do all sorts of ridiculous things."

"Probably, but honestly the most painful thing I've ever done is pole dancing," I said, watching his expression to see his reaction. I'd been doing pole for nearly five years now, and the responses I got ranged from the ridiculous to the sublime. Some people couldn't understand why I'd want to "learn to dance like a stripper", which always got them the patented Rhys special of me asking them to explain what they meant in excruciating detail until they realised the error of their ways, some people got super excited and started asking questions, and some wanted me to demonstrate for them, which was always a bit fucking weird.

"Seriously? You pole dance? I'd never have expected that but... I can see it." He smiled and my stomach flipped. "How long have you been doing it?"

"About five years. Ianto and I always said we wanted to try as many sports as possible, so we thought we'd give it a go and it kind of stuck. I've never been particularly graceful, but I can get by pretty well since I focus mostly on strength-based stuff. I'm not really a performer, although Connor—he's my instructor—seems to live in hope that I'll give competing a go one day, but I really like it." I grinned at him over the top of the frozen peas, which felt like they were starting to defrost. "It's bloody painful, though. I'm surprised I've still got any feeling left between my thighs."

Evan's eyes met mine and for a second I wondered if he was going to take the bait. But all he said was, "From Superman?"

"Mostly, and leg hangs too and..." I trailed off and stared at him as my exhausted brain put two and two together. "How do you know what a Superman is?"

He shrugged. "I did a little bit of pole at university before I really got into drag. It was fun, painful but fun. But I only had time to keep one up and drag won."

"You're a drag queen?" How the fuck had I not noticed I lived next door to a fucking drag queen? Had I been living under a rock for the past six months? "How the fuck did I not know this?"

Evan shrugged again, a tiny smile playing across his lips and a glint in his eyes. "You clearly don't pay that much attention. That and I don't tend to go out in drag a lot. Most weeks I get ready at the club I perform at, and if I do come home with my make-up on, it's usually very late."

"Can I see you in drag?" I asked. I was trying to picture Evan in drag, but nothing I imagined quite fit him. Maybe I was going too pretty and pink… there had to be alternative drag queens out there, and that seemed more likely. Although maybe he'd look cute in bubblegum pink with Barbie hair.

"No."

"Why not?"

"Because… Fine. But not tonight."

"You know I could just find you on Instagram," I said slyly.

"You can try, but I don't post photos of myself out of drag."

"Why not?" I moved the peas on my nose, trying not to wince. "Is it because of your job?"

He thought for a second and I wondered if he'd ever had this conversation with anyone. He was obviously a very private man, but there was a difference between private and closed off, and I was beginning to think Evan was the latter. I mean, he had to have friends, didn't he? But he'd been alone at the gig tonight. Did he keep all his little bubbles separate and think they'd never overlap? Or did they never overlap because he didn't let them?

My head was starting to spin and that was enough to stop me thinking. Any more thoughts could come tomorrow when I wasn't in so much pain.

"A little," he said eventually. "A few people at my day

job know, and they're all fine with it. But it only takes one asshole. And after last year…" He trailed off and shook his head. "How's your nose? Let me have a look."

I lifted the peas and wished I'd been able to get another five minutes of conversation out of him. Now I'd had a taste of what was under the surface, I wanted more. I needed to peel back the layers and see what was underneath this gorgeous, grumpy bastard because there was clearly more to him than sarcasm and snark.

"Well, the good news is your nose won't need realigning and you don't seem to have any symptoms of a more serious injury."

"Thank heaven for small mercies then. What's the bad news?"

"You're going to have some cracking bruising," he said, his lip twitching like he wanted to smile but was holding himself back. "Under both eyes and across your nose."

"I'll have to come up with a plausible story then," I said, winking at him. "Maybe a fight with a bear or something."

"As long as your brother doesn't ruin it by telling the truth."

"Too late for that. He's probably told his boyfriend everything by now." I groaned. "Still, at least it wasn't you that injured me."

"Why would that matter?"

"That's how Ianto ended up with Ben. Broke Ben's collarbone at rugby practice at the end of November a couple of years ago and then ended up helping him with his pre-Christmas to-do list since Ben runs a pub and he's always busy. And that was how they fell in love. Bit sickening if you ask me, but at least I can forever tease him about breaking his boyfriend's collarbone."

Evan looked at me and for a second I thought I might've said too much. I wasn't trying to compare us with Ben and Ianto, but it probably sounded like that. God, I'd really put my fucking foot in it.

But instead of pulling away like I'd expected, Evan actually smiled. "Sorry to disappoint, but injuries aren't really a turn-on for me. They're just work."

I laughed, ignoring the shooting pain through my cheekbones. "Ah well, good thing you rescued me instead then."

CHAPTER NINE

Eva Nessence

I HADN'T PLANNED on bringing Milo and Grace back to mine on Friday after picking them up from school, but with starting my first night shift at seven after ten days off, I really wanted to eat something before I left and it was easier to do that at mine where I could shove any leftovers into the fridge.

I wanted to check on Rhys too, because I hadn't seen him all day and there was a nagging voice in the back of my mind telling me to make sure he wasn't dead. I didn't think he was—I was sure I'd heard him moving around that morning—but my brain kept insisting that wasn't good enough.

It needed proof of life.

"Okay," I said as I helped Grace out of her car seat, collecting her lunch box and reading bag before they got left to fester on the back seat all weekend. She was six, and half the time it seemed like she'd forget her own head if it wasn't attached to her shoulders. "I need to check on my neighbour and then we'll go in. Just give me two minutes."

"I can go in," Milo said and held out his hand for my keys. He'd not long turned ten, and sometimes I forgot how big he was getting. I needed to remember he was closer to being a teenager than a toddler, even if the thought terrified me since I remembered exactly what I'd been like at fifteen. "Can I get a drink?"

"Sure. There's squash on the side or some cans of Coke in the fridge. But if you have one now, you're not having one with your tea." I glanced down at Grace as I handed Milo the house keys. "Do you want to go in too?"

"No, I wanna meet your friend," Grace said, grabbing my hand and giving me a cheeky grin.

"All right, come on then." I walked over to Rhys's door, Grace beside me, and knocked loudly as Milo opened my front door and stepped inside, kicking off his school shoes. At least I didn't have to remind him about that this time. "Milo, leave the door open. I'll just be here."

"I know. I'm not going to lock you out."

I chuckled. The pre-teen sarcasm was strong with that one.

"Why do you need to check on your neighbour?" Grace asked as we waited.

"Because he broke his nose yesterday, and I want to make sure he feels okay."

"That's nice of you."

I snorted. "I suppose. You wouldn't check on your friends if they had a broken nose?"

"I don't know." She shrugged. "Maybe. Depends how they got it."

I bit back a laugh. Damn, my niece was brutal. Although with me for an uncle, I wasn't sure what else I'd expect. Maybe I needed to learn to be slightly less salty when I was around them.

The door swung open and my choked-back laughter turned into a whistle of shock. Rhys's nose wasn't any more swollen, which was a good sign, but there was a massive purple bruise all across it which had spread across his cheekbones and under his eyes. It was so dark in places it looked almost black, and it looked more like he'd been in a cage fight with an angry tiger than a mosh pit.

"Looking good, Rocky," I said. "How're you feeling?"

"Like someone's shoved cotton wool up my nose and hit me in the face with a brick," Rhys said, grimacing. He looked down at Grace and gave her a little smile. "Hello, I'm Rhys. What's your name?"

"I'm Grace," she said. "Evan said you broke your nose. Is that why your face is purple?"

I pursed my lips, because while I loved my niece with all my heart, I wished she'd skip the "so direct she was painfully blunt" stage and learn subtlety. Although I knew adults who hadn't even mastered that, so I wasn't sure why I expected better of a six-year-old.

"Unfortunately," Rhys said. He bent down slightly so he was a little more on her level. "Would you believe me if I told you I got into a fight with a bear?"

Grace giggled and shook her head. "No."

"What about a ginormous octopus with hundreds of tentacles?"

"No," she said with another laugh.

"Oh, you want the truth then." He leant forward like he was whispering conspiratorially. "It's because I'm a secret agent and I rescued Evan from being kidnapped. I'm like a knight in shining armour, only I don't have a horse."

Her giggling turned into full-on laughter and I smiled. Rhys might be annoying but he hadn't ignored Grace or brushed her off and that made something twist and fizz in my chest, like my heart was a Mentos being dropped into a vat of Coke.

"Come here then, Mr Secret Agent," I said, beckoning him firmly with one finger. "Let me take a look at this heroic nose of yours."

"Don't touch it. It really hurts."

"I'm not going to touch it. I'm just going to look at it."

"You can look with your eyes then!"

I sighed and reached forward to grasp his jaw. "I can't look at it if you're all the way over there. Come here."

Grace giggled again, and I felt her eyes on us. Rhys grumbled but begrudgingly straightened up and leant into my touch. "How do I know you're a real paramedic?" he asked teasingly. "You could be making it up for all I know."

"Like your secret service career?"

"My involvement with any secret service operations is classified."

"Sure." I tilted his face, checking his nose from every angle. The swelling hadn't gotten worse and it didn't seem to have bled again, judging by the lack of dried blood around his nostrils. It wasn't out of line either.

"Well, Doctor Doom?" Rhys asked. "Can I be released now?"

"If I was Doctor Doom, we wouldn't be having this conversation on a doorstep in the middle of Nottingham. You'd be in my dungeon in Latveria. If I even acknowledged you at all. You're not exactly Reed Richards or Spider-Man."

"How do you know I'm not? Maybe I am and I haven't told you."

"Because I highly doubt you could keep anything to yourself," I said with a raised eyebrow as I released him.

"Ouch, that hurts." He clutched his chest dramatically. "I'm not that bad."

"On a scale of one to ten, I'd say you're a twelve. And that's a scale of annoyance, before you get any ideas."

"Am I on that scale?" Grace asked, tugging my hand. "Milo says I'm annoying sometimes."

"Is that because you interrupted him while he was in his room?" I asked, knowing full well the answer was yes.

Grace was a hurricane of energy and action, while Milo was quieter and more introverted. She was the sort of person who'd grow up being the life and soul of an enormous friend group, drawing people to her with charisma and magnetic charm, while Milo would be more like me, with a few close friends who enjoyed going out occasionally but needing time to recover afterwards. And both of them would have to learn how to live with each other and their different social needs, which was already challenging and only going to get more so as they got older.

"Only a few times. But I wanted him to play football with me."

"Do you like football?" Rhys asked.

"Yeah!"

"Who's your favourite player?"

Grace thought for a second. "Kelly Smith."

"Good choice," Rhys said, smiling brightly.

"She's really cool," Grace said.

"You got her shirt for Christmas, didn't you?" I put my arm around her shoulder and pulled her in for a tiny hug. Kirsty had been looking around for a football team for Grace to join, but it was trying to fit it around everything else since a lot of them practised and played on weekend mornings. And there was the cost to consider alongside the time.

I kept debating whether to offer to pay for it, but I wasn't sure Kirsty would accept. She'd been muttering about taking up too much of my time recently and I didn't want her to think that at all. She could have as much of my time as she needed, no questions asked, because it was the least I could do after everything she'd done for me growing up.

If it wasn't for Kirsty, I doubted I'd be where I was. She'd been more of a mother to me than our actual mother, and she'd given up everything to look after me, even though there was only five years between us. And that was something I'd never be able to repay.

"Yeah, it's so cool!" Grace was fizzing with energy and

almost bouncing on the spot as she looked up at me. "Can I play now?"

"If you can find the ball," I said. "I think it's in the garden somewhere." Garden was a bit of a stretch for the small yard attached to the back of my house, but it counted as outside space and required very little maintenance since it had been paved over at some point by a previous owner. I had a few flowerpots out there, which were filled with plants that grew well under my specific brand of benevolent neglect, and some herb boxes hung on the trellis that topped the back wall, which exploded in the summer months with every variety of herb I'd managed to cram into them. And a few that seemed to have migrated there from someone else's garden.

"Will you play with me?" Grace asked with pleading eyes.

"I'm sorry, I need to make tea. You can ask Milo."

She made an exasperated sound. "He never wants to play. He's so boring."

"I'll play with you," Rhys said and my eyes snapped to him. "As long as Evan says it's okay. And I promise I won't let the ball go anywhere near my face." He crossed his heart dramatically, like he was swearing some kind of blood oath.

"I thought you were in pain?"

He waved it off. "I'll be fine. It's not exactly strenuous." He grinned at Grace. "And it'll be fun!"

"Please!" Grace said. "Please, Evan, can Rhys come round and play? I promise I won't kick it at his face."

I looked between them, trying not to laugh when I realised they both had the same excited look on their face, like puppies waiting for me to throw a ball. "Yes, Rhys can come round. But no heading the ball, no kicking it at my flowerpots, and no kicking it at the door or kitchen window. And you can use the chalk in the kitchen to draw a goal on the wall."

"Awesome! Let me just grab some shoes," Rhys said.

"No rush," I said, but he'd already disappeared behind the door to find his trainers. I looked down at Grace. "Why don't you go inside and get changed? Your joggers and hoodies are clean. They're in the bottom drawer in your room."

"Okay!" Grace hurtled through my front door, her feet hammering on the floor as she ran towards the stairs and the spare bedroom I'd dubbed hers and Milo's. She obviously hadn't remembered to take her shoes off. I heard her talking excitedly to Milo and I chuckled.

"Are you sure this is okay?" Rhys asked, reappearing from behind the door with trainers on and a zip-up hoodie in one hand.

"Yeah, she's desperate for someone to play with and it'll stop her from annoying her brother, and that means no arguments. I love them both, but I don't have the energy to referee tonight. Especially since I have to be at work at seven."

Rhys nodded and I stepped back to let him out, watching as he patted his jogging bottoms pockets, checking for his keys and phone. "Makes sense. So are they…"

He left the question hanging in the air.

"They're my niblings," I said. "My sister, Kirsty, is their

mum. But she works at Tesco, so her shifts can be a bit all over. I do the school run a lot and the odd overnight if she's finishing really late or starting really early. Then I'll usually hang around and babysit until she gets back."

Rhys looked at me and I could see him putting the pieces together. I wondered if he'd realised that was where I'd been coming back from when we'd hooked up.

To my surprise, he didn't say anything about it. All he said was, "Well, you'll get a good laugh today. I can't remember the last time I played football, so I think I'm about to have my butt handed to me by a child."

I laughed as he closed his door and headed for mine. He paused on the doorstep just ahead of me and looked over his shoulder with a smirk on his lips. "By the way, if you wanted to put me in a dungeon, all you have to do is ask."

He winked and walked into my house, leaving me staring at him and his fucking perfect ass, wondering what the hell I was doing.

CHAPTER TEN

Rhys

"How old is Grace?" I asked Evan. I'd ducked into the kitchen to grab a drink and take a sneaky break because my broken nose was definitely affecting my ability to breathe, and pretending it didn't hurt had been a stupid move on my part.

Evan had said I wasn't allowed to do strenuous exercise for two weeks and had to avoid sports that might involve facial contact for at least six. That had sounded like torture at first, but maybe he had a point. I quite liked being able to breathe.

Evan looked over from the large pan of bolognese simmering on the hob. It smelt bloody delicious and my stomach rumbled, but I ignored it because it wasn't really my place to ask for food. I was surprised he'd let me come over in the first place. "She's six," he said. "She'll be seven in May. And Milo's ten."

I looked around for Milo, and while I could hear him moving around in the living room, it wasn't possible for us to see what he was doing.

"Why?" Evan added as he tapped the wooden spoon on the edge of the pan and put it on the chopping board next to him.

"Just curious," I said, leaning against the counter opposite him. Evan's kitchen was small, and unlike mine, built into an extension on the back of his house. "She's very good —got a lot of control of the ball."

"Yeah?"

I glanced out of the window behind me, which didn't show much of the garden but I could just about see Grace, her plaits bouncing in the air as her head moved. "Yeah. I started teaching her to do keepie uppies just to see how she got on, and she's already managed to do seven. Apparently, she wants to get to at least ten before tea."

Evan whistled quietly. "Impressive. At least, it sounds it. I'm not particularly sporty, so I doubt I could even do one."

"They take practice," I said. "I used to be obsessed with them when I was a kid. Did them all the time in the playground and at home until Tadcu threatened to take the ball away. That might've been because I tried to do them in the kitchen and broke two glasses." I chuckled at the memory. Ianto and I had really tested the patience of Tadcu, our Welsh grandfather who we'd lived with from the age of five, but he'd only really gotten cross with us when one of us had put ourselves, or someone else, in danger.

I still didn't know how he'd done it, taking on two slightly traumatised, unloved, and energetic twin boys in his fifties, but he'd done it with no small amount of grace and love. He was the only person in the world I considered my parent, and I loved him more than anything. We still talked virtually every day, even if it was just about work or the weather or whatever village gossip Tadcu had heard, especially since I'd introduced him to WhatsApp. For someone who pretended he wasn't interested in what went on in the small village he lived in on the coast of South Wales, Tadcu was a terrible gossip and I loved it.

Evan was looking at me, and I wondered if he was trying to work out who I meant by Tadcu since most English people weren't familiar with any Welsh vocabulary.

"Tadcu is my grandfather," I said. "Ianto and I grew up with him in South Wales."

He nodded, then smiled. "No wonder he was annoyed with you doing keepie uppies in the kitchen if you broke shit."

"It was only once! I did a lot worse."

"That's another thing that doesn't surprise me." His eyes roamed over me and I could see that sparkling gleam in them. The one that meant nothing but good things for me. "I bet you were a hellion."

"That's one way to say it," I said with a grin. "I'd say more like..." I glanced around and then mouthed, "Absolute twat."

Evan snorted. "You said it."

"I'll admit it. Maybe not as a kid, but as a teenager... I'm surprised Tadcu didn't throttle me." I thought back to all the stupid shit Ianto and I had done—everything from jumping off cliffs, getting drunk in the park with our friends from school until we'd thrown up everywhere, and "borrowing" Tadcu's car when we were sixteen. That was probably the stupidest thing since it was illegal, neither of us could drive, it was the middle of winter, and our parents had been killed in a car accident. It was the closest I'd ever seen Tadcu to losing it, but the disappointment in his face had hurt more than any bollocking he could've given us.

That'd been the kick in the ass Ianto and I had needed to get our shit together and channel everything we had into trying to be better. We'd always been into sport, and it wasn't long after that we'd decided we'd aim to study it at university.

We'd ended up at Nottingham Trent because Tadcu had thought a fresh start somewhere new would be good for us but Nottingham still had a direct train line to Cardiff. We'd loved the city so much we'd stayed. And now that Ianto was with Ben, who'd never leave his beloved pub, I doubted we'd ever leave. Because even if we lived apart, I couldn't imagine living more than five miles from my brother. Any further would be like ripping out part of my soul.

"I think we all did stuff we regret as teenagers," Evan said, and the expression on his face said he was speaking from experience. "It's part of growing up."

"As long as it makes you grow up and you don't turn being a dickhead into your whole personality. Oh shit, I probably shouldn't say that."

Evan chuckled. "You're fine. I doubt either of them are listening, and Kirsty and I have already had the whole swearing conversation."

There was a thump from the front room and both of us turned our heads. "Milo?" Evan called. "You okay?"

"Yeah." A loud sniff followed his words and Evan grimaced. "Can you keep an eye on that?" he asked, gesturing at the pan. "And if you want a drink, help yourself. There's cans in the fridge, squash, water, tea, coffee."

"I'll be fine. You're not going far." I waved my hand at him before he sped through the house. Something warm flickered in my chest as I watched him. It wasn't just seeing how much he cared about his niblings but how much of himself he obviously gave away. He was a paramedic, a drag queen, and regularly cared for two kids—that was a lot, however you sliced it, and even if he wouldn't admit it, I had a strong suspicion Evan was the sort of man who'd give himself to everyone else without saving anything for himself.

"Rhys?" Evan called. "Can you grab me one of the gel ice packs out of the freezer, please? There's a cover for it in the second drawer down next to the freezer."

"Everything okay?" I asked as I opened the freezer drawer and bent down to retrieve the specified pack. I'd wondered if I'd have to go rummaging through the drawers, but it was sitting on the top shelf next to a frozen loaf of bread, which was open and half-used, and a box of fruit splits.

"Yeah, Milo's twisted his ankle."

I grabbed the ice pack and found the cover, shoving the frozen gel inside. I glanced at the bolognese, but it didn't seem in danger of exploding or burning, and a quick look out the back door told me Grace was still occupied, so I hurried through to the living room.

Milo was sitting on the sofa looking like he was trying very hard not to cry. His foot was resting on Evan's thigh with his sock off and the leg of his jogging bottoms pulled up.

"Looks like it's not just me in the wars," I said as I handed Evan the covered ice pack.

"Milo is a lot less troublesome than you, though," Evan said dryly as he gently placed the pack on Milo's ankle. He looked back at his nephew and added, "Are you going to tell me what you were trying to do?"

Milo shrugged, his eyes fixed firmly on a random spot on the sofa cushion next to him. "I don't know."

"You're not in any trouble," Evan said. "I promise."

"It's stupid," Milo muttered.

"No, it's not."

There was a pause, and then Milo said so quietly I almost missed it, "I was trying to do a pirouette and I slipped on the floor."

"Were you wearing socks?" I asked. Evan's two main downstairs rooms had a polished, wood laminate floor that'd be easy to slip on. Milo screwed up his face. "It's just if you're going to do pirouettes, you'll need a bit more grip. Either from bare feet or some dance shoes."

"I don't have any dance shoes," Milo said. "I… I don't… I like watching videos on YouTube."

I nodded and crouched down beside him. Reading between the lines of what Evan had said with the babysitting and Kirsty working a lot, and from what Grace had said when we'd been outside about wanting to play more but not being able to, it was clear there wasn't much money for things like dance or football.

"What sort of dance do you like?" I asked, glancing at Evan, who was watching me with interest. "Ballet? Latin? Bit of ballroom? Or more like modern and street dance?"

Milo looked at me suspiciously as if he thought it might be a trap, which made sense because I was a fucking stranger who'd annoyed his way into his uncle's house. "I like ballet. I saw a video of a guy doing some on YouTube and it looked fun."

"Ballet is fun," I said with my best encouraging smile. "It's hard work, though. My friend Connor is a ballet dancer. He's got pointe shoes and everything."

"Boys can't do pointe," Milo said, but he didn't sound convinced, like he was testing the waters to see if I'd confirm or deny his suspicions.

"Of course they can. It just takes a lot of practice and proper pointe shoes, the ones you have to break in."

"I've seen videos of that!" Milo grinned. "Where they have to hit them on the floor and bend them until they crack so they fit."

"Sounds like somebody needs to make better pointe shoes," Evan said dryly.

"No," Milo said, shaking his head. "It's because everyone needs them different! And I try and practice. I know all my foot positions now." He wiggled his toes and flexed his other foot, which was resting on the floor. "Fifth is weird, though. I feel like a penguin."

"Is that what you've been doing in here whenever you

come visit?" Evan asked. It didn't sound like he'd known and there was a tightness in his voice he was trying desperately to hide. I didn't think it was from what Milo had been doing, but more that he hadn't known. Guilt was a powerful thing.

"Sometimes." He shrugged. "Sometimes I practice at home too."

"Would you ever want to take lessons?"

"Maybe but... they're expensive. I looked."

"Let me talk to your mum," Evan said. He was frowning and I could see the cogs whirring inside his mind. "In the meantime, you're going to sit here and ice your ankle while I finish tea. And no more pirouettes in socks."

"Okay," Milo said. "Can I keep watching videos on YouTube?"

"Sure," Evan said and handed him the TV remote. Neither of us commented on the fact Milo had said "keep watching" or that the TV was off. It was easy to see he'd turned it off before Evan had come to find him after he'd gone splat. "But only on your profile. And you know if you see anything that makes you uncomfortable, then you tell me."

"I will."

"Thank you." Evan carefully put his leg on the sofa and stood up, kissing the top of Milo's head. "I'll be in the kitchen if you need me."

I followed him out, sticking my head out of the back door and checking on Grace, who delightedly told me she'd reached ten keepie uppies, before turning back to Evan. He was stirring the sauce with a fierceness I'd never seen anyone use on bolognese and when he put some water on for the pasta, he virtually slammed the saucepan on the hob, spilling water across the surface and making the gas flame of the next burner hiss.

"Everything okay?" I asked. I knew the answer was no, but there didn't seem to be another way to open the conversation. Evan was private enough that running straight at him with questions was going to be like running headfirst into a brick wall.

He let out a low grunt, then salted the pasta water and flicked the gas on. "No, not really."

"Want to talk about it?"

"Not really." He chuckled, but it was dry and hollow. "Just… feeling like a shit uncle. How the hell did I not know Milo liked ballet? Why didn't he tell me?"

"Hey now, that's not on you," I said. "He'll have his reasons. Kids are just as complicated as adults. Maybe he didn't think you'd take it well. Does he know you do drag?"

"Yeah, but I guess to him that's totally different. Doesn't help his dad was a total knob," Evan muttered. "He used to pull all that 'you're a boy' and 'you're a girl' shit on both of them. Honestly, I'm glad he pissed off because they're better off without him."

"What happened?"

Evan glanced around and shook his head. "I'll tell you another day. I don't want…"

"It's fine," I said. "Sorry, I shouldn't have asked." He'd told me enough anyway and it was clear that even without his father's toxic influence, Milo was still struggling. "Hey, if it helps, my friend Connor actually is a dance teacher—he's my pole instructor, but he teaches ballet too. Want me to ask if there's some good free resources Milo can watch? Or if there's a place to get him some cheap shoes? I don't know anything about ballet shoes, so I'm bloody useless, but Connor will know."

"That's very kind of you but—"

"No, I know what you're going to say, and it's no trouble at all."

"But—"

"Nope, unless you have a genuine reason for me not asking that doesn't involve your pride or some absurd idea that you're annoying someone, then I'm asking."

He pursed his lips together. "Fine. Thank you."

"You're welcome." I grinned. "See, was that so hard?"

"Yes." He smirked and reached for a tall storage tub filled with spaghetti. "Are you staying for tea? I know it's early."

"Are you asking me to stay?" I had to hear him say it. Not only because I needed to know I wasn't overstepping, but because I needed him to admit he wanted me here.

"Stay," he said quietly. "Please."

"Of course."

His expression softened, and his smile was the most genuine I'd ever seen. It made something spark and fizz in my chest, and a sense of overwhelming glee started to build inside me.

I was going to tear down those walls around Evan's heart, even if I had to use a catapult and a battering ram to do it.

CHAPTER ELEVEN

Eva Nessence

"Do any of you hoes need another drink?" Eli asked, sticking his head around the living room door and giving us all the once-over. "Or should I just bring through more wine?"

"More wine, please!" Rory said from his position curled up on the end of the sofa. We were having a movie night at Eli's, with Bubblegum and me being joined by several of the other performers from The Court: drag king Moxxie Toxxic and drag queens Legs Luthor, Scary-Kate, and Slashley.

The latter two were frequently referred to as the murder twins, given their propensity to dress up as characters from horror movies, including two girls from *The Shining*. In reality, they weren't even related, just two guys who'd been best friends since forever and were permanently attached at the hip.

Their make-up skills were good enough that in drag they were virtually indistinguishable, bar a small difference in height, but out of it, they were easier to tell apart. Slash's hair changed colour whenever he got bored and he had tattoos, whereas Kate's hair was a gorgeous natural red, and his phobia of needles meant the only time he went near a tattoo parlour was when he went to hold Slash's hand.

Sparkles and I had once wondered if they were dating, or even casually fucking, but neither of us were sure since they'd mentioned boyfriends in the past and Kate had apparently been dating someone for the last eight months. None of us had met him, though, and he'd never been to one of her shows, which was never a good sign in my opinion.

Drag was such a big part of all our lives that I couldn't imagine not sharing it with the person I was supposed to be closest to. And if they couldn't be bothered to take even the smallest bit of interest in something so important to me, then what was the fucking point in even dating them?

"Can I have another Jack and Coke, please?" Moxxie asked. They were stretched out on the floor on a mass of pillows and blankets with Eli and Tristan's two Labradors, Indy and Solo, on either side of them. The dogs had decided Moxxie was their new favourite person, although that might have been because Moxxie treated them both like enormous babies and let both of them try and sit on their lap.

"Wine, Jack and Coke, anything else?"

"I'll just have a Coke, please," I said from my seat between Sparkles and Legs. Despite my initial reservations about coming, mostly because I was exhausted from work and desperate for an early night, I'd had a lot of fun so far. It was reminding me that having a social life wasn't the worst thing in the world.

Legs, wearing one of his famous neon jumpers, looked up from his phone and glanced over at Bitch. "I'll have the same."

"Can we have more vodka orange, please?" Slashley asked. He and Kate were sitting on the smaller two-seater sofa with a blanket across their laps and a giant bowl that had been filled with popcorn balanced in between them. They'd eaten most of it during our first film of the evening, *Bring It On*, which had caused Sparkles and the twins to all ask if people had really dressed like that in the early noughties. But it seemed like spirit fingers might be making a comeback.

"Okay, anything else?" Eli asked as he collected people's glasses.

"Nope," Rory said. "I think we've got everything. There's still some snacks in that bag Legs brought."

"We've got another couple of bags of popcorn too," Kate said, pointing at the bag for life by the sofa. When Eli had asked the three of them to bring snacks, they'd taken that mission to heart and now we had everything from popcorn and Pringles to jelly sweets, sour cherries, and Hello Panda biscuits. And that was on top of the homemade pizzas Eli had whipped up for us. I'd never imagined Bitch being so domestic but being settled and newly engaged seemed to have mellowed him out. It had obviously caught him by surprise too, because last week he'd been talking about buying a bread maker and then he'd had to stop and ask what the hell was going on.

I'd told him that was what being thirty-plus and engaged did to you, and he'd told me if I kept that shit up, he'd make me do another routine with him and Sparkles in latex, like the *Mean Girls*-inspired Christmas one we'd done a few years ago.

And considering how many times Bitch had mentioned the film while teaching us the choreography, I really was surprised Bubblegum hadn't seen it. Maybe she'd been lying just to see Bitch's reaction—it wouldn't be the first time any of us had done it because Bitch was kind of fun to wind up, in a loving, affectionate way.

"Do you need a hand?" I asked, because I felt guilty that Eli was running around after us. I'd have done the same if I'd been hosting, but I always felt bad about people waiting on me while I sat around and did fuck all. I'd always been the friend who offered to help cook, or wash up, or whatever else was needed, even if I was drunk out my ass.

Apparently once in my early twenties, I'd gotten really drunk at a house party along with a bunch of friends, thrown up everywhere, and then tried to offer people glasses of water and toast when they were trying to look after me. I might have been a salty bitch, but I was a polite one.

"If you're offering," Eli said. "If not, I can manage. It's only a few drinks."

"I've got you," I said as I climbed off the sofa and followed him out to the kitchen, leaving everyone else to chat about upcoming shows, new routines, and Rory's plans for a low-key housewarming party since he'd recently moved in with West.

Eli had put the empty glasses on the kitchen counter and was rummaging around in the fridge for some more cans of Coke and some orange juice.

"Where's Tristan this evening?" I asked, grabbing the bottles of Jack Daniels and vodka people had brought and opening the lids. "He didn't fancy joining us?"

"He's gone out for dinner with Dick and Ruby," Bitch said with a grin. "And sadly, I already had plans and was forced to decline the invitation."

I laughed. Richard, or Dick, was Eli's oldest brother and Tristan's best friend, and while Dick and Eli's relationship had improved over the last eighteen months, they weren't exactly close. They'd simply gotten past the "fighting in their parents' front garden like teenage boys" stage. "How sad. I bet you're devastated."

"Truly, it is the saddest day of my life. Although I will admit Ruby is adorable as fuck and I really like her. I only wish I could spend time with her without Dick, but apparently they're a package deal. Married people are so gross."

"Says the man who literally got engaged nine weeks ago."

"I'll be different. I'm a pansexual disaster and an emo trash goblin."

"You also thought about buying a bread maker."

"I can be queer and bake bread. Bread making doesn't just belong to straight people."

I chuckled. "You know, it's not a bad thing. Being married to the person you love."

"I know. It's why I'm actually really looking forward to it." Eli's smile softened as he looked fondly at the glittering engagement ring on his finger. "It's weird. Once upon a time I didn't think I'd get to have this. But now... God, I love that man so fucking much. He's so fucking cute and I just—" He let out a strange happy growl, like a feral cat, and then sighed. "But enough about me. How's things with you? Did you talk to that sexy Welsh bastard yet?"

I swallowed and picked up the bottle of vodka, looking down at the glasses and trying to work out which ones were the twins' so I didn't have to look Eli in the eye. "Er, a little."

"Sparkles said he was at that gig you went to last week. How was it, by the way? You never said." I felt Eli's gaze boring into the side of my head. His voice was sweetly inquisitive, and I knew at any second he was going to go for the kill.

"It was fun," I said. "Carmilla were fucking incredible." In truth I'd hardly thought about the gig again, not because it hadn't been good but because I'd been so concerned about Rhys.

"Really? That's all you have to say? Babe, you've been talking about this gig for *months* and I have to prod you to tell me about it? Nope, something happened and I'm guessing it had something to do with your sexy-as-fuck neighbour. My money is on the two of you banging in the Rock City toilets."

"You'd lose then. We didn't hook up."

"Seriously? Why the fuck not?"

"We just didn't." I spotted a tiny puddle of orange juice

in two glasses, which had to be the twins', and started pouring liberal amounts of vodka into them. Legs was giving them both a ride back into the centre of Lincoln, so it didn't matter if they got a bit wasted.

"Has he got a boyfriend?"

"No." I shook my head. "He's single."

I could practically hear the smirk in Eli's voice when he said, "Is he? And you know this how?"

"Because…" I sighed and put the bottle of vodka down heavily on the counter. "Because he broke his fucking nose in the pit and I ended up having to take care of him because I can't stop bloody working even if it kills me."

Eli put his arm around my waist and squeezed me tightly. "That's because you are a saint. And because you have instincts and can't help it. It's like when Sparkles has a go at us for overloading plug sockets."

I snorted, thinking about all the lectures we'd had from our resident electrician in rhinestones, and picked up the orange juice to top the twins' drinks up. I hoped they liked them strong because I hadn't left much room for the mixer. "Yeah, something like that."

"Want to tell me what happened?"

"Not really but…" I had to tell someone, and Bitch and Sparkles were the two people I was closest to. If I thought about it, they were probably my best friends outside of Kirsty, and I hadn't even considered telling her. "He was stood a few rows in front of me and when they played 'Creature of Chaos', everything got a bit wild and someone elbowed him in the face. I saw it happening and I just went for him… grabbed his hand, dragged him out of the crowd... I didn't even have any gloves." I let out a soft, amused huff. "He has a twin brother, Ianto. The pair of them were there together."

"Is his brother single too?"

"No, he's got a boyfriend. It's why..." I shook my head. It wasn't my place to tell Eli all about Rhys's family, even if it would be a good distraction. "Anyway, Rhys kept insisting his nose wasn't broken, which it was since it was bleeding everywhere, but luckily it wasn't a bad break. The first aider checked him over, I took him home and made him ice it, and we started talking. And now he won't stop."

Eli hummed and I could hear his brain putting all the pieces together. I hadn't told anyone about my hook-up with Rhys, and I wanted to keep it that way, but luckily this story sounded plausible enough to be our first proper interaction.

Putting the juice down, I risked a glance at Eli's face. He caught me looking and smiled. "You know," he said gently. "It'd be okay if you wanted to start something with him, even if it's only casual."

"I know."

"Do you?" He squeezed my waist again. "I love you, darling, but I don't think you know how to put yourself first. You've clearly got some shit going on outside of drag, and I'm not talking about your day job either. I've known you for, what, four years? And I can count on both hands the number of times you've told me really personal shit. That's fine, by the way. You don't have to spill the beans, but it's not a bad thing to let people in. I don't know what you're protecting yourself from, but you and I are both old and ugly enough to know that shutting people out never ends well. So if this annoying Welsh bastard wants to talk to you, why not let him? Why not see where it goes?"

"It's not that simple," I said, my heart racing as it considered the idea of letting Rhys in, even just a little. Because I had too much to balance, too much to do, and I couldn't afford for any of it to be thrown off-kilter. My entire life was like walking the tiniest tightrope, only there was no net to catch me if I fell.

"I know. But it doesn't have to be complicated either." Eli kissed the side of my head. "Don't put everyone and everything else first for so long you forget about yourself. You matter, Evan, and you deserve to see that. And if it takes someone else making you see it, then I'll take that."

"Thanks." The use of my name had caught me off guard, and it felt like someone had walked up behind me and yanked on the back of my T-shirt, pulling me up short and stopping me dead in my tracks.

"You're welcome," Eli said. "And who knows, maybe one day you'll actually listen to me."

I laughed and picked up Moxxie's Jack Daniels. "Does anyone ever do that?"

"No, but there's a first for everything."

CHAPTER TWELVE

Rhys

"I NEED to learn how to cook," I said, slamming Ianto's front door behind me and kicking off my trainers. It was Thursday, which meant Ben was at work, so Ianto and I were having one of our weekly "hang out, chat shit, and watch terrible movies" nights. But today I was a man on a mission.

"Are you sick of living on breakfast food and boiled chicken then?" Ianto asked teasingly as he stuck his head out of the kitchen. Out of the two of us, he'd always been the better cook. It wasn't that I'd refused to learn, since I could make the best breakfasts known to man, but for everything else I'd always had Ianto, so there hadn't been much point.

"It's not for me. It's for Evan."

"Can't he cook?"

"No, it's not that," I said as I walked into the kitchen

and immediately began raiding the fridge for a beer. "It's that he's so bloody busy I don't think he has time for anything. I mean, he can cook, but I thought if I learnt to cook, then I can help him out. You know, when he's come off a night shift or he's looking after the nibs."

I'd filled Ianto in on Evan's situation, leaving out a few of the more private details but giving him a good overview of the situation. My brother wouldn't say anything, not even to Evan. We'd always been able to tell each other everything in confidence, and if there was something we didn't know about each other, there was usually a good reason for it.

Ianto grinned at me as he stirred the Thai curry on the hob. "And you're not just using this as a way to talk to him?"

"Obviously I'm doing that too, but I want to give him a hand. The poor man looks one bad day away from a breakdown."

"That bad?"

"I think so." I found a bottle opener in the drawer and opened the two bottles I'd retrieved from the fridge, handing one to Ianto. "Not that he'd admit it, mind. He's wound so tight it's like he can't bring himself to stop. I think… I know he uses drag as an outlet, but it's still a job, and I don't know how much time he gets to sit around and do nothing."

Ianto frowned as he nodded. "Ben was like that at first. He still is sometimes. It was like he had the weight of the fucking world on his shoulders and thought he had to carry it all himself."

"How did you get him to stop?"

"I didn't, not really anyway. He had to make that decision for himself. I think me being there and wanting more helped. But I also believe that Patrick had words."

"Lord help him," I said with a wry chuckle. "I'm surprised Aaron hadn't tried."

"I think he did, but Ben ignored him. But you can't ignore Patrick. I think it's because he doesn't yell—he just goes very quiet and makes you reconsider all your life choices. At least that's what I've been told."

"I'd believe it." I took a swig of my beer, pleased I'd come to Ianto for help. I'd known my little brother would be able to do something, even if it was just reassuring me that things could change. And while I didn't think a lecture from an Irish pastry chef was going to help here, it did give me an idea of where to start.

I had to make Evan see he wasn't alone. And that he didn't have to do all of this alone either.

Was that too big a declaration after one fuck, a broken nose, and dinner together? Probably. But I'd never done anything by half.

"What do you want to learn to cook then?" Ianto asked as he picked up a bottle off the side and added a generous splash to the curry.

"I don't know... a few easy things, I suppose. Doesn't need to be fancy."

"You know there's cooking channels on YouTube, right? And TikTok. You could learn from those."

"But they're not you," I said with my best charming smile. "You're the best cook I know."

"That's a bloody lie."

"No, it's not."

"Yes, it is. You're hoping flattery will get you somewhere."

I took another swig of my beer. "Is it working?"

Ianto sighed. "Fine. But I'm not teaching you."

"How does you teaching me to cook work, if you're not going to actually teach me?" I was completely baffled by my brother's logic on that one.

"I'm going to ask Ben to do it," Ianto said. "Look, I love you but you're terrible to teach. All you'll do is argue with me and wander off when you get bored."

"No, I won't!"

Ianto shot me an unimpressed look. "Really? So, when you asked me to teach you how to make fish pie last year and you disagreed with everything I did, that was a figment of my imagination, was it?"

I opened my mouth to argue with him, then realised that was exactly his point and instead said, "I promise it'll be different this time."

"You say that every time," he said. "Which is why I'm going to ask Ben."

"How do you know I won't argue with him?"

"Because you're my brother, so arguing with me is practically genetic."

I laughed because Ianto had a point there. "Ben's my brother-in-law. Doesn't that count?" True, he and Ianto weren't engaged or married, but that didn't matter because I couldn't see them ever breaking up. There was a certainty in my gut whenever I looked at them that told me they'd be together forever.

A flush blossomed across Ianto's cheekbones and he smiled. It was cute, in an almost sickening way, that after two years together he still went all gooey when he thought about his relationship with Ben. "You still won't argue with him," Ianto said before reaching into his pocket and pulling out his phone. "Anyway, you might still get out of it. I don't know if he'll have time with everything going on."

That made sense. Ianto had mentioned that the man who owned the buildings The Pear Tree was in was looking to sell it, and that Ben, Aaron, and Josh had decided to try and buy it for themselves. It sounded like a monumentally stressful process, especially since they were trying to keep their efforts under wraps so none of the pub's staff got worried.

"If he's too busy, then don't worry about it."

"I think he'd like the distraction to be honest. It'll give him something else to think about rather than spreadsheets and paperwork."

"Are you going to ask him now?"

"Yeah, while I remember." He glanced at the curry again and then at the little rice cooker he'd recently acquired, which had a minute left on the timer. "Do you want to get some bowls out?"

"Sure," I said as I began rummaging in the cupboard in front of my head, being extra careful so I didn't smack myself in the face with anything. Until recently, I'd had no idea how many things were liable to cause facial injuries.

"How's your nose, by the way?" Ianto asked. "It doesn't look nearly as swollen."

"Thank God, because it's not like the bruising is doing me any favours." My face had now changed from a lovely shade of deep purple to a sickly yellow-green with purple splotches. I'd tried covering it up with some cheap concealer I'd gotten in Boots, but that'd made it look worse, so I'd given up. I was still getting plenty of stares at work, but they weren't bothering me as much now.

The only thing that had really annoyed me was Connor saying I wasn't allowed to do pole for six weeks despite promising him I wouldn't head-butt the pole. I'd popped in to see him after work a couple of days ago to ask him about Milo, and he'd taken one look at me and asked what the hell I'd been up to. After recounting my sordid tale and asking my questions, he'd given me some shoes for Milo to try, a list of free resources, and a stern dismissal from pole. Although he had said if I did want to keep up my flexibility and strength, to go to his adult barre class.

I was so bored I was tempted to say yes, even though I knew it would be agony. If anyone thought ballet was easy, they needed to take one of Connor's classes and try to get out of bed the next day. My legs had felt better the day after our first Ironman.

"I guess it could have been worse," Ianto said.

"True, but since the worse options are everything from needing surgery to severe brain injury, I'm not sure that's helpful." I put the wide bowls on the counter and began rummaging around in the drawer as the rice cooker beeped.

"Has Evan still been keeping an eye on you?" Ianto

asked. He was trying to make the question sound innocent but I knew my twin far too well for that.

"Most days. He doesn't seem to trust me to keep out of trouble."

Ianto snorted as he opened the rice cooker, picking up the little plastic paddle to break the cooked rice up. "He knows you better than I thought."

"Very funny. Your sympathy is appreciated."

"I'm sorry, but I'm not sure you need sympathy for that," Ianto said. "Besides, isn't it a good thing he's checking on you? It means you get to see him more. And it shows he cares."

"I don't think it's care," I said, doubt rising in my voice. It was something I'd been thinking about for a few days and I wasn't sure if I was just trying to convince myself he didn't care. Because while deep, deep down I wanted him to care, the rest of me wanted to run screaming at the idea. There was a reason I hadn't had a serious relationship since I was seventeen, and it was why I'd dumped everyone who'd ever attempted to get close to me.

Evan caring about me would only end in tears.

While I wanted his friendship, and his dick, I didn't want anything else.

And I was well aware that sounded hypocritical as fuck considering I was asking Ianto to teach me to cook so I could take care of him. I wasn't going to argue with my brain, though, because that would involve doing some serious self-reflection and unpacking all the things I'd shoved into a box and hidden in the darkest corner of my mind. It was much easier to keep doing whatever the hell I wanted, having some fun, and enjoying my life.

"What is it then?" Ianto asked. "If it's not care."

"I don't know… professional pride? Common courtesy? It's probably because if I died, he'd think it was an inconvenience."

"Really? That's what you're going with? That's the biggest load of bollocks I've ever heard of."

I turned my head and stared at him, not sure how to respond. Ianto had called me out on my shit before, but very rarely on anything related to relationships.

"Look, I know you've got some shit going on in that heart of yours, and I've never pushed because quite frankly I didn't think you'd listen to me," Ianto said. He raised his voice as he continued. "But if you seriously think checking on you every day isn't Evan caring about you, then you're a bigger fool than I thought. And I'm not saying you have to marry the man, but for fuck's sake, Rhys. You're asking how to cook for him, you've fucked at least once—"

"Only once."

Ianto ignored me and carried on. "He checks on you and you've met his niblings, which by the sound of it not many people have." He sighed, whatever anger he'd been holding melting away. I probably deserved to be shouted at, though, because he wasn't wrong. "I'm not going to tell you to just get over what you're carrying around, but please, at least be open to the possibility of *something*. And I think you want to be, even if you pretend you're not."

"Why do you think that?" I asked, knowing the answer but wanting to hear him say it. Because if Ianto said it, it would be real. And then it would be so much harder to hide from.

Ianto smiled at me softly. "Because even though you think you're asking for cooking lessons to be helpful, I've never, ever known you to do anything like this for a man who wasn't me."

CHAPTER THIRTEEN

Eva Nessence

Seven in the morning was always worse when seen from the wrong side of a twelve-hour shift. Thank fuck that had been my last night shift for a while because it felt like I'd done far too many of them recently. Or maybe it was because every night shift was starting to feel like it lasted twelve days instead of hours.

How the fuck I expected myself to keep doing this for another twenty, thirty, or even forty years was beyond me. Especially if I wanted to keep doing drag.

I was supposed to be on stage that evening and even though it was the thing I'd been clinging to for the past two days, now it was here, all I felt was stress and exhaustion. I loved performing, but recently my drag career seemed to be taking more and more of a back seat to everything else in my life. I wasn't sure what had changed, because it had never felt this difficult to juggle everything before, but maybe I was finally approaching the point of no return. Burnout was bearing down on me with all speed, and this time I didn't think there was anything I could do to stop it.

And it fucking sucked.

"Are you just getting home?"

The question made me jump and I realised I was stood in front of my door, key in hand, staring into space. How fucking long had I been standing here? I turned to see Rhys beside me, dressed in a skin-tight T-shirt and running shorts, ink spilling out from underneath them and down his well-muscled thighs. He was putting ear pods back into their case and although he was smiling, there was an intensity in his gaze that suggested something more.

"Er, yeah," I said with a hollow laugh. "Is it that obvious?"

"The uniform's a bit of a giveaway."

"It's not going to help my case that I'd forgotten I was wearing it, is it?"

"No," Rhys said. "Long night?"

"Is that the polite way of saying I look bloody knackered?" I asked, grinning at him as I finally managed to put the key in the lock. My bed was calling me, but my stomach was also reminding me I hadn't eaten in hours. I'd taken a pack-up to eat during my break, but that had been somewhere in the early hours of this morning and a lot had happened since then.

"Would you prefer me to say that instead?"

"Maybe." I noticed Rhys was still watching me. "Something wrong?"

"When was the last time you had something to eat?" he

asked, a frown settling on his face as he looked me up and down. Had my stomach rumbled that loudly? Or did I just have the look of someone ravenous?

"About two? Around then anyway."

I'd never seen Rhys look so scandalised. You'd have thought I'd told him I'd kicked a puppy. "Two AM?"

"Yeah, that was my lunch break."

"We're fixing that right now," he said firmly before pointing at the door. "Open the door and I'll make you some breakfast before you crash."

"You know I can cook for myself?"

"I don't fucking care. You've done a twelve-hour shift and look about ready to drop, so get in the bloody house and let me make you breakfast."

My heart did a funny skip-thump and I rubbed my chest, wondering if it was because I was oddly touched by his demanding gesture or simply because it had been a long, stressful night and I was exhausted. Maybe it was time to stop thinking.

I turned the key and opened the door, stepping inside and moving out of the way so Rhys could get past me. He marched straight towards my kitchen and I found myself stopping to watch him instead of taking my boots off. He obviously didn't know where anything was because he opened multiple cupboards and muttered to himself while peering inside them. As I bent down to start unlacing my boots, he'd opened the fridge and all I could hear was an unimpressed hum.

"When was the last time you went shopping?" he called.

"Last week," I said as I pulled my first boot off. "I was

going to go again this afternoon." If I'd gotten around to it. I should have just ordered a delivery from Tesco, and then I wouldn't have had to leave the house again.

"Right," Rhys said, striding back out of the kitchen with more purpose than I'd thought possible. "Leave the door open. I'll be back in a second."

"Where are you—"

"I'm going to raid my fridge so I can make you a proper breakfast burrito."

"You don't need to do that."

"I don't care. I'm doing it anyway." He grinned at me as he pulled open the front door and stepped outside, leaving me staring at the space where he'd been. Who the fuck was this man? Every time I was with him he seemed to throw me for a loop. He wasn't only annoying but apparently stubborn too. And demanding.

And cute as fuck, but I wasn't going to acknowledge that thought. I wanted to try and focus on the things about him that annoyed me because then it would be easier to keep him at arm's length.

I didn't have time for a relationship or romance or any of that shit, and keeping Rhys at a distance was the only way to stop me from falling into a cunning trap laid by my heart. Or maybe it was by my dick. Either way, I needed to keep up the sarcastic, salty barricade I'd built around myself.

. . .

Eli might have said things didn't need to be complicated, but that didn't mean I had to make them simple either. There was room for emotional nuance here.

Or maybe that was another way of my brain turning loop-the-loops to try and justify itself.

The only problem was Rhys seemed determined to steamroller, climb, destroy, and break through every single one of my defences. And there were only so many times I could reinforce them before they crumbled into dust.

I was still stood lost in thought when he returned a few minutes later carrying a packet of large flour tortillas, a box of eggs, some peppers, onions, mushrooms, a pack of bacon lardons, a whole block of cheddar, a giant potato, a can of pinto beans, and a bottle of chilli sauce. It was a lot of food and I wasn't sure how he was juggling it all in two hands.

"Do you need a hand?" I asked slowly as Rhys kicked the door shut and somehow kicked his shoes off.

"Nope," he said, looking at me excitedly over his mountain of supplies. "If you wanted to have a shower while I make these, then now is a good time to go and get naked. God, I never thought I'd be suggesting you get naked without me watching but I suppose there's a time for everything."

He walked towards the kitchen, resuming his one-man mission and leaving me standing in the front room. "I don't hear any getting naked," he said as he reached his destination. Then he turned and smirked at me. "I don't see any getting naked either. Need a hand?"

"No, I'll be fine," I said, finally jolting into action.

"That's a shame. Maybe later." Rhys winked as he

pulled a knife out of the block and grabbed one of the onions. "Oh… do you have any allergies? Or is there anything I've got here you don't like?"

"No… that all looks fine. What're the beans for?" I thought I knew but it was just out of reach.

"I was going to make refried beans," Rhys said. "I know you can get them in a can, but they're pretty easy to make yourself. They taste better too." He began chopping the onion with easy precision as he continued. "By the way, don't expect this sort of cooking from me regularly. I only know how to make good breakfasts. For the rest of the day, you're on your own."

"That's okay. I can make dinner. And I'm pretty sure even you can make sandwiches." I yawned and felt something pop in my chest. My muscles felt like lead and I didn't know how much longer I'd be able to resist the call of my bed.

"Go and have a shower," Rhys said. "That'll wake you up a bit. And these won't take long."

I wanted to argue with him, but it felt like I'd be doing it just for the sake of arguing. With one final look at Rhys, who'd moved on to slicing a pepper at speed, I turned and headed for the stairs.

Dumping my dirty uniform in the washing basket, I turned the shower on to the hottest setting I could physically stand before climbing into the bath and stepping under the spray. I winced as the scalding water drenched my skin. It felt good, though, like it was washing away my stress and the top layer of my exhaustion, stopping my internal battery from flashing red.

My bathroom was built above my kitchen in the same extension that had been added to the house well before I'd bought it. The paint was chipping and so was the plaster, and every time I consciously looked at it, I reminded myself the room really needed decorating. It was another thing on my "when I get around to it" list.

But that wasn't what I was thinking about as I reached for the bottle of shower gel resting on the end of the bath.

It was that I could hear Rhys singing.

It was hard to make out the exact song, but maybe it was because I was so focused on his voice. It was warm and rolling, his Welsh accent adding a richness that sank into my soul. I wanted to listen to it for hours, until the water ran cold and my skin went numb.

The scent of frying bacon and vegetables wafted in under the door, making my mouth water. I'd been expecting to come home to beans on toast, not fucking breakfast burritos. I hoped my stomach didn't get any ideas because this wasn't going to happen regularly.

At least, I didn't think it was.

But if Rhys was involved, then who the fuck knew. The man was a wild card.

I washed quickly and climbed out of the shower, wrapping a towel around my waist before heading to my room to grab an old hoodie and a pair of grey joggers. I didn't bother with any underwear because I'd be going straight to bed after breakfast and it wasn't like Rhys hadn't seen my dick before.

By the time I got back downstairs, Rhys was plating up the most enormous burritos I'd ever seen, complete with a little salsa of onions and tomatoes scattered across the top and drizzled with chilli sauce and grated cheese. From the state of the cheddar on the side, I guessed there was a lot more inside the burritos since the block was about half the size it had been.

"Feeling better?" Rhys asked when he looked up. "You look a bit more human."

"I'm feeling it too," I said, smiling gratefully. "This smells amazing. Thank you."

"You're welcome. It's the least I could do. And considering what was in your fridge, I'm not sure what you were planning on eating if I hadn't been here."

"I don't know, probably just beans on toast."

Rhys scoffed. "That's not breakfast."

"It's served me pretty well for the past ten years."

"Is that how long you've been a paramedic?" Rhys asked as he handed me one of the plates along with a knife and fork. "Do you want a drink? I wasn't sure if you'd drink tea this time of day."

"There's some orange juice in the fridge," I said. At least, I thought there was. "And I've been a paramedic for eight years now. It's what I went to university for…." Fuck, time went quickly. I hadn't thought it had been that long, but I'd had my twenty-ninth birthday in February, so it had to have been. I shook my head and chuckled at myself. "I've definitely been having beans on toast for breakfast for longer than ten years…"

Rhys shook his head. "At least it's not pilchards in tomato sauce. Or anchovies." He pulled a face. "Tadcu loves them but I fucking hate them. I got used to the smell of smoked kippers but anchovies are on the permanent no list."

"I've never been a fan of fish for breakfast either."

"I'll put that in your list of good qualities then," he said, winking at me. He gestured towards the dining room. "You go and sit down. I'll join you in a second once I've grabbed that juice."

"Join me?" It seemed silly to ask, but I couldn't stop myself. For some reason I needed confirmation, but for what reason I didn't know.

"Yeah, if that's okay?"

I grinned, my heart doing another of those strange skip-thumps. "Yeah. I'd love that."

CHAPTER FOURTEEN

Rhys

WATCHING Evan devour every crumb of his breakfast burrito warmed all the nooks and crannies of my heart, even the parts that were trying to avoid it. After my conversation with Ianto, I'd been determined to keep my distance and not let my emotions trick me into something I wasn't ready for.

But seeing him standing on the pavement staring into space and looking like he was two seconds away from falling asleep had made all those protective instincts I'd honed through years of looking after Ianto kick into gear. And when he'd said he hadn't eaten, that had been the cherry on the cake.

I might not have been able to cook much, but I was the fucking king of breakfasts. It was the most important meal of the day. True, eating it at the end of a shift didn't make it Evan's breakfast, but it'd at least be better for him than fucking beans on toast. And if that was what he ate regularly, I'd be here making him burritos more often.

"That was amazing," Evan said with a contented smile as he put his knife and fork down. "Thank you."

"You're welcome," I said. "Wasn't much really."

"Don't lie. You love the praise."

His gaze enveloped me and I swallowed. Had I begged that much when we'd fucked? Or was my desperate need for approval simply written above my head in great big red letters that said praise whore? "It's always nice to be appreciated," I said finally, unable to tear my eyes away.

"I definitely appreciate it. And despite your protestations, you can cook. There's not much difference between making that and something like fajitas or enchiladas."

"I suppose, but if you buy a kit for those, all you have to do is follow the instructions. Even I can do that!"

Evan chuckled softly, the sound reverberating through me and making me shiver. "Can you?"

"If they're worth following," I said, trying to ignore the way my cock twitched in my shorts. I'd only come over here to feed him, not fuck him, and I'd accomplished that. Evan needed sleep, not me trying to get into his joggers, despite the fact the first thing I'd noticed when he'd come back downstairs was that he wasn't wearing boxers.

His dick print had been really fucking obvious and I'd nearly swallowed my tongue just looking at it.

Evan smirked and leant across the corner of the table, putting his elbow on the wooden surface and resting his chin on his fingers, which were curled into a loose fist. "Tell me, what sort of instructions do you follow?"

I forced a casual smile, trying desperately not to take the bait. "Fitness ones... safety ones... especially around the sea. I grew up by the coast, so I know how hazardous it can be."

"Very good," he said in a smooth, dangerous tone that made me shiver. "What else?"

"Cooking ones. Sometimes."

"Any others?"

"What others are there?"

"Plenty." He leant closer, lowering his voice so I had to strain to listen, my whole body focused on every word. "Like me telling you to strip for me... slowly. So I can savour every moment as I watch you undress. Telling you to touch yourself for me. Giving you exact instructions on how to play with your nipples and your balls and that tight hole of yours because I want to hear you whimper. Making you ignore your cock even though it's hard and aching because I want to see how long you can listen to me before you break. Giving you a toy to play with and telling you exactly how I want to watch you fuck yourself with it. How hard and how fast to ride it... making you stop just when you reach the edge... making you hold yourself there even when your body is screaming for more... Would you listen to those instructions?"

"Yes," I said eagerly, practically throwing myself across the table in a desperate need to be closer to him.

"All of them?"

"Yes."

He let out a low, approving hum that made my stomach twist in delight. "Good." He reached out with his other hand, letting his fingers brush along my jaw, his thumb resting in the middle of my bottom lip. Not stroking. Not teasing. Just resting there. Waiting. "You're such a needy boy, aren't you? So eager for praise… for someone to notice you and give you all the things you tell yourself you can't have or pretend you don't want. Tell me, what secret fantasies are lurking inside you, just waiting for someone to notice?"

"I… er…" I didn't know what to say. It wasn't often I was stunned speechless, but this was one of those times. I wanted to tell him, the words clinging to the tip of my tongue. But I was holding back. Because how did I know he wasn't going to use them against me?

There was only one man in the world I trusted with my secrets. And even he didn't know these.

Evan hummed again, caressing my face. "Shall I guess? And you can tell me if I'm right."

I nodded, pressing my chin into his hand.

"Good." His eyes met mine and for a moment he was silent. But I was hooked on every breath he took. "You're needy and desperate, and you crave praise and attention. You want to be cherished and worshipped, but there's a filthy, slutty side to that too. I think you want to be used… filled to the brim with cock and cum, letting men fuck you over and over as they tell you just how perfect you are."

My body tensed and I felt my eyes widen, just for a split second, as I fought to control my expression. How the fuck did he know? Did this man possess bloody psychic powers or something? How on earth did he get all that from looking at me?

"Mmm, you really do like that idea, don't you?" He leant even closer until I could see all the details of his face with perfect clarity. "The only problem is, I don't share. But we could fill you up with plenty of toys."

I whimpered, my patience snapping like a twig. I surged across the table towards him and his hand pulled me in, our mouths meeting in a clashing, hungry kiss. The plates and crockery clattered as at least one of us bumped against the table, but the sharp sound didn't stop us from kissing like it was our last morning on earth.

Evan stood, pulling me upright by the front of my T-shirt and dragging me around the edge of the table until our bodies collided. My fingers slid under the bottom of his hoodie, desperately seeking bare skin. Evan groaned as I ran my hands across his abdomen, his own hand reaching for the hem of my running shirt.

"Upstairs," he growled, nipping my lip for good measure and practically making me melt into the floor.

"Y-yes," I said. I wasn't sure why he didn't simply bend me over the table, but then again it didn't seem like the sturdiest piece of furniture and the last thing I wanted was for it to collapse when Evan was balls deep inside me.

He stepped back and my hands slowly slid out from under his hoodie. He reached down and caught my wrist in his fingers, smirking as he pulled me towards the stairs. Fire burned in his eyes like our kiss had sparked life into him, and any tiredness I'd felt from my run evaporated in an instant.

We climbed the stairs quickly and I was pleased when he pulled me through the door to the front bedroom, but the satisfaction of being right about which room was his was forgotten as soon as he turned me around and pushed me backwards onto the bed. I made an undignified squawk as the back of my knees hit the edge of the mattress and I tumbled onto my ass.

"Very graceful," Evan said with a soft chuckle as he pulled off his hoodie.

"Next time I'll push you onto the bed and you can demonstrate how to do it gracefully then."

"You're assuming I'd let you push me anywhere." He dropped the hoodie onto the floor, giving me my first proper view of his body. Fuck, he was gorgeous. Lean and toned but with a softness to his body that made my mouth water. I wanted to press kisses all across his chest and down his stomach, licking the dips in his hips that ran straight into his joggers. There was a dusting of dark hair there too, but his chest was bare and I wondered if he shaved it for drag.

His joggers were already tenting as his half-hard cock pressed against the grey fabric and I silently thanked whoever had decided that men looked better in grey joggers because his dick print was giving me life.

"You're very sure of yourself," I said teasingly, keeping my eyes on his hands. If he was going to keep stripping off, I didn't want to miss a second. I hadn't gotten to see enough of his dick last time, and it was a fucking crime.

"I am. And you like it." He wasn't wrong. "Get undressed," he continued. "Time to prove you can follow instructions."

"And what happens if I don't?"

"Then we enter a fabulous place called 'find out'," he said in that low, dangerous voice that fucking killed me. "If you don't like something, you can say no. But if you refuse because you think being a demanding brat will get you more attention, then I don't think you'll like the consequences."

I swallowed, my cock throbbing in the tiny, constricting pair of boxers I'd put on under my shorts. Worst underwear choice ever. "I… I think I might."

"Do you really want to find out? Or would you rather have some fun?"

"I want to have fun," I said. "But you should know telling me there'll be vague consequences is like putting a giant sign above a red button of doom that says Don't Press. I'm going to press it."

"Don't you have any self-control?" he asked, raising an eyebrow and folding his arms.

I shrugged. "Yes. But not in this situation."

He chuckled. "I suppose I walked into that." He stepped closer, pushing his knee between my thighs. Kneeling on the mattress, he leant down over me until I had no choice but to lie down and let him pin me to the bed, his hands on either side of my head. My heart was racing, desire coiling in my stomach. He was so close I could easily steal a kiss. "How about this… if you don't do what you're told, I'll spank you, fuck you with one of the toys in my drawer, one I'm sure will make you scream… and make you stop just before you come. You won't get my cock or my cum. And sure, you could finish yourself off when you go home, but you and I both know it won't be the same."

He leant closer until his lips were virtually pressed against mine. "So, are you going to do as you're told?"

I whimpered again, nodding furiously.

"Say it."

"I'll do as I'm told."

"Good," Evan said, kissing me deeply and claiming my mouth with his tongue. I melted underneath him, his single word of praise like a drop of cold water on a hot day. But then he was gone and I whined pitifully as he stood looking down at me with hungry eyes. "Then do as you're told and take your clothes off."

CHAPTER FIFTEEN

Eva Nessence

I'd never seen a man get naked as fast as Rhys did.

He practically ripped his T-shirt off, exposing all that delicious, tattooed skin I wanted to run my tongue across. Then he lifted his hips and grabbed the waistband of his shorts, yanking them down roughly, releasing his cock, and finally showing me what the tattooed wing I'd been so focused on belonged to: two swallows, one on each of his hips, curving down the line of the muscle.

He threw his clothes off the bed and toed off his socks, leaving himself utterly and perfectly naked. He was so damn beautiful and there was an ever-growing list in my head of deliciously filthy things I wanted to do to him.

I hadn't expected him to be so affected by what I'd said downstairs, but if Rhys had a poker face, it was clearly non-existent when it came to being told what a needy, desperate slut he was. And fuck… I loved that.

I'd always been good at reading people—it was what made me a good paramedic and an acerbic drag queen—but using my skills on Rhys to make him melt into the palm of my hand was heady in a way I'd never experienced. It was powerful and beautiful and something I'd take great care and delight in using. After all, with great power came great responsibility.

A smile played across my lips as I reached for the waistband of my joggers, slowly inching them down. Rhys stared at me, desperation written across his face. I wondered how much he wanted to tell me to just get on with it.

"You know, I've seen snails move faster than you," he said and I bit back a laugh. "There's teasing and then there's this." He waved his hand at me. "This is bloody torture."

"Do you want me to apologise?"

"You can do that by taking those off and getting your ass over here. I'm fucking dying."

"Oh, poor baby," I said dryly as I slid my joggers over my thighs and let them pool around my feet. I cupped my cock in my hand and slowly began to stroke myself. "Are you suffering?"

"I bloody am."

"Do you need me to kiss it better?" I knelt on the bed, putting my knee back between his thighs as I looked down at him. He was spread out beneath me like a fucking buffet. All I had to do was work out where to start.

Rhys grinned up at me. "It wouldn't hurt."

I brought my other knee between his thighs, spreading his legs wider as I leant down over him, resting on my hands. My core muscles protested strongly at this unexpected plank, which was probably a sign I needed to do more exercise. It was another thing to go on my list of things I'd get around to one day. Maybe I'd see if Rhys could take me to his pole classes. It would be fun to go back to and much more exciting than something like running.

I brushed my lips against his, so lightly it barely counted as a kiss. Rhys's hand came up to cup the back of my neck, pulling me down. "More," he said with a groan, pulling my bottom lip between his teeth. I moaned, my tongue darting out to slide over the seam in his lips, demanding entry to his mouth. His body radiated heat underneath me, and every point of contact felt two seconds away from self-combusting. It might be a myth, but I was willing to bet Rhys and I could prove the entire scientific community wrong.

Rhys groaned and pushed up against me as I deepened the kiss, his erection rubbing against mine and sending need spiralling through me. I wanted to bend him in half and slide deep inside his perfect, tight hole and pound him until he couldn't do anything but scream out my name as he came. Those tattoos would look so pretty covered in cum.

I broke the kiss and trailed my mouth across his jaw, running my lips down his neck and tracing his collarbone with my tongue. Rhys moaned as I moved my mouth lower, kissing down his sternum until my face was between his pecs. My eyes met his for a moment as I lifted my head. The silver balls on the ends of his nipple bars glinted in the morning light, and I wondered what sort of sounds he'd make if I teased them with my tongue.

There was only one way to find out.

Rhys gasped as I slowly licked one nipple, dragging my tongue deliberately over the hardening nub and feeling the solid bar running under his skin. I'd never considered getting my nipples pierced, or any other part of my body apart from the simple ones in my ears I'd gotten for drag. Despite spending half my life around needles, I wasn't the biggest fan of them going into me. But I'd happily spend all my time exploring Rhys's, especially with the sounds he was making.

"Do you like that?" I asked before wrapping my lips around the nub and sucking gently.

"So fucking good," Rhys said, arching his back and pushing his chest up. "You can do it harder."

"Are you sure?"

"Y-Yeah. It… it feels so good."

I sucked a little harder, then used the tip of my tongue to tease one end of his piercing, making him groan. I pulled his nipple between my teeth, the gasp he made sending shivers through me. Rhys's fingers tangled in my hair as I released him and began to kiss across his chest. After all, I wanted to play fair.

And I wanted to hear Rhys groan again.

I dragged my tongue firmly across his other nipple before nipping it with my teeth and soothing it with another kiss. Rhys gasped at every flick of my tongue and press of my mouth, grabbing my hair tightly like he needed some sort of anchor. He was so much fun to play with, I could have spent all day there, licking and sucking and teasing every inch of him.

But the exhaustion I'd felt earlier was starting to creep back in around the edges, and no amount of good food or fabulous sex was going to stave off my tiredness forever.

When I looked up, Rhys was watching me, pleasure and concern mingling on his face. "You're tired," he said.

"What's new?"

He rolled his eyes and muttered something under his breath I didn't understand. Then he grinned cheekily. "Do you speak Welsh?"

"No," I said. "But now I'm wondering if I need to learn so I know when you're talking shit about me."

Rhys laughed and pulled me towards him, sitting up enough that he could kiss me easily. "That's no fun."

"I guess it's something you and your brother do?"

"For years. Drives some guys nuts."

"And that's why you do it?"

"Obviously," he said. "That and if they can't possibly function without knowing every single thing we say, then they're probably a piece of shit." I kissed him again, revelling in the softness of his lips. "If you're tired, we can stop."

"No," I growled. "I don't want to stop. Do you?"

"No. But since you're tired, I've decided I'm taking over. And I'm not letting you argue with me."

"And how do you expect to do that?"

"Like this." He winked and threw his legs around my waist, rolling the pair of us over with a surprising amount of speed and force until I found myself flat on my back with

Rhys straddling my hips, looking down at me with a smug smile of satisfaction.

"Very clever," I said, sliding my hands up his thighs. One of them had an intricate-looking horse skull tattooed on the top, with what looked like a sheet or cloak attached to it and a crown of flowers and plants with ears poking out the top. I'd never seen anything like it before. "What are you going to do now you've taken over? Do you have plans for your power?"

Rhys traced one finger over my chest while he thought. I wondered whether he actually wanted to take over, or if he only wanted to take care of me. Was the illusion of power enough for him?

"Do you want some ideas?" I asked as I inched my hands a little further up his thighs, stroking my thumbs over the muscle.

"Depends what they are."

"Firstly, I'd suggest we move further onto the bed since my legs are hanging off and it's uncomfortable."

"Agreed. My toes keep catching on the edge of the mattress and I don't need any more bruises."

I chuckled and before he could say any more, I grabbed his waist, holding him in place as I wiggled further onto the bed, using one foot to push myself around so my head was closer to the pillows. It wasn't the most dignified movement, but Rhys was too busy laughing and making jokes about being a cowboy to notice.

"What other ideas have you got?" he asked, leaning down to kiss me. His whole face sparkled with infectious delight, and it felt like someone had struck a match in my chest and started lighting fireworks. I couldn't remember the last time I'd felt anything like it and it made me hesitate. I kept telling myself nothing could happen between us because adding anything more to my plate would cause me to break it.

But this man, with his sparkling eyes and wild smile and utter determination to annoy his way into my life, had kicked in the door, tackled me to the floor, and announced his intention to stay. Whether I liked it or not.

And, loath as I was to admit it, I *did* like it.

I'd never had anyone try to fight for my attention like that before.

"Plenty," I said slowly, swallowing down my doubts and forcing myself to focus on the gorgeous, naked man sat on my lap. His ass was pressed against my cock and if I rocked my hips, I felt it slide roughly between his cheeks. Rhys groaned as I ground slowly up against him, my hands still holding his waist. "I think you should sit on my chest so I can suck your cock while you open yourself up for me. And then I think you should sit on my cock and ride me hard until I'm covered in your cum."

Rhys groaned and kissed me deeply. "Mmm, I like your ideas. I just have one more."

"Oh? Is there something you want?"

"Yes," he said, his voice breaking as I rolled my hips again. "I want you to come on my face."

"Are you sure?"

"Yeah, otherwise I wouldn't have asked." He grinned and nipped my lip playfully. "It's hot."

The image of Rhys's face dripping with my cum materialised in my mind and I had to agree with him. And now I needed to see if the reality was as good as my fantasy.

"There's lube in my bedside drawer," I said, gesturing towards it with one hand. "And condoms. You'll have to get off me to get them."

"Unless you want to wiggle closer to the edge so I can reach?" he asked.

"No, you can get up. And when you've got them, you can straddle my chest and let me play with your cock."

"You drive a hard bargain," Rhys said. He kissed me softly before sliding off my lap and rolling across the bed. I watched him, unable to stop myself from smiling at his ridiculousness. I'd thought this was going to be another hot, heavy, quick fuck where we both got off as fast as possible, but somehow it had slowed… and I was realising how much I liked that.

Being with Rhys wasn't only sexy. It was fun.

He retrieved the lube and new box of condoms I'd bought as a just in case thing, tossing the box onto the duvet beside me as he knee-walked across the bed. He threw one leg across my chest and I slid my hands around his thighs to pull him closer to me. His erect cock jutted out in front of him, the silken head swollen and leaking.

A small part of me had still hoped he'd have some interesting piercings for me to play with, despite not seeing or feeling any when I'd bent him over the sofa, but his cock and balls were smooth and free of any ornamentation. I wrapped my fingers loosely around his shaft and drew it closer to my lips. "Is it weird I was almost expecting you to have your dick pierced? Or tattooed."

Rhys laughed as he tilted his hips forward, his body begging for me. "No. I've thought about it but doing an Ironman with pierced nipples is uncomfortable enough. I'm not riding a bike for a hundred and twelve miles with a ladder of barbells down my balls. And as much as I love getting tattooed, there is no way in hell I'm putting a tattoo gun anywhere near my dick. Especially not as you have to be hard for them to tattoo you."

I grinned, holding his cock millimetres away from my lips. "I didn't know that."

"Next time we're together I'll show you a video," he said as he pushed his cock into my hand, desperate to reach my mouth.

Our eyes met as I ran my tongue slowly over the soft skin, lapping up his precum. He groaned softly, his chest heaving. His body was so expressive, every touch drawing a reaction out of him.

I wrapped my lips around the head of his cock and slowly sucked it into my mouth. Rhys moaned, his head tipping back for a moment as he relished the sensation. He still had the bottle of lube in his hand and I was tempted to remind him what he was supposed to be doing. But if I did, we'd start rushing again and now we'd slowed down, I couldn't think of anything worse than this ending quickly.

Rhys tried to thrust his hips forward but my hands gripped his thighs and held him still. I wasn't going to let him take what he wanted. Where was the fun in that?

I pulled myself slightly more upright, my core muscles protesting as they were forced to hold me in position, but it allowed me to suck Rhys deeper without totally gagging.

Now I'd had a taste of his cock I wanted as much in my mouth as I could fit. I'd never been great at deep throating, and even though I'd tried to train away my gag reflex with no small number of bananas and dildos, it persisted.

Thank fuck Rhys didn't have some monster cock or there was no way he'd ever get more than the first four inches sucked.

Rhys let out a sweet groan that made my dick pulse and stomach flip. I tightened my lips around him, working his cock in and out of my mouth and tasting his precum as it dripped onto my tongue.

I slid one hand up the back of his thigh and onto his ass, dipping my fingers into his crack to tease his hole. He gasped and tried to push back into my hand, then suddenly remembered he was holding the lube. He clicked the bottle open and poured a generous amount on his fingers before dropping it on the bed. His hand bumped against mine as he reached behind himself and slid his slick fingers between his cheeks.

"Fuck," he said with a groan as he began fingering himself open. I wished I could watch him, but I wanted to watch his face too and see all of those beautiful expressions. He was so open, so unguarded… it was enthralling in a way I couldn't describe. The way he took what he wanted, with no hesitation, was something I'd rarely allowed myself to experience.

Even when I took control during sex, I was always aware of the other person's pleasure. Very rarely did I take anything for myself.

Maybe it was something I needed to start doing more of.

I could hardly take my eyes off him, even when they started to water and burn. I took my hand off his thigh and wrapped it around his cock, pumping his shaft as I sucked the tip.

Rhys gasped and pulled back, panting. "That… fuck, that's… you have to stop or I'm going to come. I know that's the aim, but if you don't stop, we'll be missing out on a crucial step in the middle."

I snorted, nearly choking on my own saliva. "A step? You make it sound like an instruction manual," I said as I let his cock slip from my lips.

"You did say I needed to get better at following instructions," he said with a sly smile. He pulled his hand out from behind him and slowly began to wiggle down my body until he was hovering over my cock.

"I think I said you don't follow them at all."

"Did you? I wasn't listening." He leant down and grabbed the box of condoms from next to me and pulled the top open. Thank fuck I'd remembered to take the plastic wrapping off the box when I'd put them away because it would've been so awkward if Rhys had been forced to do it now.

He grabbed a condom out and ripped open the foil wrapper, reaching down and rolling it onto my cock without even looking. There was still a little lube on his fingers, which he smeared on my shaft, and before I could ask if he wanted more, he'd grasped my cock and lined it up with his slick, open hole. Somewhere in the back of my mind, I remembered him saying something about liking it to burn, but that thought was quickly washed away by a flood of sensation rushing through me as Rhys sank down on my cock.

I'd forgotten how tight and hot and *fucking perfect* his ass was.

My hands shot out to grasp his thighs, my fingers digging into the firm muscle as he took every inch of me deep inside him. Our groans and desperate breathing mingled together in the still air, and for a moment I couldn't think about anything except him.

Rhys didn't even give me a chance to catch my breath before he began to move. He circled and rolled his hips, the movement deep and filthy, making his ass rub against the top of my thighs. I gripped his legs harder as I fought the urge to take control and fuck up into him because I desperately wanted to see what Rhys would do.

What did he want from me? What would he take?

"Fuck, your cock feels so good," he said, pulling his bottom lip between his teeth and running his hands down his chest. He teased his nipples as he rolled his hips again before sliding his fingers down further to caress his cock. "Fucking love it inside me."

"Your ass… shit, it's so tight."

He smirked. "You like it?"

"I… fuck, I love it."

"Good." He leant down and brushed a teasing kiss across my lips. "I think I'll take that control now. But you have to tell me when you're going to come… because I want your load all over my face."

"You, fuck, you might not have to wait long."

He smirked as he sat back onto my cock. "If it's less than

two minutes, you owe me at least another round. Maybe two."

I chuckled. "I'll aim not to disappoint you."

Rhys snorted and laughed, the sound catching me off guard. He raised himself up slowly until I was barely inside him, then slammed back down hard. He gasped, a wild smile on his face as he began to ride me.

All I could do was hang on and enjoy the show.

Heat bubbled under my skin as his channel squeezed my shaft, the sensation threatening to overwhelm me. Rhys bounced faster on my cock, the sounds dripping from his lips getting louder and needier with every move he made. He tilted his hips to adjust his position and cried out with wanton delight as he slammed down onto me.

"Oh fuck, right there," he said. "That's it... fuck!"

I slid my hands up his body to grip his hips, holding him in place and starting to guide him up and down. "There?" I asked as he cried out again. "You like that?"

"That's a... bloody stupid question," he said with a breathless gasp of delight. "Feels fucking amazing."

"Don't stop. I want to watch you come."

He grinned but if he was going to say something smart-arsed and clever, it got lost in amongst the groans as I pulled him down onto my dick. I held him there for a second, thrusting my hips up to drive my cock into him until I was balls deep. Rhys groaned. "Again," he said. "Fuck me. Please."

"Well... since you said please..." I grabbed his hips and rolled us over, flipping him onto his back with my cock still buried inside him. I grabbed the backs of his thighs and pushed them up, practically folding him in half as I got my knees under me and began to drive my cock into him hard and fast, nailing his prostate with every thrust and making him cry out.

His screams of delight and the way his ass was squeezing my cock made the heat bubbling under my skin reach the boiling point, and I felt the familiar burn of my approaching orgasm start to run down my spine.

"Rhys," I growled out. "I'm getting close."

"Me... me too."

"Touch yourself," I said. "I want you to come while I cover you with my load."

He groaned, his hand flying to his cock and starting to jerk it. I thrust inside him again and again, pushing myself as close to the edge as I dared. Then, just when I was approaching the point of no return, I pulled out and ripped the condom off my cock.

"Come here," I said, kneeling up and pumping my cock. "Show me that pretty face."

Rhys moaned as he sat up, hurriedly shuffling closer to me. He tilted his face up, sparkling eyes filled with need. "Please, Evan. Come on me."

The desperation in his voice was all it took to send me over the edge, and a broken moan slipped from my lips as my cock shot ropes of hot cum across his beautiful face. It dripped down his forehead, nose, and cheekbones, catching on his lips and the piercing in his eyebrow. I'd tried to avoid his eyes, but from a glance I could see some clinging to his eyelashes.

It was the hottest thing I'd seen in a long time, and the

sight of it would be burned into my memory for years to come.

"Your turn," I said with a growl, watching as Rhys jerked himself. On a whim, I reached down and pushed two fingers into his ass, fucking him hard and curling the tips up to rub against his prostate.

Rhys cried out, his ass clenching around my fingers as his body stiffened and he pumped cum across his hand, the thick liquid spilling down his skin and dripping onto the bed. His chest heaved and I slowly eased my fingers out of him. Then I reached for his hand, the one that was covered in cum, and slowly lifted it to my mouth.

"Can I?" I asked, letting his fingers brush across my bottom lip.

His eyes fluttered open, cum still clinging to the ends of his lashes. Once we were finished, I was going to take him to the bathroom and gently wash his face, making sure I cleaned him up with all the care and attention he deserved.

"Yes," he said.

I opened my mouth and sucked his cum-covered fingers into it, slowly licking his cum off his skin and savouring the salty taste.

Then I leant forward and kissed him softly, my hand cupping his jaw, drawing out this moment between us for as long as possible.

CHAPTER SIXTEEN

Rhys

"So what the fuck can you cook?" Aaron, The Pear Tree's head chef and resident asshole with a heart of gold, grinned as he leant against the polished kitchen counter on the other side of the large island between us. His fox red hair was pulled back into a bun and his tattoo sleeves spilled out from under his chef's whites. I'd only met him a few times, so I had no fucking clue why he and his husband, Josh, The Pear Tree's other head chef, had offered to teach me to cook.

Ianto had conspicuously forgotten to mention that fact when he'd told me to come to the pub on Wednesday morning, which made me suspect he was in on the whole thing.

Then again, I knew he'd had a couple of lessons from Aaron, Josh, and Patrick, so it couldn't be that bad.

I wasn't exactly starting from the same point as Ianto, though…

"Mostly breakfast things: fry-ups, breakfast burritos,

those thick American pancakes, a full Welsh breakfast, and then anything that's in a jar or comes with instructions on the back of the box," I said. Maybe I should have known how to do more, but I'd always had Ianto and he'd been happy to swap cooking for me doing the washing up.

"That's not bad," Josh said. He was stood closer to me, with a warm smile lighting up his dark eyes. He was wearing a similar pair of chef's whites that had a cluster of pears embroidered on the chest pocket. "Your brother made it sound like you were a walking disaster."

I laughed. "That's a bit fucking rude of him. I won't be making him any more Christmas breakfasts." Although maybe that was what Ianto wanted since he'd hinted I should stop letting myself into his house. In that case, I'd keep doing it.

"If you can make those, you can learn to make plenty of shit," Aaron said. "It depends on how fucking complicated you want to make it. Who are you trying to impress?"

"Not that complicated." I smiled and shook my head. "I'm not trying to impress anyone. I'm just trying to help someone out."

"Who?" Aaron asked.

"Don't push, asshole," Josh said. "Rhys doesn't have to tell us anything."

"What? I'm only asking. If we're teaching him to impress someone, that's different from teaching him to feed himself."

"May I point out, you impressed me with cheese toasties," Josh said with a wry smile as he folded his arms across his chest. "That's not exactly Michelin star shit."

Aaron shrugged. "Eh, you were fucking easy to impress."

"That's because I was young and impressionable and I didn't know what a pain in the ass you'd turn out to be."

"Sucks to be you then, dickhead, because you fucking married me," Aaron said, shooting his husband a wink. Watching them was hilarious and I almost wished I'd brought popcorn. Ben had said they bickered almost constantly, even on their best days. Ianto had described it as some weird form of foreplay, and from the sexual tension simmering between them, I could well believe they were two seconds away from dropping everything and fucking against the kitchen wall.

"This doesn't look like a cooking lesson," Ben said, sticking his head around the door at the other end of the kitchen. "Morning, Rhys. You okay? How's your nose?"

"Yeah, not bad." I gingerly touched my nose, which was still bruised, but now that the purple spots had faded it looked slightly less like I had some kind of pox. Instead, the skin had faded to a sickly green, which made it look like I was trying out Halloween make-up about six months early. "Still a bit sore."

"It's looking better, definitely less swollen." Ben nodded at Aaron and Josh, who'd gone suspiciously quiet. "Are they being helpful?"

"Since when am I anything but helpful?" Aaron asked indignantly and Ben sighed.

"Would you like me to give you a list?"

"Yes, actually, I would."

"Don't be a wanker," Ben said. "Or I'll teach Rhys to

cook and you can come and wade through nine years of spreadsheets."

"Fuck no, that's your job. I'll stay here." Aaron looked at Josh and grinned. "I've got some ideas. What about you?"

"About food or spreadsheets?" Josh asked. "Because if it's the first, I've got a list. If it's the second, I'd rather peel ten tons of potatoes than look at spreadsheets."

"That can be arranged if you want," Ben said and Josh laughed.

"No thanks, I'll be fine. But I will make you some lunch when we get closer."

"I accept your bribery," Ben said. He looked back at me. "Any problems, I'm just in the office at the end of the corridor. Ianto said you're not working until after lunch, so he's going to swing by once he's finished and I thought we could all have lunch together?"

"Sounds great," I said. Ianto and I were on opposite shifts at the gym today, with him on a short early and me on a late. I didn't mind lates too much because they gave me most of the day to get stuff done before I started work. Ianto and I both taught classes and had personal training clients we slotted in around that. Luckily, we both had set classes, so our schedules didn't change too much, which made it easier to plan client sessions, our own training, and whatever things we did outside of that, like pole and Ianto's Saturday morning rugby.

"Hang on, I thought I was just making lunch for you," Josh said.

"You're a professional chef," Ben said dryly. "I'm sure you'll figure it out."

Josh flipped him off and Aaron laughed as Ben disappeared, his footsteps echoing up the corridor as he headed for his office. Then Josh turned to me and said, "If you're looking to help someone out and you want things that are pretty easy to make but still really fucking tasty, then I've got a few ideas. Some of them will reheat too, maybe even freeze if you've got enough leftovers." He walked over to one of the big fridges at the end of the kitchen and retrieved a whole chicken. "First up, I'm going to teach you how to make my mum's chicken curry."

"Fuck yes," Aaron said, clapping his hands together. "Wait, will we get in trouble for sharing the recipe?"

"Only if my aunties get their hands on it," Josh said.

"Am I being charged with a secret family recipe?" I asked with delight. We'd had a few family recipes growing up that my grandmother had left written on some old notecards, including one for Welsh cakes that Tadcu made every year on St. David's Day.

"Something like that," Josh said. "Mum's chicken curry is legendary in our family, and although she technically got the recipe from my nan, she's tweaked it over the years until it's her own."

"It's the best chicken curry you'll ever have," Aaron said. "Seriously. If you give that curry to this mystery man, he will shag you. I guarantee it."

"You speaking from experience there?" I asked as Josh put the chicken on a red chopping board and pulled out some large knives.

"A hundred percent," Aaron said.

"I'd say you're not hard to impress but you're picky as

fuck about other people's cooking," Josh said as he started breaking the chicken down into pieces. He looked over at me and added, "I'm not expecting you to do this. We tend to buy whole chickens and this curry works best with chicken legs. You can use skinless, boneless chicken thighs too, or even chicken breasts if you need to. Now, usually this will serve about five or six but I'll show you how to make it for two or three."

"Can I make notes?" I asked, pulling my phone out of my pocket and opening the notes app. I'd meant to bring a notebook with me, but I hadn't been able to find one before I'd left the house.

"Please do," Josh said as he neatly lined up the pieces of chicken. "Aaron, can you grab me some onions, please? And some garlic."

Despite their bickering, it was easy to see how well they worked together in a kitchen and the level of respect they had for each other.

Aaron showed me how to dice an onion quickly and easily, which was much neater than the way I'd been hacking away at my onions until tears streamed down my face, and Josh showed me how to fry them off slowly until they went beautifully golden.

It wasn't as hard to make the curry as I'd imagined, and Josh gave me plenty of help. I'd imagined he'd show me how to do everything without letting me get my hands dirty since it was a professional kitchen, but instead he and Aaron watched me carefully and guided me through every step.

For two well-regarded chefs, they were surprisingly patient and kind.

"Holy shit," I said as I took the first bite from the bowl of curry Josh handed me. "That's fucking incredible."

"Told you," Aaron said. "Fucking shaggable."

I wondered what Evan's reaction would be if I made it for him. If it was anything like the other morning, I'd be in fucking heaven. If I thought about it, I could still feel his cum landing on my skin and dripping down my lips.

"You did a good job," Josh said with a pleased nod as he stole a spoonful out of the bowl Aaron was holding. "You can serve it with rice, naan, some yoghurt. You can just buy naans or get them from your local takeaway. I can teach you how to make them too, but I don't think we'll have time today. I'll send you the recipe, though, because it's not hard to follow."

"Thanks," I said, taking another huge mouthful of curry. I knew I was supposed to be having lunch with Ben and Ianto, but I didn't want the curry to go to waste. "I really appreciate it."

"You're welcome," Josh said with a satisfied smile. "Aaron's going to show you something else before you go, but we can work out another day for you to come back."

"Seriously?"

"Yeah, if you want to." Aaron grinned and pointed his spoon at Josh. "I know he's a bit of a dickhead, but he's a reasonable chef."

"Said the biggest asshole I've ever met," Josh said.

"The most loveable asshole you've ever met."

Josh rolled his eyes and nudged Aaron gently with his

hand, their fingers brushing against each other. You could almost see the sparks running between them.

"Can I ask you a question?" I hadn't planned on asking them anything, but now I'd thought of the question, I needed to know the answer.

"Fire away," Aaron said, handing Josh the bowl of curry and walking over to a small sink to wash his hands.

"How do you make it work? With both of you being so busy. It's not like you work nine-to-five jobs, or even Monday to Friday, and I…" I trailed off because I wasn't sure what else to say. I hadn't been planning on baring my soul to two men I hardly knew, but maybe they'd understand.

It wasn't that Ianto wouldn't, because Ben was here as much as Aaron and Josh, but he was also my twin and knew all my secrets. It sometimes made it hard for him to be objective because he'd always take my side.

Josh and Aaron exchanged a long look for a second, and then Aaron said, "Let me guess, this mystery man you're helping out works long hours? Stressful job?"

"Yeah," I said, deciding it would be easier to get an answer if they had the full picture. "He's a paramedic. And a drag queen. And he does a lot of babysitting for his sister. I think his schedule is pretty set—it's just busy."

Aaron snorted as he dried his hands. "Busy sounds like the wrong fucking word. Exhausting would be better." He pulled out some different knives and grabbed a shopping bag I hadn't noticed from the pass at the other end of the kitchen. "And usually, that sort of shit isn't feasible long-term."

Josh nodded. "We make it work because we've fallen down the rabbit hole of doing it wrong. Trust us."

"I've been sober for nearly eleven years," Aaron said with a quiet seriousness I'd not heard before. I realised he was sharing something deeply personal with me, and I was oddly touched to get a glimpse at the man behind the chef. "Professional kitchens can be pretty unforgiving. The long hours, the stress, the tempers... I know a lot of people who ended up using because it was the only way to get through the days. I think it's different now. At least, I fucking hope it is. It is here anyway."

He shook his head. "My point is stressful, exhausting shit isn't something you can do forever. Everyone's breaking point is different and people cope with different levels of shit. Sometimes you have no option but to keep going because it's about fucking survival. But sooner or later, everyone breaks."

"It's what you do to survive too," Josh said quietly. "Some people don't need anything. Some of us..."

I nodded, not needing to know more. "Is there anything I can do?"

"Depends," Aaron said. "Is he a stubborn fucker?"

"Yeah." I chuckled softly. "He seems to think he needs to do everything. And getting help isn't an option."

"Sounds familiar," Aaron said with a pointed look at the kitchen door closest to Ben's office. "I'd say force yourself into his life but apparently that's not a good approach. I got told off last time I did that."

I raised an eyebrow as a few things about the December Ianto and Ben had gotten together clicked into place. I'd always had a sneaking suspicion other forces had been at work but Aaron had practically confirmed it. He grinned when he looked at me and just said, "There was a group chat. We had a hashtag and everything."

I laughed. "If I'd have known, I'd have helped. The pair of them were bloody sickening. Still are, to be honest."

"I think all you can do is be there," Josh said. "He might not want you. He might resist every single step of the damn way, and maybe you'll have to back off or admit you're not going to work. But maybe you'll get lucky. And if he does burn out, then at least you'll be there to catch him."

I nodded. It was similar to the advice Ianto had given me, but it was good to hear it from other people who understood. "Cheers, I appreciate it."

"No worries," Aaron said. He reached into the bag on the counter and started pulling various things out. "Now, I'm gonna teach you something that's not on our menu but it's the absolute tits and I fucking love it. It's Mrs Chen's Oyster Chicken." He grinned. "I met Mrs Chen in Sydney when I lived there for a year. She ran a dim sum restaurant and taught me this recipe, along with how to make dumplings—although apparently I can't fold dumplings for shit. Anyway, in honour of Mrs Chen, I'm gonna teach you how to make this. Then maybe I'll get universal bonus points for butchering so many Siu Mai."

CHAPTER SEVENTEEN

Eva Nessence

"Beloved Eva," Bitch said, throwing his arms around my waist and putting his head on my shoulder as I sat at the dressing room make-up counter, foundation sponge in hand. "How are you? You look tired."

"Do you begin all your conversations with observations about people's faces?" I asked with a grin and Bitch laughed, kissing the side of my head noisily. He was still in street clothes, having only just arrived while I'd gotten here early because I was always worried about the traffic between Nottingham and Lincoln. Once upon a time, I'd only given myself the time Google had predicted it would take me to get here and I'd ended up with fifteen minutes to get into full drag.

Never again.

"How else am I supposed to start them?" Bitch asked, squeezing my waist tightly.

"The hello was a good start. Although I'm not even sure you said that."

"I did call you beloved, though."

"That usually means you want something." I arched an eyebrow. "What is it?"

"I have an idea I want to run past you," Bitch said. "And don't worry, it's not some totally harebrained scheme."

"The fact you have to clarify it isn't a good sign." It also meant it definitely *was* some ill-thought-out, madcap scheme. But that didn't mean it would be a totally terrible idea either. Bitch was a dreamer but he was also very clever, and both of those qualities working together was a beautiful and dangerous thing. He was similar to Peachy Keen, another of The Court's queens, in that way. And if the pair of them ever got an idea together, then the rest of the world was fucked.

"I think it's a very good sign. It means I've thought it through." He glanced around like he was somehow expecting someone to be hiding in the clothing racks on the other side of the room. We were expecting more people that evening, specifically the murder twins and Sparkles, but none of them had arrived yet. Or maybe they had and Bitch had seen them before they'd come into the dressing room and sent them to get ready elsewhere.

Bitch released me and flopped in the chair next to mine, digging his make-up bag out of the backpack he'd been wearing along with a wig cap, a bag of bobby pins, and a velvet headband that he'd use to hold the cap in place. "It's an idea I've started thinking about. Well, I've done more than just thinking at this point. There are spreadsheets and

Word documents coming out of my eyeballs. They're colour coded and everything."

I chuckled. "Impressive."

"I know, Lewis would be so proud of me." Lewis, one of Bitch's many siblings, was a PA to several high-profile professional cosplayers as well as his husband, the actor Jason Lu. Bitch had always said Lewis's collection of highlighters, coloured pens, and notebooks would put any stationery store to shame.

And knowing that made me realise how little I'd shared about my own life with him. Or with any of the people here.

I'd always thought distance was a good thing, that it gave me the separation between all the facets of my life I needed to keep everything in balance. But suddenly, I wasn't sure it was the right decision. These people weren't only my colleagues, they were my friends. But I'd been keeping them at arm's length for so long I had no idea where to start when it came to sharing.

"My sister is the same," I said, focusing on my reflection in the mirror. I didn't want to see Eli's surprise at me finally sharing something personal. Otherwise I knew I wouldn't keep going. "She loves notebooks and craft stuff. She doesn't get a lot of time for it, but she likes making scrapbooks. It means I'm never short of ideas for her birthday."

"Honestly, having a sibling with a clear and obvious love for something is perfect," Bitch said as he stuffed his hair under his wig cap and began ruthlessly pinning it in place. "Although I find when it comes to you being the one with the interests, you do have to train them to get the right things or you get the weirdest shit. But these days it's how I get ninety percent of my make-up."

The knot in my chest that had been sat there for years slowly began to loosen the first few threads.

"What's this idea then?" I asked as I reached for my concealer and dabbed some on my face before starting to blend the fuck out of it. My make-up skills had improved drastically over the years, but I wished I had more time to practice.

"Have you heard of those drag pantos?"

"Yeah—it's basically an adult pantomime where the whole cast is made of drag performers." Pantomime was a British institution performed in theatres up and down the country every Christmas, with everyone from local amateur groups to full, high-budget cast productions putting one on. They were basically retold fairy tales or classic stories, like *Sleeping Beauty*, *Cinderella*, *Peter Pan*, *Aladdin*, *Dick Whittington*, and *Jack and the Beanstalk*, but performed in a camp, colourful, funny, and interactive way with musical numbers, audience participation, romance, plenty of innuendo, and copious amounts of glitter.

They also usually included various gender bending or drag roles, like the panto dame or Cinderella's ugly sisters being performed by men in drag, and sometimes the leading man was a woman in tiny shorts and tights, although having a principal boy was becoming less common as celebrities were cast in all the main roles.

With so many pantomimes available, production companies increasingly looked for famous names to increase ticket sales. I didn't blame them, though, and anyone who got involved in panto deserved plenty of credit because they were intense runs with short rehearsal times and a lot of shows.

"Exactly! And most of them run in big cities like London and Manchester, and *if* they come on tour, it's not usually to places like Lincoln. Although I think they sometimes go to one of the Nottingham theatres." He'd finished putting his wig cap on and was rummaging in his make-up bag for his concealer and whatever eye shadow palettes he wanted to use. "Anyway, I was thinking maybe we could do one round here. It would obviously be a smaller scale than some of the bigger ones, but I might have found a drag production company willing to support it."

"Seriously?" The production company would be a big deal because he'd not only need to cover costs but get things like costumes, a script, a director, and a whole production team. Bitch really had been considering this seriously. "How did you manage that?"

"I was chatting to Mercy a couple of weeks ago about it. She did *Cinderella* at a theatre in London over the winter and really enjoyed it, and I said I wished there were more of them, especially smaller ones with local talent. I mean, there are plenty of amateur pantos, so it wouldn't really be that hard to put one on, even if we just did it ourselves," Bitch said.

Mercy, or Madam Mercy, was a drag queen who'd done very well on *Drag Stars UK* a few years ago and had invited Bitch on a couple of variety show tours after seeing clips of her performing online. "Anyway, we ended up talking a bit more about it and we're going to try and run one round here this winter. Maybe Lincoln, if we can find a theatre. If not, we might have to try Nottingham."

"That would be amazing," I said, picking up my contour stick—because even though I went for a very gothic look, I still needed my face to have shape.

"I'm glad you think so. Because I think you should audition."

My head whipped around and I stared at him, splotches of contour all over my face. "Audition?"

"Yeah, I think you'd be good in panto. We're going to do either *Sleeping Beauty* or *Dick Whittington*, and I think you'd make an excellent villain or maybe something smaller if you're not as keen on that much stage time. But either way, I want you to audition because you've got great stage presence, you're easy to work with, and I think you're fucking fabulous. And it's my show, so what I say goes. Obviously, you'll get paid too. I just need to work out contracts and costs and how much we can afford."

"Eli, I…" I didn't know what to say. The idea of being in a drag panto was amazing, but my brain was already adding up the amount of extra work it would be, whether I'd be able to get the time off, and how it would fit in with the rest of my life. If it was only a few days, then maybe I could swing it, but any longer and it wasn't going to be feasible.

And it would depend on the rehearsals.

It would depend on a lot of little things. If it did end up being in Nottingham, I might be able to bring Milo and Grace to rehearsals, although if it was going to be aimed at adults, that wasn't going to work because they were both too young. And Kirsty always ended up working a lot of extra shifts in the run-up to Christmas too.

"You don't have to give me an answer now," Bitch said, putting his hand on my thigh. "You have time to think about it. But I will keep nagging you."

"Can I get more details, please?" I asked as I turned back to the mirror, trying to ignore the squirming in my stomach. "Like potential dates, rehearsals, which theatre you're using, all that shit. I need to look at everything and work out whether it's possible."

"Of course, I'll send everything across." There was a pause as I felt Bitch's gaze boring into the side of my skull. "Is everything okay, babe? And I mean that seriously. Are you all right?"

"Yeah, just busy." It was the truth, even if it was a stunningly understated one.

"Are you still working full-time?"

I nodded slightly as I continued blending. "Thirty-seven and a half hours a week. That's what I'm contracted for anyway. It sometimes works out a little different depending on my shift patterns but it all comes out in the wash."

"Have you ever considered doing less?" Bitch asked and I appreciated the fact he wasn't trying to circle around it. His directness was always something I'd liked, even if it could be a pain in the ass at times. "You're a fucking incredible performer. You could be doing so much more. And I know you love it—otherwise you wouldn't drag your ass all the way up here two or three times a week."

"It's complicated."

"Is it? Or are you making it complicated?"

Once again, I didn't have an answer.

And the sharp knocking at the door stopped me from having to think of one.

"Babes, can we come in yet?" Bubblegum called. "We need to put our shit down."

"Legs and Peaches kicked us out of their dressing room," Kate added. "Apparently, we make too much mess."

"You make too much fucking mess in here," Bitch yelled. "And their room is bigger than ours."

"Tough shit," Slashley said as she opened the door and stuck her head around it. There was fake blood dripping down her face, and it looked like the murder twins were aiming to live up to their name tonight. "You're stuck with us."

"Quick, find something to bar the door," Bitch said with a laugh as the three queens piled inside with all their shit in hand. How they needed so much stuff was beyond me. Then again, I'd turned the entire top floor of my house, which was a large, loft-style bedroom, into a dedicated space for my drag. It was bigger than my bedroom, with custom wardrobes, huge shelves for my wigs, and a craft table.

But my drag was important to me and I didn't want to half-ass any of it. I'd worked too hard over the years and my craft deserved to be treated with respect. Drag wasn't just a job to me; it was an art form, a release, a chance to do something different with my life and break out of the chains that had confined me. It was an opportunity to forget my responsibilities and be someone else for a little while.

Eva Nessence had come from my love of all things dark,

gothic, and beautiful. She was regal and elegant and wore beautiful gowns inspired by all those gothic music videos I'd been obsessed with as a teenager. I'd watched them more times than I could remember on the computers in the school library while pretending I was working on some project or another, dreaming of running away to those broken castles and faraway forests.

Everything had felt so impossible back then, but life was so much more complicated now than it had been when I was seventeen.

My love of the gothic had continued, though, and Eva was still here, still strong, and still beautiful.

I just wondered when she'd begun to feel like work instead of something I lived for.

The problem was I didn't know how to get back to that or if it was even possible.

I rummaged in my bag for my powder, trying to distance myself from the thoughts buzzing around me like angry wasps. But deep down, I knew I couldn't run from this. The weight of everything was starting to bear down on my shoulders, and I'd either have to deal with it.

Or be crushed.

CHAPTER EIGHTEEN

Rhys

I'D TOLD myself I wouldn't stoop so low as to start stalking Evan online, regardless of how badly I wanted to know the details of his life. But that had clearly failed because here I was, sitting at a front-row table in a drag club in Lincoln, waiting to watch him perform.

I wasn't quite sure how I was going to explain this one to Evan. Maybe I'd get lucky and he wouldn't look in the audience. Then I'd be able to sneak out the front door and get away before he even knew I was here. I'd hoped by coming alone I'd be able to go incognito, but it had taken me much longer than I'd anticipated to get here and by the time I'd gotten inside, the only free seats were near the front.

Luckily, the other three men at the table had been very warm and welcoming and hadn't seemed to mind a total stranger plonking their ass down in the spare seat. From what I gathered, they all played for a local rugby club. One of them was the boyfriend of one of the queens and two of them lived with another.

"Have you been to one of the shows before?" asked West, the boyfriend. He had a vaguely familiar face but I couldn't figure out why because I didn't support any English rugby teams.

"No," I said, sipping the Coke I'd gotten before I sat down. Since I was driving home, I wasn't going to drink, and a clear head would help me figure out the nearest exit if I needed to make a quick break for it. "This was a bit of a last-minute decision. To tell you a secret, I'm here because my neighbour is one of the queens but they don't know I'm here, so I was trying not to draw attention to myself."

West suddenly looked surprised. "Wait… are you Eva's neighbour?"

"Yes?" I wasn't sure if admitting it was a good thing. I'd only worked out Evan's drag name after some serious Instagram stalking last night. I couldn't even remember how I'd found it, but I'd started with local drag nights and Nottingham Pride and gone from there, lying in bed staring at endless photos and scrolling through countless profiles until I'd found him. Or her. I'd been quite proud of myself. And tired, since it had taken me until two in the morning, but I wasn't going to think about that. "How did you know?"

"Er, she's mentioned you a few times," West said, picking up his drink and glancing away like he wasn't sure if he should have said anything. "To Bubblegum at least."

"Legs too," said Mason, one of the other guys. "You

wouldn't happen to be the Welsh bastard with the terrible taste in music?"

A bark of laughter burst out of me. It sounded like I had a reputation, and I took a strange delight in knowing I'd been getting under Evan's skin for a while. Maybe I really could annoy my way into his life. "That's me. But I don't think my music is that bad."

"Just loud, apparently," Mason said with a grin.

"Didn't Legs say it was weird mash-up shit?" asked the third man, who'd introduced himself as Jonny. He frowned as he ran his thumb up and down the side of his pint. "Like techno-metal? He said Eva won't stop grumbling about it." He glanced at me and grinned sheepishly. "Sorry. I'm sure it's great, if you like that stuff."

"I do but it doesn't sound like many people are fans." I felt a bit bad because while I loved getting under Evan's skin, if it had been that awful, why hadn't he said anything earlier? And if I hadn't pushed him into snapping at me, would he still be stewing and letting his resentment build?

"I'm glad you guys are talking, though," West said, giving me an adorably warm smile. "And I'm sure Eva will be pleased you showed up to surprise her."

I wasn't so sure, but I didn't want to burst West's bubble. And luckily, I didn't have to because someone randomly came up and tapped me on the shoulder, and when I looked around, I saw a man in a tight black T-shirt with green hair and a tongue piercing.

"Hey," he said. "Sorry, this is random but are you Rhys?"

"Yeah, can I help you?"

He grinned and beckoned me with one hand. "Yeah, Eva asked you to come backstage."

Shit.

Fucking bollocks.

I'd been caught.

And since I had no fucking poker face, everyone at the table could see me looking like Bambi in fucking headlights.

Evan was going to fucking murder me and nobody would ever know where to look for me since I hadn't even told Ianto where I was.

"Sure," I said, because I couldn't exactly say no to him. I drained the last of my Coke, stood up, said a quick goodbye to everyone at the table, and followed the green-haired man to a door beside the stage.

Inside was a set of stairs, which I climbed rapidly, and at the top of them, waiting for me, was a queen straight out of my gothic dreams.

I'd seen countless pictures of Eva Nessence on Instagram, but none of them could hold a candle to the reality.

Eva was tall and graceful with long dark hair that cascaded down her back and the most beautifully made-up face with smoky eyes and blood red lips that I wanted to kiss. She was wearing a deep-red dress with a sheer corset-style bodice, long sleeves, and a flowing skirt that I could just about see an enormous pair of spiked-heel shoes underneath.

And on top of her head was a bejewelled black crown that sparkled in the low light.

Eva wasn't simply a queen—she exuded power and

radiance, and all I wanted was to drop to my knees in front of her and worship the ground she walked on.

She was watching me with a glowering expression that made my stomach twist, and I couldn't tell if she was pleased to see me, angry, or a little of both.

"Hey," I said, giving her an awkward smile.

"What are you doing here? Actually, my first question is how the fuck did you find me?"

"Just a smidge of Instagram stalking." I held my thumb and forefinger apart. "I wasn't actually expecting to find you, but I recognised you in a picture from Nottingham Pride last year."

Eva frowned. "You recognised me in full drag?"

"Of course," I said softly. "I'd know those eyes anywhere. They're stunning." And they'd stolen my heart along with my soul. It should have terrified me, and maybe it did, but I was too in awe of my queen to notice.

She reached up and touched her cheek almost self-consciously, and I saw she was wearing long pointed nails painted the same dark red as her dress. I wondered what they'd feel like scraping across my nipples, teasing my balls, and running down my back.

"Why?" she asked.

"Why what?"

"Why did you find me? Why are you here? I don't…" She trailed off and I took two steps closer. "I don't understand."

"Do you want me to go?" I didn't want to, but if Eva didn't want me here, then I wasn't going to intrude.

"No. I just want to know why."

I took another few steps closer. I could hear other people moving around, the sounds of voices and the swell of music. But as far as I was concerned, it was all taking place in another universe, far away from Eva and me.

"I just... I know you try and keep things separate, and you don't let people in," I said. "Fuck, if anyone understands not letting people in, it's me. Apart from Ianto, I've kept everyone at arm's length for fucking years. But I also know drag is important to you. It has to be, even if you don't talk about it that much. Because I don't think you'd keep doing it if it didn't mean something to you. And I wanted to understand, wanted to see." I shot her a half smile. "I was kind of hoping you wouldn't actually see me. How did you know I was here?"

"West," Eva said. "He messaged Sparkles, and Sparkles couldn't keep a secret if her life bloody depended on it."

"I heard that!" cried an indignant voice from the direction of the stage. I didn't look to see who it belonged to and just laughed when they continued. "And don't blame my boyfriend. He's too sweet to be blamed. He was only asking me if I knew Rhys was coming."

"Sparkles, I love you but you're not part of this conversation, so sod off."

"You shouldn't have mentioned me then! What was I supposed to do, pretend I wasn't here?"

"Yes," Eva said acerbically with a dark smile that made my knees weak. "I'm trying to have a private conversation."

"Nothing private about it," said another voice. This time I could see the speaker since they were walking towards me. They had fake blood dripping down their face, which was so realistic it made me do a startled double take. "If you don't want any of us involved, you need to take it upstairs. Wait... when are you on? You're after us and Sparkles, right?"

"Yeah, before Bitch and Peaches," Eva said.

"Then you've got about thirty minutes, maybe forty if we stall," said a third voice, which belonged to another queen with fake blood on her face who was the spitting image of the other queen except for maybe a head shorter. They had horror movie-psycho twins vibes and I was digging it. It reminded me of the creepy twin costumes I'd done with Ianto over the years.

"Thanks," Eva said. She reached out and grabbed my hand, her nails gently catching me and sending sparks shooting across my skin. A tiny smile pulled at the corner of her mouth as she added, "Come with me."

I didn't get a chance to ask where before she started pulling me towards a large set of concrete stairs. When we reached them, she released my arm to pick up her skirt, lifting the hem off the floor like some Victorian lady so she could climb the stairs without treading on it. Though I was more worried about the set of spikes she was wearing—they looked fucking lethal and one good stamp would send them straight through someone's foot.

That idea probably shouldn't have turned me on as much as it did.

Once we reached the top, Eva led me to one of the wooden doors, knocking on it sharply before sticking her head around it. "Babe," she said to whoever was inside.

"Can I borrow the room? I won't be long." The person on the other side of the door said something I didn't catch, but Eva's reply made it obvious they were talking about me. "Yeah, he's just behind me. Pierce went and got him."

"I'm sorry," I said. "I didn't mean to cause such a fuss. I can go."

"No," Eva said. "You're staying."

I let out a surprised snort. "Bossy much. You can't order me to stay."

"Yes, I can." She turned and smirked at me, a gleam in her eyes that I'd only seen right before we fucked. "You're in my castle now, and I'm in charge."

"Kinky, I like it," said a voice from behind the door. Another drag queen appeared, looking exactly like one of the noughties MySpace emo girls complete with jagged bangs and fingerless arm-warmers threaded with ribbon. I recognised her from some of the photos on Eva's Instagram. She was carrying a pair of shoes in one hand, with her phone tucked into them. "I'll be in Peaches's room if you need me. Have fun. If you get cum on my make-up, you're replacing it."

She blew Eva a kiss and strolled off towards the stairs and Eva let out a long, slightly tortured sigh.

"You know," she said as she pulled me into the dressing room and shut the door, clicking the lock into place, "they're going to be torturing me about this for weeks. It's been four years and I've hardly told them anything about my life."

"I could have just left," I said as Eva slowly backed me up against the door, towering over me like some infernal goddess. "You drew all the attention by dragging me back here."

"I know…" She leant down until we were nose to nose and I could see every detail of her face. Her make-up was heavy and seemed to amplify every expression, like I'd held up a microscope. "You've broken through half my boundaries like they're made of wet cardboard. And that should piss me the fuck off but… I've never met anyone so interested in me they literally hunted me down before. It's a little creepy."

I chuckled breathlessly, my heart racing. She had me totally pinned against the door as she lifted one finger to run her nail along the underside of my jaw. God, why was that so fucking hot? "Good creepy?"

She smirked. "Just this once, yes."

Then she kissed me hard and it felt like all the life was draining out of my body.

I'd told myself I was never going to fall for anyone. But I'd fallen for Evan so fucking hard nothing could stop me.

And whatever happened next, I'd be falling without a parachute.

It was going to be a wild fucking ride, and I almost didn't care that it would probably kill me.

CHAPTER NINETEEN

Rhys

I could get drunk on Eva's kisses. And if she kept on kissing me the way she was, I'd be a fucking puddle on the floor in less than five minutes.

The door was a hard, cold wall against my back and there was some sort of hook digging into the back of my neck, but I didn't have words to say how uncomfortable it was. If it was a choice between being uncomfortable and making out with Eva, I'd choose the second a million times over. In fact, there was no fucking universe where I'd say no.

I was a little confused about how we'd ended up here because Eva seemed both pissed at seeing me and really glad about it. From the sound of it, nobody in her life had ever come to see her in drag before because she'd always kept them separate, and that saddened me because if drag was that important to her, then she shouldn't be hiding it.

Although hiding it was probably the wrong word. Disconnection would be better.

Evan had disconnected all the parts of his life, trying to keep all the bubbles separate for some strange reason I couldn't even begin to fathom. Which was probably why I'd charged straight into the middle of this strange three-ring circus because I hadn't even known it was a thing to begin with.

At some level, I understood keeping the two professional parts of his life apart, especially if any of the management weren't understanding or supportive, but to keep his friends or family in the dark was something else entirely. Maybe it was because I'd always shared everything with Ianto, so keeping secrets from someone I loved was a completely alien concept to me. I'd have to try and talk to Evan about it, or more likely pry the truth out of him with three feet of rope and some fucking dynamite.

Later, though.

When I wasn't being kissed senseless by a gothic drag goddess.

"You're too fucking sexy for your own damn good," Eva said with a growl as she broke away from me, wiping the corner of her mouth with her thumb. Her lipstick was smeared and she reminded me of a vampire who'd been feeding. It was another thing that had no right to be as fucking sexy as it was. "I'm supposed to be talking to you."

"We can talk later," I said, stepping slightly forward to get away from the hook digging into my neck and discovering my legs had turned to jelly. "I'm quite fond of you kissing me."

Eva grinned and raised a perfectly painted-on eyebrow at me. "You're incorrigible."

"You started it. I wasn't the one who kissed me."

"Yes, well…" She sighed, folding her arms and unfolding them again. "You're the one who showed up out of the blue looking like that."

I glanced down at myself, trying to work out what was so special about a nice pair of jeans, a shirt, and some decent boots. Maybe it was because I spent most of my life in shorts, joggers, and gym shirts, but most of them were pretty nice. Ianto had made me get rid of my very comfortable pair of joggers when the holes had become indecent, at least in his opinion. "Is the shirt doing it for you?" I asked with a sly smile. "Do I need to wear one more often?"

"No, I'd never get anything done. And neither would you."

"Sounds fun, though."

She huffed but there was still a glint of desire dancing in her eyes. And maybe something that could even be fondness. "You're such a pain in the ass, you know that?"

"You might have mentioned it once or twice."

"I don't get why you care so much. Like, why the fuck would you want to find me? Why the hell would you come all this way? Don't you have anything better to do on a Friday night?"

"Not really, no," I said. It was my turn to glare at her, but it was more imploring than angry. Why couldn't she see? Was Evan that determined to keep people shut out? "And like I said, I'm here because drag is important to you. It's obvious from the way you talk about it, even if that's barely at all. But since you don't talk about anything personal, I figured anything you did mention must mean everything."

"Seriously? That's a bold assumption."

"I'm right, though. Otherwise you wouldn't have gotten so flustered. You wouldn't have fucking cared that I'd shown up unless it properly meant something," I said. "And I've come all this way because, whether you like it or not, I *like* you. You're infuriating and frustrating and you seem to think your whole life should be a secret, and when someone shows an interest, you have no idea what to do. I've told you why I'm here three times now, but it's like you don't believe me. Do you not think you're worth the attention? Is that it? Or are you worried your house of cards is going to collapse if you even consider letting someone in? Because I've seen your life and it's exhausting, but that's because you insist on doing everything yourself. The world won't end if you ask for help."

Eva stared at me, shock and anger warring with surprise across her face. I didn't think she'd expected me to challenge her. I hadn't been expecting to do it myself, but I had to say something. I'd never forgive myself if I sat idly by and watched Evan burn himself out until he was nothing more than a burnt crisp.

"You don't know me," Eva said finally. She was trying to sound angry but there was something about her tone that didn't quite convince me, like she wanted to be angry but couldn't get all the way there. "You're just—"

"I'm just someone who cares," I said, stepping closer to her and reaching out for her hand. "You're right, I don't know you. Not really. But I want to." I squeezed her hand and closed the gap between us, looking up into those beautiful, bright eyes framed by extraordinarily dramatic lashes. "Do you want to know a secret?"

"A secret?"

"Yes. I know I'm annoying, but it always gets me what I want. And usually, after a few hours, or days, maybe even a few weeks, I run away. You see, I got my heart broken at seventeen and ever since then I've thrown away everything that could potentially become a relationship because it's easier to do that than consider opening myself up to someone," I said. It was the first time I'd ever admitted that out loud, and I wasn't completely sure why I was even saying it. Maybe I was hoping that on some level, my words would resonate.

Or maybe I'd just sound like a self-centred jackass. It was hard to tell at this point.

"Why are you telling me this?" Eva asked.

"I don't know. I guess I'm hoping it'll show you that you mean something to me. It doesn't have to be a big deal. In fact, I'm not sure I want it to be. Otherwise I might run for the hills."

Eva chuckled dryly. "Maybe I should declare my love for you now, then, save us both the trouble."

"You could, but I know you wouldn't mean it," I said. "Especially not now you've said that."

"Drat, you've foiled my cunning plan."

I laughed. "I'm sorry for the inconvenience."

"No, you're not."

"You're right, I'm not." I leant forward and kissed her

softly. I was already wearing enough of her make-up; it wouldn't hurt to wear more. "Look, I'm not saying this has to be something big and dramatic and all that. I'm only saying I like you and I want you to let me in, just a little."

"Do I get a choice here?"

"Of course. I've already offered to leave. You're the one who kidnapped me and locked me in your dressing room."

"You weren't kidding about annoying me into wanting you, were you?"

I shrugged. "It's already worked at least once. I think about it every time I look at my sofa."

Eva snorted and shook her head. Then she smiled, her other hand coming up to cup my jaw. "Every time I lie in bed, I think about you in it... the way you rode me... how you begged for my load all over your beautiful face. I can't get you out of my head no matter how hard I fucking try. It's like you moved in and claimed bloody squatter's rights."

"Good," I said. "Because I'm staying."

"Until you get bored or scared and then run away?" Eva raised an unimpressed eyebrow. "How does that work? Is it supposed to make it easier, knowing you're probably going to break my heart?"

I swallowed, a pang of guilt echoing through my chest. "Maybe... maybe not... but I'll tell you something else. You're the first person, besides Ianto, that I've gone to any sort of lengths for. And I didn't realise it until the bastard pointed it out."

"So what, are you telling me I'm special? How many other people have you given this speech to?"

"None," I said. "Cross my heart. I'm a dickhead, but I'm not that much of a prick."

"I'm not convinced," Eva said. "But I appreciate your honesty. Most of the men I've dated have promised me the moon and stars. You've only promised you'll probably dump me and in the next breath told me I'm special. Which makes you more fucking irritating than ever because I should be running screaming down those stairs and having you thrown out the stage door."

"But?"

"But," she said with a growl of frustration. "I can't fucking do it because you're the first man who's ever made me feel like I somehow matter. Like, we're barely dating and you're *here*. And I should be pissed as fuck at you, and I am, but you're charming as hell and I can't stop myself from wanting you. All this shit is probably going to go up in flames but fuck it, for once I don't care if I get burned."

"You never know. Maybe it won't," I said, for my sake as much as hers. I knew I'd probably run. I always did. But this time something felt different, and a small part of my heart hoped maybe this time I wouldn't sink my own ship. That I'd give myself a chance. "Either way, we'll have some fun. And the sex will be fantastic."

"You're an asshole," she said, kissing me forcefully.

"I know, but I'm a charming asshole."

She sighed and broke away, turning to the mirror and letting out a huff of frustration. She stalked over to it and grabbed a packet of wipes, pulling a couple out then throwing the pack to me so I could clean up my face, before turning back to the mirror and starting to tidy up the mess that was her mouth. "What are you doing after this?"

"After what?" I asked, confused by the sudden change in direction.

"The show. The one you bought a ticket for."

"I don't know, why?"

"Want to go and get McDonald's? I'll be fucking starving by the time I'm done. And then maybe… you can come back to mine?"

I grinned. "I'd like that. Shall I go back to my seat then?"

"You can," she said as her reflection smiled at me. "Or you can watch from the side of the stage. Get a close-up. Then we can leave straight afterwards instead of waiting for the end of the show. Unless you want to watch the others? They're actually pretty good. Although you'd only be watching me, Bitch, and Peaches."

"I can see them another time. As long as I get to see you," I said. "I don't think I've told you how beautiful you look yet, have I? I'm not even sure beautiful is the right word. It's more like fucking stunning. I've never seen anyone who looks so good in a crown."

Eva turned and looked at me, a flush breaking out on her pale cheeks as she reached up and touched one of the crown's bejewelled spikes. "You think so? I was worried it was too much."

"You look like an empress," I said. "It's perfect."

The smile that blossomed across her face branded itself on my heart, and I knew if I tried to run, Eva's heart wouldn't be the only one getting broken.

CHAPTER TWENTY

Eva Nessence

GETTING McDonald's after the show while still half in drag wasn't that much of a rare occurrence. The unusual part was sharing it with someone who wasn't a drag performer.

But here I was sitting in a booth at McDonald's with a Big Mac and fries, sipping my Diet Coke with Rhys sat opposite me, alternating between dipping chips and deep-fried mozzarella balls into sweet chilli sauce. If I looked hard enough at this situation, it probably counted as a date. It made me feel like I was seventeen all over again, sitting opposite Darren Wilson and hoping he'd be up for shagging me in the back of his car before he took me home.

I was a classy teenager.

And why I was thinking about Darren Wilson and not this whole mess of an evening was anyone's guess. Probably because I wanted to avoid thinking about how my carefully planned and separate lives had all come crashing together in one big colourful mess. It was like someone had just chucked a load of paint across a canvas and called it art, only that art was my life.

My conversation with Rhys in the dressing room was still playing in loops around my mind, and I couldn't decide whether I liked any of it. Add into that the drag panto discussion I'd had with Bitch, and my brain was two seconds away from a nuclear meltdown.

The one thing I clung to, in all the mess, was the fact Rhys was here.

Against all the odds, despite all the barriers and my desperate attempts to keep him away, he'd found Eva. Because he knew she was important to me. And it stunned me to think how much he cared.

It made me want to reach out in some way, ask more, connect with him. But how to do that was still a mystery since I wasn't great at sharing and didn't know where to begin with asking him to do the same.

"What are you thinking about?" Rhys asked as he gently nudged his foot against my ankle, drawing me out of my head and away from the rabbit hole I'd been about to climb into.

"Just… stuff." I waved my hand and reached for my burger, knowing that if it went cold, it would be like eating cardboard.

"Want to elaborate on that?"

"Not really," I said, taking a large bite and chewing slowly. Rhys was watching me, waiting patiently, and when

I swallowed I found myself adding, "Eli asked me to be in a drag panto he's putting together."

"That sounds like fun," Rhy said with an encouraging smile as he reached for more chips. "I'm assuming it's like your standard panto but everyone's in drag and it's full of blatant sex jokes rather than sneaky ones that go just over the heads of the kids? And I'm guessing there's not kids in the audience either."

"Pretty much."

"You're not sure about it, are you?"

I frowned at him. "Is it that obvious?"

"Yes and no." He sat back in his seat and looked at me carefully while I took another bite of my burger. "I don't think you'd have brought it up if you weren't considering it, and I'm very happy to be your sounding board, but I think you're also worried about how it will fit into everything else. There's wanting to do it, and there's being able to."

I put the remaining half of the Big Mac back into its box and took another sip of my drink. I didn't want to like that he could read me so well, but I couldn't deny it made things easier. I couldn't dance around if Rhys had already hit the target, and I was too tired to argue with myself. Since he'd already steamrollered through most of my walls, it seemed ridiculous to try and keep him out any longer.

It made me think of a cartoon where the walls of the castle were in a heap on the floor but the door was still standing, and yet the character still insisted on people using the door.

And if I wanted to connect with him, purposefully this time, I had to push myself out of my comfort zone.

"I think I want to," I said. "But I don't think I can. I mean, I can get all the details and try and make it work, but I don't want to disappoint Eli by turning up late or having to leave early. Besides, the holidays are always busy at work, and I know I'll be exhausted from dealing with everything because no matter how many years I do, I never get used to some of the shit we see. Plus, Kirsty works a lot around Christmas, and I can't stick Milo and Grace in the car and bring them to rehearsals."

"Why not?"

"It's not exactly appropriate. I know everyone would love them, but as you said, there'll be a lot of swearing and sex jokes and…" I sighed. "It's just better if I say no. Then I can't disappoint anyone."

"Except for yourself," Rhys said pointedly.

"That's not important."

"Being disappointed and unhappy with your own life isn't important?"

"Not if I have other things to put first," I said. "I love drag, and being Eva means everything to me, but I have other responsibilities. I can't fuck Kirsty over like that, not when…" I shook my head. That was another story for another time.

But apparently, I wasn't allowed to let it go.

"Not when what?"

"It doesn't matter."

"Yeah," Rhys said. "I think it does." He reached across the table and brushed his fingers against mine, while under it he hooked his ankle around my foot. I couldn't escape. "Please."

"Similar story to you, I guess, except swap the dead parents for a dad who left when I was six and a mum who decided she'd rather go out partying than look after her kids. Social services did fuck all because my mum was around just enough to keep up appearances, but if it wasn't for my sister, who was only fucking eleven when all this kicked off, then who the hell knows where I'd be. Kirsty gave up everything for me, her childhood, her whole fucking life. She got a job at sixteen, she made me go to school, she told me I was going to university if it was the last thing she did. She was my mother... and now she's got two kids and she's still struggling and I just... I owe her *everything*, Rhys, and I can't forget what she did for me. And I'm not suddenly going to turn round and tell her she's on her own. She won't let me do much, but she will let me babysit and if that's all I can do to repay her, then I'll babysit every damn day."

"Hey," Rhys said softly, and I realised my eyes had filled up with tears. "It's okay. I promise."

I sniffed and reached for a napkin, trying to dab my eyes before I actually started crying and ruined what was left of my make-up. "This is why I don't tell people about my life," I said, trying to sound sarcastic and realising I only sounded defensive and miserable.

"I'm glad you told me."

"Are you now going to tell me I shouldn't let that stop me living my dreams?"

He smiled. "Maybe. But I also know life is complicated

and so is family." He squeezed my hand again. "So, you want to do drag. You need to make it fit with your family things... what about changing your job?"

I dropped the screwed-up napkin on the table and reached for the other half of my burger, not quite sure why we'd suddenly jumped from my youth to my career. "My job?"

"Your day job. You work full-time, right? Any chance you could go part-time? Would that cover your bills?"

"I don't know. I've never really thought about it." It sounded strange, considering I'd always wanted more time for drag, but reducing my hours at work had never factored itself in as a plausible option.

I knew the East Midlands Ambulance Service offered part-time positions, but I'd never thought about applying for one. I really liked my shift pattern, my station, and the people I worked with, and there was a huge risk going part-time would change all of that. I didn't want to find myself stuck out at the arse-end of Lincolnshire working nothing but nights and weekends because that would defeat the whole purpose of changing in the first place.

"Maybe it's worth giving it some proper thought then," he said. "Because if you can make it work and get to do more of the things you love, then why not do it? You only get one life, and if you get the chance to live your dreams and not be miserable, why wouldn't you take it? Unless you like being miserable, that is."

"Aren't you a ray of sunshine?" I asked with a grin. My heart fluttered, something it had started doing on a semi-regular basis, and I resisted the urge to thump myself in the chest like I was an old computer that needed rebooting.

"And you're a miserable bastard."

"We're a right fucking pair, aren't we?"

"We are," he said, his foot sliding up my calf. "And I like it."

We finished eating, Rhys thankfully changing the subject to the show, and my heart kept fucking fluttering as he talked about my performance. I didn't think I'd been that good, but from the way he was waxing lyrical, it sounded like I'd just won a bloody Oscar, Tony, Brit Award, and a BAFTA all at once.

Next time I'd make sure I got out of my own head. Then I'd fucking stun him.

"Where are you parked?" Rhys asked as he headed out of McDonald's and into the cool spring night. His fingers slotted easily into mine and I almost tripped over my own feet in shock. I couldn't remember the last time anyone over the age of ten had held my hand.

"Just, er… back near The Court. There's a little car park that belongs to some of the nearby offices, but Phil made a deal with them to let us park in there for free after six," I said, gesturing vaguely in the direction of the club with my free hand. "What about you?"

"In the multi-story by the Brayford," he said. "Not far from you at all."

He started walking, gently pulling me along with him, and I followed, feeling more unsteady on my feet than ever despite the fact I'd swapped my heels for trainers when I'd hastily gotten changed before we'd left. Usually, I was the one in control of everything, but at that moment it felt like the whole world had turned upside down.

The streets of Lincoln were full of people heading out for the night, but everyone ignored us for once and I was glad I didn't have to deal with another night like last November when a group of drunk dickheads had harassed us, causing poor Sparkles to go into shock, Bitch to break the ringleader's nose, and me to pick up the pieces.

But unlike with Rhys, I'd had no inclination to help the drunk bastard with blood on his face. Which was technically contrary to my duties as a paramedic, but I'd excused myself by reminding my brain I wasn't on duty and poor Rory had needed more help than the drunken cockwomble.

"If I'd known you were coming, I'd have given you a lift," I said as we got closer to The Court, sidestepping a group of girls all dressed to the nines. "Then we wouldn't have had to bring two cars."

"It's okay. The plan wasn't for you to notice me anyway," Rhys said.

"How? You were literally sat in the front row."

"That wasn't my plan! There were no other seats."

I laughed. "You'd make a fucking awful spy."

"Probably, but I'd look good in the suit, though." He drew me to a stop, pulling me in for a soft kiss. "You know, I think we should pick up where we left off earlier. Before you started asking me twenty questions."

Heat bubbled in my stomach as I remembered the way his body had felt through the thin material of my dress. I'd been so tempted to make him drop to his knees and suck me off, but the idea of trying to put myself back together before I went on stage, combined with my spiralling thoughts, had been enough to shove that temptation to the back of the queue.

But now I was only wearing jeans, a T-shirt, and an old denim jacket. And my dick wasn't shoved behind skin-tight underwear and two pairs of tights.

"We should," I said as I wrapped my arms around him, not caring that we were in the middle of the street. "And I really don't know if I can wait until we get back."

Rhys chuckled softly against my mouth. "Are you suffering? Do you need me to take the edge off before we drive home?"

"Are you offering?"

"Yes. Are there any cameras in this car park of yours?"

"Maybe, but it's dark and I can always move my car."

He smirked. "I don't care if anyone sees me sucking you off in the front seat."

"As long as you're not going to fuck me on the back seat, otherwise this whole evening will be like the night I lost my virginity all over again."

Rhys snorted with laughter, the sound bursting out of him and causing a few people further down the road to stop and look at us. He rested his head on my shoulder as his whole body shook. The sound was infectious and I couldn't stop myself from chuckling along with him.

"I was a classy teenager," I said. "As you can see."

"Are you trying to tell me you're better now?"

"No, obviously not." I laughed and kissed him again. "We can't get caught, though, because the others will *never* let me live it down. I'm supposed to be the smart one."

Rhys grinned and grabbed my hand, towing me back towards the club and making me yelp in surprise. "Don't worry, I'm good at sucking dick. You won't last long enough for anyone to catch you."

"I can't decide if that's a threat or a promise." Either way, I liked the idea. It was reckless and silly, and I shouldn't be doing it. But for once, I was going to say fuck it to being sensible. I deserved to enjoy myself every once in a while.

Rhys and I rushed down the street giggling like teenagers and stopping every few steps to kiss each other senseless. It was like we couldn't get enough of each other. I dragged him around the edge of The Court, avoiding the people queuing up to get into the club night after the show and sneaking past the stage door in case someone burst out and caught us.

The car park was deserted and dark except for a few streetlights dotted around the edge and a couple of lonely ones in the middle that cast a paltry glow over the potholed tarmac. I'd left my car in the corner out of the way, which now seemed like fate because anyone walking past wouldn't see us. Although I doubted anyone bar the other members of The Court would be around here at this time of night, and none of their cars were parked beside mine.

I pulled my keys out of my jacket pocket and unlocked my tiny, battered hatchback. Rhys opened the driver's door and pushed me onto the seat before running around to the other side and I laughed as I watched him because he was practically skipping. My heart raced and my stomach flipped, joy and desire coursing through me. I couldn't remember the last time I'd had such wild, careless fun.

Rhys threw himself onto the passenger seat and grabbed the front of my jacket, pulling me in for more deep, heated kisses that set my body on fire. His tongue pushed into my mouth and he nipped my bottom lip as his other hand reached for the button on my jeans. The front of my car was cramped, so getting my jeans open and down far enough to pull out my cock wasn't easy or graceful, but all we did was laugh, our lips meeting in more hungry kisses.

Rhys reached down and shoved his seat all the way back, giving him room to wiggle into position. He grinned at me as he wrapped his fingers around my aching erection, grazing his thumb across the leaking head. "I've been wanting to do this for ages."

"What?" I asked breathlessly as he started to pump my cock slowly. "Suck me off in the front of my car?"

"Just the sucking off part, although the car is a novel touch. Not done this in a while."

I wanted to laugh but the sound died on my tongue as Rhys lowered his head and wrapped his lips around my cock. I bit back a groan as he slid me deeper into his mouth, the wet heat and the press of his tongue sending pleasure racing through me. Rhys had said he'd make sure I didn't last long, and I believed him. The man sucked dick like a fucking god.

Rhys's head bobbed up and down as he worked my cock, wrapping his fingers around the base of my shaft so every inch of me was encased in heat. His saliva dripped down my skin, running down my balls, and the car filled with filthy, wet sucking sounds that were fucking music to my ears.

My hand rested on the back of Rhys's head as I fought back countless moans, my breath coming in deep pants. I wanted it to last because I wasn't ready for this moment between us to end. I knew we'd likely go home and fuck until the early hours, until we were both dripping in sweat and cum and too exhausted to move. But that was different… planned… and there was something strangely intimate about Rhys blowing me in the front of my car. It had been a long time since I'd felt this kind of desire, that burning need-you-right-now feeling which consumed every waking thought.

Rhys groaned and swallowed around me, the vibrations making pure pleasure drip down my spine. I was getting close and at this rate, nothing was going to stop me from coming down his throat.

"Rhys," I said, my low voice sounding like a shout in the confines of the car. "I'm… fuck, I'm close."

He tilted his head up, his eyes meeting mine for a moment. He looked so beautiful like this, slick pink lips stretched wide around my cock, cheeks flushed, and eyes shining. It made me want to paint his face with my release and lick it off before pushing my cum into his mouth with my tongue.

Fuck, I was definitely doing that later.

Rhys hummed around me and swallowed again, sucking me deep into his mouth, and that was all it took. I grabbed his head, my hips bucking up as my orgasm hit me, and I filled his throat with my cum. Pleasure ripped through me and blood pounded in my ears as Rhys gently slid my cock out from between his lips, licking up the last drops of my release that clung to my slit.

I reached out and grasped his jaw, pulling him towards me because I needed to kiss him. I needed to taste myself on him.

"You were right," I said softly. Breathlessly. Completely undone by him in a matter of minutes. "Nobody caught us. And you're really fucking good at that."

"I know." He kissed me again. "Feel better now?"

"Maybe? I think I might need a few minutes before I drive home, though. I'm not sure it's safe. And…" I punctuated my words with another kiss. "I really want to repay the favour."

"Later," he said. He was practically sitting in my lap now but he still didn't feel close enough. "I want you to take me apart."

"I will, I promise."

"Good." He brushed his lips against mine and I sighed, the tension that had been sitting in my chest all evening finally easing. "Have dinner with me."

I startled, not sure I'd heard him right. "What?"

"We should go out for dinner together," he said, brushing a stray lock of hair off my face. "Not just for McDonald's, somewhere nice. And before you start grumbling about having time, you let me know when you're free and I'll book something."

I opened my mouth to say no, that the offer was lovely but I didn't have time. But instead I said, "That sounds great. I'm off on Thursday night if that works? I finish work at six if you don't mind waiting for me to get back and do a quick change?"

"I'll be waiting." He kissed me softly and I wondered how one man could undo me so completely I'd consider giving up everything for him.

CHAPTER TWENTY-ONE

Rhys

I HADN'T PLANNED on taking Evan to The Pear Tree for dinner, but the decision had been taken out of my hands by Ianto. As soon as I'd told him I was looking for somewhere, he'd immediately messaged Ben and we'd had a table booked for us before I'd even realised what was happening.

So here we were, on a Thursday evening, tucked in a corner of the dining room at a lovely table for two with drinks, a basket of sliced sourdough, and a little dish with two different types of butter in it. The restaurant was packed, and I wondered if Ben had magically conjured up a table just for us. It was something he'd done in the past for people he cared about, and I made a mental note to not only tip well but give him a big hug before we left.

I'd wondered if he was going to hover and eavesdrop, reporting everything that happened to Ianto, who was probably blowing up his phone with a desperate need for details. But Ben, and the rest of the staff, had been nothing but professional and it reminded me why The Pear Tree was such a bloody good pub.

"This is really nice," Evan said as he glanced around the dining room, which despite the large windows and high ceilings had a warm and cosy feel. "I've never been here before. I'm surprised you managed to get a table."

"It helps when your brother-in-law owns it," I said, reaching for the pint of very good locally brewed beer they had on tap. "I'll be honest, the decision to come here was slightly taken out of my hands. I love my brother, but he isn't half interfering."

Evan chuckled. He looked a little pale and the dark circles under his eyes looked more pronounced than usual, but I wasn't going to mention it because I knew he'd brush me off with the excuse that he'd had a long day. "That's nice, though. That he cares so much."

"Yeah, for all my complaining I don't know what I'd do without him. I think it'd feel like I was missing something."

"Is it weird? Not seeing him every day."

"Not as bad as it used to be," I said as I sipped my drink. "The first few months were the worst, mostly because I didn't want him to know how much I missed him. He was so happy about moving in with Ben, and I think if he'd have known how miserable I was, he'd have moved straight back in. And I wasn't going to ruin the best relationship he'd ever been in because I couldn't cope. I think he knew, though… we've never been able to hide anything from each other."

"Are you two very alike? Bearing in mind I've only met him once and you had blood pouring out your nose."

"Yes and no. He's always been the romantic one. And the nosy one. I'm the one who just does whatever he feels like," I said with a wry smile. "Also, he fucking loves Christmas. His house always looks like a kitsch glitter factory vomited all over it."

Evan snorted and reached for a piece of sourdough. "Are you the family Grinch then?"

"Not that bad, I just like Christmas at Christmas. Not in the middle of fucking November."

"I like Christmas more these days because Milo and Grace get so excited about it. I sometimes have to work, depending on when my shifts fall, but I'll always try and get over and see them. I know Milo figured Santa out a few years ago, and I think Grace has nearly twigged, but we still do stockings and stuff. I do one for Kirsty, and she does one for me, and then we do presents for the kids."

"That's nice, that is. We usually get Tadcu over and spend a few days together. Ben works, so Ianto spends time with him in the evening, and I usually make us all breakfast. And the last few years, we've come here for lunch."

"I can imagine it looks lovely at Christmas," Evan said, looking around the dining room again.

"Yeah, they do a proper job." I smiled as I watched him. Since last weekend, we'd seen each other every day, at least in passing. I'd made him breakfast once, he'd made me dinner, and on Tuesday I'd gone round while he was watching Milo and Grace after school. I'd shown Milo some of the YouTube videos Connor had recommended, and we'd used the back of Evan's sofa as a barre to do some basic ballet.

It'd all felt so normal, like something we did every day.

Evan and I hadn't labelled what any of this was, but since we kept ending up in bed, there was definitely an "and benefits" thing going on. Usually, I wouldn't have wanted any more than that and I'd have drawn the line at everything outside of sex, but here I was, organising romantic date nights and trying to find the words to ask what the hell we were doing.

I'd always thought I didn't want another relationship, but maybe I'd been running away for other reasons than getting my heart broken at seventeen. Deep down, I'd always been afraid a serious relationship would take me away from Ianto, and I couldn't allow that. My little brother had needed me, and I hadn't been about to let anyone come between us.

But now that he had Ben and all his romantic fantasies were coming true, I was left with the realisation that I was alone. And while we'd always need each other, maybe we needed each other a little less than we had once upon a time. We'd always be there for each other, in our unhealthily codependent way, but maybe I needed to start thinking about what I wanted to do with my life rather than worrying about Ianto's.

Not that I'd ever really stop worrying, but maybe I could do it less.

"What're you thinking about?" Evan asked, gently nudging me with his foot under the table. "You look very serious."

"Sorry." I shook my head. "I was just thinking about my brother." I glanced around because the last thing I wanted was for Ben to overhear, even though I was sure he'd understand. "Do you ever think about all the things you put off because you don't put yourself first?"

Evan raised an eyebrow as the corner of his mouth twitched. "Yes, you know I do. You literally told me off for it last week."

"I know, but I'm very good at looking after other people and terrible at doing it for myself."

"I'd never have guessed," Evan said dryly, a playful glint in his eye. "You don't seem like the caring type."

"It's a curse being such a selfish bastard."

"You're an avoidant one too."

My retort was suddenly curtailed by the appearance of two members of the wait staff carrying our starters, because we'd decided that while we were here we might as well go all out.

I'd gone for a spiced crab salad because it'd been ages since I'd had crab, and Evan had ordered what sounded like a very fancy version of French onion soup made with Lincolnshire Poacher cheese, chunky sourdough croutons, and a certain type of onion we'd had to google sneakily because to us an onion was an onion.

"Damn," Evan said once the staff had walked away. "This is fancy. It's literally like the opposite end of McDonald's."

"Is it too much?"

"No, it smells incredible. It's just not what I'm used to."

He grinned. "Keep this up and I'll start becoming an expensive date."

"No more car park blow jobs then?" I asked in a low voice, trying to pretend I was more interested in my salad and the gorgeous half a crab sitting on top.

"I said expensive, not classy."

I laughed, feeling something bubbling in my stomach that felt like *more* than joy. Only I didn't know how to explain it. "I'll remember that."

"Are you going to tell me what you were thinking about?" Evan asked as he dipped his spoon into his dish, lifting out a steaming spoonful of onions and cheese. Next time we came here, I was going to order that. Although as soon as I tasted the crab, I knew I'd be dreaming about it for weeks. Maybe I'd get both.

I took another mouthful of crab while I thought. "Ever since we were little, I've always taken care of Ianto. I'm only seventeen minutes older than him, but with everything that went on… he was such an anxious kid, and I wanted to protect him. And I kept doing it as we grew up because I just wanted him to be happy."

"And now he has Ben," Evan said softly. "And he doesn't need you."

"Yeah… I mean, we're always going to be close. I can't see that ever changing. But I'm realising I put things off because of Ianto. I think I used taking care of him as an excuse because I was so scared of leaving him behind. I couldn't see myself having a serious relationship with someone because, what if they didn't understand? What if they wanted me to choose? I'd always pick Ianto, no question about it. And it never seemed worth the effort. Or the potential heartache."

"And now you're thinking about the fact he's moved on, and you're still here. Waiting. And you want to pretend everything is fine, but suddenly you can have things you never thought about and you don't even know where to start. How do you undo a lifetime of putting someone else first?"

"I don't know if I can," I said, pursing my lips together. "I think I'll always need someone to take care of. Is that bad?"

"No, I don't think so. Not if you find the right person," he said. He smiled again, and my chest fluttered. Behind all the salt and the snark and the desperate desire to keep people out was someone kind and caring. Who I thought needed to be loved more than anyone I'd ever met. "You just have to find someone who doesn't mind you smothering them with love."

"Some people like that."

"They do. And some people wouldn't admit it, even if they want it. They'll fight you every step of the way."

"Ah well, good thing I'm annoying and don't know how to take no for an answer." I grinned and Evan chuckled softly. "You think I'm annoying now, but you haven't seen anything yet."

"Oh joy, just what I needed. Am I going to need to build a moat outside the front door?"

"I don't know if the council will give you planning permission for that," I said, cleaning the last of my starter off my plate. I really could eat a whole bucket of that salad.

Maybe if I asked nicely, Josh or Aaron would teach me how to make it, just a less fancy version.

"Damn," Evan said. "I guess I'll just need more deadbolts for the door."

"I'm still getting inside. I'll come in the back."

Evan snorted. "Oh, will you?"

"Of course," I said. "You can fight it, but I know you like me. And it's okay to admit that. I won't tell anyone."

He nodded and swirled the last of his soup with his spoon. "I know… and I do. But I—"

"You have so much else going on," I said. "And that's fine. Just…" I laughed. "Just let me want you, dammit. Let me try to be part of your life. You might like it."

"Trust me, I already am," he said, a soft vulnerability in his voice. "I'm trying, I promise. But I've never let anyone in before. It's fucking scary."

"Bloody terrifying." I reached over the table and caught his hand in mine. "But maybe we can be scared as fuck together? Two against one and all that."

"Who are we fighting?"

"Ourselves?"

"Shit, we're fucked then," Evan said, snorting with laughter.

"Maybe, but at least we can go down together."

Evan interlaced his fingers with mine and squeezed. "Together. I think I'd like that."

CHAPTER TWENTY-TWO

Eva Nessence

No matter how many times I was called out to one, dealing with a multi-vehicle collision was never easy. Especially when children and motorbikes were involved.

Today had included both.

I'd learnt to compartmentalise things over the years, to talk it out with people and accept I couldn't bottle everything up and pretend it hadn't happened. I'd seen some truly horrible things over the course of my career, like anyone who worked in medicine or the emergency services, and it had taken me a long time to learn how to deal with them.

I drove home on autopilot, my body already craving the routine I'd developed to help me deal with days like today: shower, food, mind-numbing comfort television, and sleep. Lots of sleep. Sometimes I'd do something mindless like hot glue rhinestones to shoes, but I didn't think I had the energy to do that today.

I pulled the car onto the edge of the pavement outside my house and switched off the engine, staring into space for a long minute before I glanced at my phone. And groaned. There were two missed calls from Kirsty.

Shit. Was I supposed to have been babysitting today? No, she wasn't on nights.

That probably meant it was an emergency.

I hit the call back button before I could think better of it.

"Hey," Kirsty said. "Sorry, were you at work? I didn't mean to bother you."

"Yeah, I've just finished."

"Rough shift?"

"Not the best," I said, leaning into the back of the seat as Kirsty clucked softly in the warm way she'd always done when things went wrong.

"I'm sorry, honey, anything I can do? Do you want to talk about it?"

"No, not really." I sighed and rubbed my forehead. My head had been pounding all afternoon and now it felt like it was splitting at the seams. I couldn't remember the last time I'd had anything to drink, though, so that was probably what was causing it. "Everything okay with you?"

"It's fine. Don't worry about it," she said.

"No, come on. What is it?"

"I was going to ask if you wouldn't mind babysitting for a few hours tonight. I, er… there's this shift leader job going and I put an application in a couple of weeks ago. I didn't think I was going to get it, but my manager insisted I give it a go, and now… now they want to interview me." She sounded shocked, like she couldn't believe the words she was saying. But she should because if anyone deserved that job, it was my sister. Fuck, she should've been doing it years ago. "I can tell them no, though. I'm sure they'll be able to rearrange it."

"That's fucking incredible," I said. "And you're not changing it. Bring the monsters round. I'll be fine."

"Are you sure? Because you can say no. I don't want to stress you out."

"I'll live. I'm not letting you turn this down."

"Okay. I'll be over in a bit then? Want me to bring you some food?"

"Nah, we'll figure it out," I said, which was code for ordering pizza or some other form of takeaway because there was no way I was cooking tonight. We said goodbye and as soon as I'd hung up, I groaned and rubbed my face. I really didn't fancy looking after the kids, but I couldn't let Kirsty turn down this opportunity. Hopefully, Milo and Grace wouldn't care if we just vegged on the sofa with movies and pizza.

I heaved myself out of the car, grabbed my bag, and sloped towards my front door, trying to shake the itching irritation under my skin. I'd survive without my routine for one night, and Kirsty wasn't going to be more than a few hours. I could crash as soon as they left.

As I fumbled for my keys, I heard the sound of another car pulling up and turned to see Rhys's bright red Citroen, another groan of frustration welling up in my throat. As much as I was really starting to like him, I couldn't deal with him tonight. But since he was already climbing out of his car, I wasn't going to have much choice.

Ignoring him would only make things worse.

"Hey," he said as he slammed his door. The sunshine in his tone was like a cheese grater on my soul. "Perfect timing."

"Yeah, something like that," I said as I fumbled for my keys, trying to squash my rising anger. Rhys didn't deserve to have me round on him simply because he was in the wrong place at the wrong time.

"Bad day?" he asked and I froze.

"It was shit. Absolutely shit."

"Want me to leave you alone?"

"Maybe…" I sighed, tipping my head forward until it was almost resting on the door. I *hated* asking for help, but if I was going to do it, now was the time. "Kirsty's coming to drop the monsters off, though. She's got a job interview. And I…" I couldn't find the words to ask for what I needed, but Rhys seemed to know.

He walked up behind me and gently plucked the keys out of my hand, unlocking the door and putting his hand on my arm to nudge me inside. "No worries, you go and shower and I'll make some dinner. Do you think the kids will have eaten?"

"Maybe? I don't know, I forgot to ask," I said. "I was just going to order pizza."

"It's okay. I can make something. And I'll make enough in case Milo and Grace are hungry."

I turned to look at him and realised he was still in his gym gear with an Ironman hoodie and a pair of shorts that hugged his tattooed thighs. He was so casually gorgeous it stunned me for a second. "Are you sure?"

"Of course, otherwise I wouldn't have offered." He tilted his head, studying me carefully. I thought he was about to start digging, but all he said was, "If you need anything, I'm here."

"Thanks." I gave him a brief smile before I headed towards the stairs, kicking my boots off in the process.

The shower was blissfully hot and I found myself staring into space as the water pounded down on my back. I made myself breathe deeply, working through some of the quiet mental exercises I'd come to love over the years. They helped me to process and start to let go, to live with the weight of what I'd seen and package it carefully in a little box to put away. I'd done my best today and that was all I could do. I wasn't a superhero and I didn't have magical healing powers like Rapunzel. I just had my training, my experience, and the support of my crew.

In the background under the sound of the shower, I could hear Rhys pottering around in the kitchen. There was no singing today, though, and I wasn't sure if I was grateful for the silence or wanted him to fill it.

I spent longer than necessary in the shower, and I was only starting to throw some clothes on when I heard a knock on the door. "Shit!" I muttered, scrambling to pull my joggers up. I hadn't told Kirsty that Rhys was here and I didn't know how she'd feel about him answering the door or leaving the kids with him.

My feet thundered on the stairs as I rushed down them, nearly crashing into the wall at the end. And when I straightened up, I realised everyone was stood by the front door watching me.

"Hey," I said casually. "Sorry, I was…"

"Don't worry about it," Kirsty said. Her smile was sweet but there was a twinkle in her eyes that told me to expect questions later. She looked smart in black trousers and a red jumper, her long dark hair pulled back into a slick ponytail. "Your boyfriend said you were getting changed."

Boyfriend? Oh fuck. I glanced at Rhys, who was carefully avoiding my gaze. "Yeah, it's been a long day."

"Was it a bad one?" Milo asked with a shrewd look I was sure I'd seen on my own face. He was much more astute than I gave him credit for.

"Not the best," I said with a fixed smile.

"It's okay," Grace said, running up to me and throwing her arms around me. "We'll look after you."

"Thank you, sweetie." I put my arm across her shoulders and leant down to kiss the top of her head.

"Okay, I'll be back in a couple of hours," Kirsty said. "Be good for Evan and Rhys, please."

There was a chorus of affirmations and wishes of good luck as she headed out the door, and as soon as it was closed, Grace grabbed my hand and towed me over to the sofa. "You have to sit down," she said firmly, practically shoving me onto the seat. "With blankets. And—" She ran over and picked up her backpack, unzipping it and pulling out her rather battered stuffed lion, the one I'd given her when she was born. "You need Marvin too."

She climbed onto the sofa beside me, putting Marvin the lion gently in my lap as she reached for the blanket carefully folded across the arm. My heart melted because this was what I did for her when she was sick. The blanket was an enormous faux-fur one I'd grabbed from Home Bargains one Christmas. It had fleece on one side and was nearly twice Grace's size. She wrestled with it for a second, then said, "Milo, can you help, please?"

"I've got you," Rhys said, gently taking it off her and shaking it out. "You sitting down too?"

"Yes. Evan needs hugs." She scooted along the seat until she was tucked up beside me, the sweet scent of her tropical fruit shampoo wrapping around me.

"Okay then, one blanket fort coming right up." Rhys waved the blanket dramatically before draping it over us. "Milo, are you staying in here? If not, I'm making dinner if you want to help."

"I'll help," Milo said.

"Wait!" Grace threw her arms up as the two of them turned to leave. "We need to put the TV on. We have to watch *Moana*!"

I didn't object, despite the fact I'd seen the film so many times I could quote the entire thing line for line with my eyes closed thanks to Grace's obsession with it as a toddler. My eyes drifted closed as the opening music started to swell, the warm weight of the blanket across my lap and Grace pressed in beside me. In the background, I heard Milo and Rhys talking and the sizzling of something on the hob. Whatever it was, it smelt delicious.

A deep, slow breath slipped out from between my lips as I felt more of my stress and anxiety begin to loosen. It wasn't what I'd planned for the evening, but it also wasn't as bad as I'd imagined either. Having Rhys here helped. He'd taken the weight off my hands without even asking, and now he was cooking us dinner. I was sure he'd said he didn't know how to cook, though…

"Evan." Rhys's voice was soft and I realised I'd dozed off under the blanket. My eyes were heavy and my head was pounding, but when I looked around, I saw him holding out a steaming bowl of curry and rice, a small naan tucked into the side. "Do you want something to eat?"

"What's…"

"It's Josh's mum's chicken curry," he said. "I made some for all of us, even though apparently some people have already had dinner."

Grace giggled and I realised she was resting a small bowl with a little bit of curry and rice carefully on her lap, a strip of naan in her hands that was already half eaten. "But I'm hungry. And it smells really good."

"Soon you'll be asking me what's next," Rhys said as he handed me my dinner. Grace was right—it smelt amazing. "Like the owl who was afraid of the dark."

"What's that?"

"It's a book, and it was one of my favourites when I was your age."

Grace laughed again as Milo appeared and sat down next to her, holding his own bowl of curry. "That was *ages* ago. You're really old now."

"*Really old*? I'm not as old as your uncle. He's ancient. Practically grew up with the dinosaurs."

"How charming, especially because you're older than me. If I'm ancient, what does that make you?" I asked dryly, dipping my spoon into the curry and taking a small bite. Fuck me, that was good. Rhys must have seen my face because he grinned at me knowingly.

"Good?"

"Eh, it's all right," I said with a shrug and a grin. "It's amazing. Seriously. I thought you said you couldn't cook?"

"Ah, well, I took a few lessons," he said nonchalantly, once again avoiding my gaze. "Thought it might come in useful. I guess it did."

I watched him wedge himself onto the other end of the sofa, joking with Milo and Grace to squeeze up like we were all marshmallows in a jar, my heart soaring into the sky on wings Rhys had given it.

CHAPTER TWENTY-THREE

Rhys

Spending my evening curled up on the sofa with Milo, Grace, and a dozing Evan hadn't been my intention after a long day of back-to-back classes and personal training sessions, but it turned out to be exactly what I needed.

It was like being back home in Wales and it soothed a sore spot inside me I hadn't realised I'd been carrying around. I'd known I was lonely without Ianto, but I hadn't acknowledged just how painful that loneliness was. I wasn't the sort of person who coped well on their own. I needed company, and the idea of going back to my empty, quiet house made my stomach turn.

So I wasn't going to.

Evan woke up again when Kirsty returned to pick the kids up, and the two of them chatted for a bit while I washed up, Milo standing behind me and using the kitchen counter as a barre while he practised pliés. He'd been doing it while I made dinner too and seemed intent on spending every spare second dancing.

"Milo, can you find your shoes, please?" Kirsty asked, appearing in the kitchen doorway. She looked a lot like her brother, with the same dark hair and bright eyes. Milo sighed and finished his plié, and I chuckled as I watched him go. "Thanks for watching them tonight," Kirsty continued. "I wasn't sure about bringing them. Evan has a tendency to downplay how bad things are."

"It's no trouble," I said, drying my hands on a nearby tea towel. "They're a good pair. Grace just treated Evan like he was ill."

Kirsty nodded, her smile warm and full of quiet pride. "She tries. I told her Evan might not feel great… it's hard to explain serious things like that to her. Or maybe I'm just trying to protect her."

"Nothing wrong with that, I don't think."

She nodded again and glanced over her shoulder, looking at where Evan was playing with Marvin and making him sit on Milo's head. "Thanks for taking care of him too. He's a bugger for trying to do everything." She huffed out a laugh and it was clear she knew her brother almost better than he did. "He just… he seems to think he owes me or something. I keep telling him he doesn't, but nothing changes. It's like he has this weight on his shoulders and he doesn't know how to get rid of it, so he keeps carrying it around. I love him, but I wish he'd let go a little. He doesn't need to do everything."

"I've told him the same thing," I said, taking a few steps forward until I was almost stood next to her. It made it easier to lower my voice slightly. "I don't know if he'll listen to me, but my plan is to keep on annoying him until he does. He'll give in eventually. Then he might start enjoying life a little."

Kirsty looked at me shrewdly with the same expression I'd seen on both Evan's and Milo's faces. It almost made me laugh. "Good," she said. "Keep annoying him. He needs it. He'll hate it, but it'll be good for him in the end."

"I'll do my best." I grinned, glad I had Kirsty on my side. One way or another, I'd get Evan away from the knife edge he was walking between burning out and surviving.

We said our goodbyes and once they were gone, I dragged Evan back to the sofa, flopping down next to him. The TV was on in the background and I realised how much I wanted to do this every day with him. I'd never be able to give this man up, no matter what happened. And if I had to, it was going to crush me.

"What were you talking to Kirsty about?" Evan asked, putting his arm around my shoulder and kissing my temple. "Were the two of you plotting against me?"

"Now why would you think that? We were just having a friendly conversation about what we'd been up to this evening."

Evan hummed suspiciously. "I'm not sure I believe you."

"That's on you then," I said, turning my head to grin up at him. He looked tired, like he was two seconds away from falling asleep again. "Do you fancy going to bed?"

"Is that a hint?"

"No, it's a bloody question. And by the way, I've

decided I'm staying tonight. We don't have to have sex, but I don't fancy going home, so I'm just going to stay here."

"Do I get a choice in this decision?"

"Not really, no." I leant up and kissed the side of his face. "You only get to decide if we go to bed now or later."

"What's the time? Wait, fuck that, I don't care. Can we go to bed?"

"Of course." I patted his thigh. "I'm just going to nip back to mine and grab my toothbrush and my phone charger. I'll be back in two minutes—then I can lock up behind me."

He opened his mouth like he was about to make a point about me going home and coming back again but obviously decided I'd win anyway and he couldn't be bothered to argue. "Okay, I'll be upstairs."

It didn't take me long to nip next door and grab a few bits, but since I wasn't going far, I didn't need more than the bare minimum. I locked my door behind me and stepped back inside Evan's to discover he'd put his keys on the back of the sofa for me since his door had a double lock. I smiled to myself at the level of trust and as I picked them up, I realised I couldn't remember the last time I'd slept over at a man's house without sex being the explicit purpose of the visit.

With the obvious exception of Ianto's house, but he never counted in any of my relationship realisations no matter how close people said we were.

When I went upstairs, Evan's bedroom door was open and he was stretched out in bed scrolling through his phone in the gentle glow of his bedside lamp. He was shirtless, but I couldn't see if he was completely naked because of the duvet. Either way, he looked gorgeous like this—all relaxed and off guard. This was the man very few people got to see, and yet somehow I'd lucked out and ended up getting to be part of his life. How long it would last I didn't know but I was determined to make the most of every moment.

He glanced up and smiled at me. It was a tired smile, full of world-weariness and exhaustion, and I wanted to kiss that all away.

"The bathroom is all yours," he said, then gestured to the bed. "Do you want a specific side?"

"Well, since you're sat there, I thought I'd take the other side," I said.

"And there was me thinking you'd want me to move."

I closed the distance between the door and the bed, leaning down to kiss him softly. He tasted like peppermints, and the scent of something deep and botanical flooded my senses, which I assumed was his skincare. It made me want to bury my nose under his chin and breathe it all in until it faded away.

"I'll be back in a minute," I said, forcing myself to pull away.

"Okay." He nodded and smiled. Up close, the exhaustion was even more obvious. His skin was pale, almost pallid, and he looked peaky. I wondered if he was getting ill. "Thanks for tonight. You didn't have to help."

"Yeah, I did. We're dating now."

His cheeks flushed. "Sorry, I didn't realise she was going to say that. You can ignore her."

"Nope, it's official now. You're stuck with me." I kissed him softly and he chuckled.

"Is this another decision I don't get a say in?"

"Not unless you really strongly object," I said. "And then I want to hear reasons. I'll make you do a PowerPoint presentation if I have to."

"At least it's not a two-thousand-word essay complete with references."

"I mean, I'd take that because I'm interested to know what sort of references you'd come up with."

He snorted. "I'd ask Ianto for your dating history and go from there."

"That's bloody rude," I said, trying not to laugh as I kissed him again. "Just be grateful this isn't like *Scott Pilgrim* and I don't have seven evil exes for you to defeat."

"I think there'd be a lot more than seven," Evan said with a wry smile, his hand coming up to cup my jaw as he drew me in for another kiss. "Don't worry, I'd have more than seven too. Maybe we could just set them on each other? Although why do I think you'd want to stay and watch what happened."

"Of course. I'll make sure I get popcorn too. We can be like Roman emperors lording it over them. I'll practice my thumbs down for when we get bored."

"How violent are you expecting this to get?"

"Have you met any petty twinks? They'll get violent if you push them. And at least one of my exes had acrylics, and he used to keep them sharp."

Evan smirked. "I bet you liked that, didn't you?" I felt my cheeks heat and tried to glance away, but he was holding my jaw tightly. "Maybe next time I'm in drag, I'll leave my nails on for the rest of the night. I've got quite a few pairs I think you'd like."

He kissed me deeply, his teeth gently tugging my bottom lip and making me groan. "Go do your teeth," he said. "Then come back here and get naked."

"I thought you wanted to go to sleep?"

"I said I wanted to go to *bed*, and technically I'm there. Are you really going to argue with me?"

"Fuck no," I said, stealing one more kiss before I dashed off to the bathroom. Evan had some toothpaste I could pinch and I took some extra time to quickly wipe myself down since I hadn't showered since getting back from work.

When I got back, Evan was still sat up in bed scrolling through his phone, only this time there was a bottle of lube, a box of condoms, and a large red and black dildo resting on the small table next to him. He looked up at me and smiled expectantly. I quickly began to throw my clothes onto the floor, dumping them in a pile where I'd be able to grab them in the morning.

"Come here," Evan said, throwing the duvet off himself. He was gloriously naked and I let out a delighted groan at the sight. I didn't need any more encouragement to throw myself into his lap, wrapping my arms around his neck and kissing him deeply.

"What do you want?" I asked in between kisses, feeling Evan's cock hardening against my ass. I was tempted just to reach for the lube, slick myself up, and slide onto his dick but it looked like he had other plans.

"I was going to suggest you fucking yourself on that dildo for me while I watch, then—"

"Does this plan end with you also fucking me?" I asked, grinding down on his lap. "Because if it does, then yes."

"It can do." His mouth twisted into a smile as he slid his hands down my spine to cup my ass, sliding his fingers into my crack and pulling my cheeks apart. "Why? Do you really want my cock?"

I pushed back into his hands and then tilted my hips forward, pressing my erection into his stomach. "Does that answer your question?"

He chuckled darkly and sat back, looking at me with reverence and desire. "Yes, but tell me anyway."

"I want your fucking cock," I said, pressing my lips to his and breathing the words into his mouth. "Fuck me, Evan."

He groaned. "Why don't we just skip the dildo tonight? I need to be inside you."

"I'm not going to argue," I said, shooting my hand out and trying to grab the lube without looking. It took me a moment to find it, and I nearly sent the dildo flying in my desperation, but soon I had it in my greedy hands. "Want to open me up?"

"Yes."

I grinned and held out the bottle. "You'll have to let go of my ass then."

"This is where I wish for extra hands," Evan said, the corner of his mouth pulling into a smile as he let go of me with one hand to retrieve the bottle. "Think of all the things I could do to you."

"I don't think we'd ever get out of bed." I pushed my hands back into his hair as he reached around me. The bottle clicked open and he let go of me with his other hand. I felt his hands moving behind me as he slicked his fingers, but I didn't look because the anticipation of his fingers on my hole was making my body thrum.

I gasped as he ran two wet fingers down my crack to tease the sensitive skin of my hole, circling it languidly like he was planning on teasing me for hours. But just as I was about to protest, he pressed one finger past the puckered ring of muscle.

My hands tightened in his hair as I groaned, loving the feeling of having something inside me again. I'd always known I wanted to bottom more and fully explore the needy, desperate, slutty side to myself, and Evan was making all my dreams come true. With him, I didn't feel like I had to pretend to be someone I wasn't or play a certain role, and he didn't make any assumptions about me based on my appearance or my hobbies.

He'd seen straight inside my horny fantasies and had no problem letting me fulfil them.

I moaned as he pumped his finger in and out of me, barely giving me a moment to breathe before he added a second. The burn sizzled under my skin, adding a new dimension to the pleasure filling every inch of me, and I craved more.

"Is this okay?" he asked in a calm voice that almost sounded like he was talking about the fucking weather while he curled his fingers inside me, stroking them across my prostate while I gasped and whined. "Do you want me to slow down?"

"D-Don't you dare," I said, huffing out the words with a mixture of laughter and determination. "Don't stop. I… fuck, I want more."

"More?" Evan's voice had a sweetly amused tone, like asking for more might be dangerous. But fuck, I wanted it.

"Yeah." I kissed him hard, digging my fingers into his hair. "More."

He growled, nipping my lip and wrapping his hand around my waist, holding me in place as he pressed a third finger inside me. I gasped into his mouth, the stretch and burn so perfect I wanted to melt.

He thrust his fingers deep, rubbing them over my prostate and making my cock twitch. I pushed my hips back, grinding down onto his hand and riding his fingers as my erection rubbed against his abdomen, leaving precum on his skin.

"Desperate, aren't you?" Evan murmured, trailing kisses down my neck. "Don't worry, I've got you."

In a moment, he'd pulled his fingers out of my ass, his hand tightening around my waist and lifting me up. Then he tugged me down, and I groaned as the blunt head of his cock pressed against my hole.

"Y-Yes," I said, moaning as I sank down on his dick, taking every inch of him until my ass was resting on his thighs. Evan was still sat up, propped against his pillows, and was perfectly positioned to reach up and pull me into a possessive kiss, giving me a moment for my body to adjust.

Then he grasped my waist tightly with both hands and

began to move my body, pulling me up and down on his cock, using me as nothing more than a hole to fuck.

My groans filled the room as he turned me into his toy, fucking me hard and deep with his perfect cock. My body felt like it was floating on a cloud of pure pleasure, shuddering in delight at the idea of him using me to relieve his stress and worry.

His cock hammered against my prostate and I knew I wasn't going to last long if he kept that up. It felt too fucking good, especially with my erection trapped between us, the friction of our bodies sending me closer to the edge with every move.

Evan slid one hand between us, grasping my cock tightly and making a fist for me to fuck as he used me. "That's it," he said. "So good for me. You take me so well."

"Feels… fuck, I love your cock," I said. "Want, uhhh, I want you to fill me. Fuck, give me your cum."

"Yeah? Want me to fill you up?"

"Yes!" I groaned loudly, right on the precipice of release. And as Evan slammed deep into me, I came with a shout, my body tensing as my orgasm rushed through me. My cock pulsed, spilling cum between us, and with another hard thrust, Evan growled and shot his load deep inside me, our mouths meeting in a messy kiss as the high of our orgasms made our bodies sing.

It was only when we started to come down from our high and I felt Evan's cum dripping from my hole as he slid out of me that I realised we hadn't used a condom.

I could see from the horrified look on his face that Evan had realised it too.

"Shit," he said. "I'm sorry… fuck, I'm sorry. I got the box out and—"

"It's fine," I said, kissing him softly.

"It's not."

"Really?" I raised an eyebrow as I looked at him. "I trust you. And I trust if there was something I needed to know, you'd have mentioned it."

He opened his mouth, his expression telling me he was about to argue, but all he said was, "No, there's nothing. You're the only person I've been with in a while. And I had a test last year."

I grinned. "A while?"

"This year," he said under his breath. "As you can tell, I don't get out much."

"I'm flattered," I said. "And I had a test a few weeks ago, about when I decided I wanted you. I've always tested regularly anyway, especially because I tend to go through men pretty quickly."

He chuckled. "Should I be flattered then, that you haven't run screaming yet?"

"Maybe." It could still happen, but I doubted it. I didn't feel any of the usual terrified itch under my skin pulling me away. If anything, I wanted to get closer.

"Should I be flattered you actually decided to fuck me?" I asked.

"You were pretty hard to resist," he said, smiling as he rolled me off him. "That first time…"

"Mmm, that was fun. I knew you wanted me." I winked and leant over to kiss him.

"I did. Resistance was futile."

"It always is."

He kissed me again, pulling me into his arms and rolling on top of me so we could kiss and kiss until our lungs gave out.

No, whatever happened, there'd be no running away this time.

I was in far too deep for that.

CHAPTER TWENTY-FOUR

Eva Nessence

The first thing I noticed when I woke up was the pounding in my head that seemed to be splitting my skull from the inside out. It made me want to curl up in a ball and go back to sleep in the hope I could stay unconscious until the pain had passed.

The second thing I noticed was the hot weight sprawled across my chest that wasn't just from the duvet. Rhys was an adorable, drooling deadweight, his dark hair stuck out at odd angles and his plush mouth hanging open as he snored softly. I hadn't realised sharing a bed with him was going to mean being smothered.

I gently tried to shift him off me because now I'd noticed he was there I was finding it hard to breathe. My throat was scratchy too, but I didn't know where that had come from. I really hoped I wasn't getting ill because I didn't have time for any of that bollocks. But gently didn't seem to do anything—instead it made Rhys snuggle harder into me, pinning me to the bed and throwing a leg over me for good measure.

"Rhys," I whispered as I attempted to roll onto my side, hoping that would get rid of him. "Rhys!"

"Hhmm? Wassup?" He lifted his head slightly, barely opening his eyes. There was drool clinging to his lip and strange lines standing out on his skin where he'd had one hand under his cheek. He looked gorgeous, in a rumpled, unguarded sort of way. If I hadn't felt like shit, I'd have pinned him to the bed and kissed him until he didn't know how to speak.

"You're squashing me."

"Huh? Sorry." He rolled off me and burrowed into my side instead, tucking his head into my neck. His breath tickled my skin and made me shiver. Then I coughed. Rhys sat up, eyes flying open as he fixed me with a suspicious look. "You okay?"

"I'm fine," I said, feeling like the furthest thing from it. "Just getting full capacity of my lungs back."

He grinned sheepishly. "Sorry, I didn't mean to squash you."

I patted the mattress, trying to get him to lie down again. Because if he was lying down, he couldn't look at me like he was now, like he was *this* close to tying me up and interrogating me about whatever possible symptoms he thought I might have. And while I wasn't opposed to the tying-up part—fuck, I even had some nice cuffs in my drawer—I wasn't keen on the rest. Rhys looked at me for a long second and then snuggled back into my arms.

"Just for a minute," he said quietly. "Then I have to get up. I've got clients to teach this morning."

"And I've got an eight-hour shift to do," I said. After yesterday I was eternally thankful today was my short day.

"Are you sure you're up for it?"

"Yeah. The days after the bad ones are never great, but it's my job. Gotta get back on the metaphorical horse."

"I didn't mean that," Rhys said, gently prodding me in the chest with the tip of one finger. "If you're feeling ill, you shouldn't be going to work. You don't want to give it to someone."

"I'm not ill," I said. "I'm just tired." I didn't know how long I was going to try and deny it, and Rhys had a very good point. Usually, I was a stickler for not going to work while ill since it would be so easy to spread a cold to our vulnerable patients, but I didn't want to believe I was coming down with something. Because if I was, it would throw a spanner in the works of so many things.

Rhys hummed, making it obvious he didn't believe me. I braced myself for him to start arguing with me, but all he said was, "All right, but you should eat something before you go in. What time do you start?"

"Eight."

Rhys glanced at the old-fashioned alarm clock on my bedside table. It was the only thing that could disturb me when I was dead to the world. The glowing red numbers read six thirty-three, meaning I technically didn't have to get up for another twelve minutes. "How long does it take you to get there?"

"I don't know, twenty minutes? Thirty if the traffic is

bad. Depends on the time of day." And the day of the week, the month, and the time of year. During the school holidays or the middle of the night, I could make the drive in ten but if I hit the wrong time of day, I'd be stuck crawling along while Nottingham's traffic lights slowly drained my patience.

"Okay, I'm going to start cooking," Rhys said, leaning up to kiss me and then throwing himself out of bed with more energy than necessary for this time of the morning. "Can I borrow some clothes? I didn't grab any clean ones."

"Knock yourself out," I said as I pulled myself into a sitting position so I could get a better view of his body. Waking up to Rhys naked in my bed every day was something I'd easily get used to. I flicked the bedside lamp on, the warm glow allowing me to see his tattoos in all their glory.

One day I was going to stretch him out and map every single one with my tongue as he told me about them. I assumed he'd gotten some because they were pretty or he just liked the design, but I was also sure that some had a deeper meaning and I wanted to hear the stories behind them, peeling back the layers on this beautiful man who shone like summer sunshine and lit up every room simply by being there.

It had frustrated me when Kirsty had automatically assumed we were together, but maybe it was the push we'd needed. Otherwise, I got the feeling we'd have danced around each other for months before one of us had said something. And I doubted it would've been me.

I still wasn't convinced I could make this work or that I

could be the man Rhys needed, but I wanted to try. I'd stretched myself so thin lately I finally understood what Bilbo Baggins meant when he described himself as butter stretched over too much bread, and a relationship wasn't going to suddenly stop that feeling. It might even add to it. But for once I wanted something for myself.

Maybe Rhys was right when he'd said I needed to weigh everything up and look at my options. I'd never considered going part time and the idea of even asking terrified me. But maybe I'd think about it. I just needed to get this batch of shifts finished with and reach my next ten-day break, and then I could relax a bit. I could think about Eli's panto offer then too. He'd sent me some details and they were sitting in my inbox, unopened as a reminder to read them.

"Any requests?" Rhys asked, looking at me over his shoulder as he fished a pair of joggers out of my chest of drawers. "Or will it be the 'whatever's in the fridge' special?"

"I don't think I'll have any choice but to request the special," I said as my eyes focused on the beautiful round swell of his ass. "Since my usual breakfast is toast or whatever cereal I've had in for the monsters."

He chuckled as he pulled the joggers on and I mourned the loss of his bare butt. "I'll see what I can do then."

"Thanks," I said as he grabbed one of my hoodies and tugged it over his head. The sight of him in my clothes made something possessive rumble in my chest. I'd always thought it was hot when my boyfriends wore my clothes, but seeing Rhys in them dialled the feeling up to eleven and

I started wondering what he'd look like in some of my band shirts and favourite hoodies. I thought about coming home and finding him face down on the bed in one of my T-shirts and a jock, ass plugged and waiting for me. Or even a pair of backless lace panties…

"What are you thinking about?" he asked, walking over to the bed and leaning down to kiss me.

"You. And how fucking hot you look in my clothes."

"Yeah? You like the idea of me being yours?"

"Fuck yes." I reached around to squeeze his ass, groaning at the feel of the firm muscle under my fingers. "Can I ask you something?" My words ghosted over his lips and Rhys groaned as I claimed his mouth. "How do you feel about panties? Or lingerie?"

"I think I'd look hot in it," he said. "Why? Are you thinking about me in lace panties and stockings?"

"Mmm, yes. And my T-shirt."

Rhys moaned softly. "Yes… mmm, yes. We're definitely doing that."

"I'll add it to the list," I said. "Along with using all the toys."

"Y-yes. Please. And…" He trailed off and tried to pull away, like his next thought was one he didn't want to admit.

I squeezed his ass again, holding him close. "What do you want? Tell me. What fantasies are you thinking about?"

"Have you ever… You know those…" He sighed and bit his lip. I'd never seen him so shy or flustered, and I wondered if he'd ever admitted whatever he was thinking about to anyone but himself.

"I promise I won't judge you," I said softly. "There are some things I don't like, and you know I don't share, but I won't judge you for your desires."

"Have you ever seen those fuck machines?"

A smirk curled at my lip and a delicious feeling of wanton desire spread through my chest as the possibilities exploded in my brain, temporarily pushing away my splitting headache. "Yes, I have."

"I've always wanted one. Thought they looked kinda fun… you know, like a gang bang without all the extra people."

I growled and kissed him deeply. "Fuck, you'd look so pretty strapped down and fucked with one. Using all my toys to stretch you open, adding my load to make you sloppy and then using more toys until my cum drips down your thighs… making you come over and over until you can't give anything else." Rhys groaned, practically melting into my arms. "Is that what you want?"

"Y-yeah," he said.

"Thank you for telling me," I said, reaching up to cup his jaw as I pulled my head back to look at him clearly. I needed him to see what his words meant to me. "I mean it. Sharing your fantasies is hard, but I'm glad you did."

"Thanks for not being weird about it." He was trying to joke it away but relief was clear on his face.

"Of course. It's hot and one day I'm going to make it come true for you." I leant in to kiss him again just as my alarm blared, making the pair of us jump out of our skins like startled cats.

"What the fuck?" Rhys gasped, clutching his chest as I

hit the button on the alarm to silence the shrill beeping. "Please don't tell me you wake up to that every day?"

"It's the only thing that works."

"Jesus Christ, that's bloody horrible." He was still grinning and his cheeks were flushed, but whether it was from the shock or our previous conversation I didn't know. "I'm going to be having nightmares about that." He shuddered dramatically. "Right, you better find some clothes then and I'll go and see what you've got in your fridge."

"Thanks." I watched him leave and as his footsteps echoed on the stairs, I flopped back into bed. I really didn't feel like going to work, but I still didn't want to admit there was something wrong. I was sure I'd be fine once I got going.

Slowly, I heaved myself out of bed and set about finding some clean uniform as the pounding in my head returned.

CHAPTER TWENTY-FIVE

Rhys

Clinging on to a metal pole with nothing but my underarm, side, inner thigh, and back of my shin for the first time in six weeks while trying to perfect a Broken Doll was the perfect distraction from thinking about Evan.

My muscles burned and the skin at every single connection point felt raw, and I already knew that by tomorrow I'd have some cracking bruises to show for it. It was good to be back, though. I hadn't realised how much I'd missed pole until I'd walked into the studio that evening.

"That's it," Connor said. He was spotting me, although if I fell there wouldn't be much he could do. I'd either have to catch myself on the pole or drop onto the padded mat at the bottom. "Extend your right leg a little further… good… Now straighten it and keep your toes pointed."

"Is this the time where I joke nothing about me is straight?" I asked with a breathless laugh.

"Nope, this is the one time where it needs to be." Connor smiled sweetly. "Okay, perfect! Lower yourself down slowly. That's getting a lot better."

I lifted my head, which had been tilted backwards, and grasped the pole with my right arm, which had also been extended, pulling myself into a pole sit. I gave myself a second to reacquaint myself with being upright before swinging my legs down and dropping gently onto the mat.

"I'll do it again in a minute," I said as I stretched, proud of myself for the progress I'd made. I'd never been able to hold it for that long before. "Do you think one of you can take a picture?"

"I can. As long as you hold still and pretend to look graceful," Colin, one of the other people in our small advanced pole class, said. He'd only joined us about eight months ago after moving up to Nottingham to start his PhD, but he'd been dancing for years back in Bristol. He had waist-length auburn hair he usually wore in a plaited crown, sparkling green eyes, and a willowy frame that moved effortlessly around the pole. He'd seemed to be on the quieter side when he'd first joined, although with Ianto, Connor, and me around that wasn't exactly hard, but recently he seemed to be coming out of his shell a bit more, revealing a sharp tongue and devilish smile. I liked him a lot.

"Easy for you to say," I said, walking over to pick up my water bottle. "I don't think you've ever not been graceful a day in your life."

Colin laughed, climbing up off the floor where he'd been stretching and pouring liquid chalk onto his palms.

"Put me in a pair of heels and you'll see *the* least graceful person on the planet. I'd make Bambi look like an Olympic gold medallist."

"You have got to come to my heels class then," Connor said as he cast his eye around the room to check on everyone else. Since the class wasn't huge, Connor had time to give us all individual attention while we worked on our moves, which meant nobody escaped his eagle-eyed scrutiny. "Next Saturday. It's for beginners, and I promise it'll be fun. You can come and shake that booty."

"What booty?" Colin asked as he reached for his pole, which was next to mine, and gracefully began to climb. "I haven't got one."

"We can soon sort that," I said, looking at Colin's small butt with a professional eye. "I could give you some specific exercises to do if you wanted to grow it."

"Maybe. I don't know if I'd actually do them, though. This is about the only exercise I get."

I watched carefully as Colin swung his legs around to the same side of the pole and began to invert himself, wedging the metal pole into his waist and armpit while hooking his shin around. His left hand rested on the pole behind his head, providing a little extra support as he dropped his head back, his spine arching softly. "How does that look?"

"Very good," I said, walking slowly around him to get a better view since Connor had walked over to spot Ianto, who was working on his Ayesha with an elbow grip. "Just point your toes. Where's your phone? Do you want me to take a picture?"

"Please. It's just the green one." He tilted his head at the mint green phone case resting on the floor, sounding so relaxed you'd have thought he was practically asleep. I grabbed it off the floor and tapped the camera icon on the lock screen, stepping back to take a few shots from various angles. Once I was done, he pulled himself up and twisted into an invert with split legs before walking himself down to the floor.

I handed him his phone, hoping I'd gotten some good pictures. "How often do you come here?" I asked, because if Colin was capable of doing all of that, he had to have some serious strength and muscle condition.

He shrugged. "Most days. I prefer dancing to the gym. And it's a nice break from work."

"At least you're taking breaks and not working yourself into the ground."

"Oh, I do that too," he said softly. "I haven't met a ton of people since I moved, so I mostly come here or to my office at the university. My housemates are nice but they're all PhD students too, and they're in the same department, so they all know each other." He shook his head and smiled. "Ignore me, I sound really miserable."

"You do, but that makes me want to adopt you. And you should know I'm what you might consider pushy—my boyfriend said I mowed through his boundaries like wet cardboard. God, that makes me sound like a proper fucking menace. I promise I'm not that bad—if you tell me to back off, I will. Evan just needed a push."

"And by push you mean annoying him until he gave in and stalking him on Instagram until you found out where he was performing," Ianto said, wandering over with a wicked smirk on his face. I assumed Connor had released him for a moment's break.

"Er, excuse me, can you not make me sound like a walking red flag, dickhead?" I asked, flicking the cloth I used to wipe the pole down at him. "I'm trying to convince Colin to be friends with us, not make him want to run screaming."

"He'll do that anyway as soon as he spends time with you."

"With *us*," I said. "You're just as bad as me. We're twins, remember?"

Colin chuckled. "At least you're honest about your faults?"

"Trust me, this isn't even half of them," I said with a wink before turning back to Ianto. "And I'll have you know Evan was very pleased to see me."

"I still can't believe you went without me! I wouldn't have told anyone." He huffed and folded his arms, and I felt a pang of guilt.

I'd explained my reasoning to Ianto multiple times now, but we both knew me going to The Court alone wasn't the real issue here. It was the fact we were slowly pulling apart from each other and there was nothing we could do to stop it unless we leant fully into codependency and literally lived in each other's pockets. But neither of us wanted to acknowledge what was happening because admitting it would make it so much more real.

"I know, but we're not exactly subtle."

"You got caught anyway, so going with me wouldn't have changed anything."

"I think I'm missing something," Colin said, looking between us as he picked up his water bottle, which was a similar mint green to his phone case and covered in rhinestones.

"Rhys's boyfriend is a drag queen and instead of just asking him about his drag like a normal person, Rhys tracked him down on Instagram and turned up at one of his shows," Ianto said with amusement. "Apparently he was trying to be subtle, only instead of staying at the back, he sat in the front row right in front of the stage."

"In my defence, that was the only available seat," I said. I reached for my bottle of liquid chalk, determined to try my Broken Doll again, complete with a straight leg and perfectly pointed toes.

"Your boyfriend is a drag queen?" Colin's face was lit up with wonder. "That's so cool!"

"Yeah." I smiled, my chest filling with pride. "Eva Nessence—she's my gorgeous gothic princess. You a big fan of drag?"

Colin nodded. "I've... er, yes."

"We'll have to all go to a show then," Ianto said. "Pole night out."

"Oh my God, I am so coming too!" Connor said, bouncing up next to us. "We're doing it and it'll be amazing. Also... why are you all stood around doing nothing?"

I picked up my phone and handed it to Ianto. "I'm not doing nothing. I'm going to do my Broken Doll again."

"Let's see it then." Connor gestured to the pole. "And then see if you can pull up into an invert. If you're feeling really confident, we can start working on a flow with a few moves together. There's quite a nice but difficult series with Broken Doll, an Inside Leg hang, and either a Meridian or a Jallegra—I can show you in a minute, but it'll take quite a bit of practice."

"Let me make sure I can do this first," I said. Because as much as I wanted to try the sequence Connor was talking about, I'd grown much more aware of my limits and abilities over the last few years and although I always wanted to push myself, I didn't want to break something while doing it. My nose had only just healed and I didn't fancy turning more of my skin lime green and purple.

Reaching for the pole, I began to climb, feeling the cold metal against my skin. My muscles burned from the long session and a day of teaching, but I was determined. I let out a breath as I slowly inverted myself, wedging the pole in place under my arm and into my waist as I wrapped my left leg around and straightened my right. Connor gave me a couple of pointers as I stretched out my right arm and made sure my head was tilted back, allowing my back to arch.

"That's it! Perfect!" Glee filled Connor's voice and he clapped wildly. "Ianto, take pictures!"

I held myself still, embracing the feeling in my body and pointing my toes as much as fucking possible. "Can I move now?"

"Yes," Connor said. "Invert, please. Spread those legs nice and wide."

I snorted and Ianto laughed. "How did you know my brother is a bottom?"

"Hey!"

"Oh please, like it's supposed to be a secret," Ianto said.

"I'd say fuck you, but that's a bit far even for us," I said as I pulled myself into the invert, spreading my legs as requested and keeping my toes pointed. Ianto was taking more pictures but suddenly he stopped and looked up at me with concern.

"Your boyfriend is calling."

"Evan?" Concern laced through me and I dropped my legs down out of the invert.

"Unless you've suddenly got another one," Ianto said and before I could add anything else, he'd answered it. "Hello? Rhys's phone, this is Ianto. Hello, Evan, you okay, love? He's just coming down off the pole. Hang on."

I landed on the mat and held my hand out. Usually, I'd never take a call during class but I didn't think Evan would've called unless it was an emergency. "Hello, everything okay?"

"Sorry," Evan said. He sounded fucking terrible. "I'd forgotten you had pole tonight. I'll let you go."

"No, it's fine," I said quickly, not wanting him to hang up. Beside me, I saw the other three wandering off, pretending they weren't listening. "What's wrong? You don't sound well, love."

"Er, I'm not feeling great. I think I'm getting a cold."

A cold sounded like a fucking understatement if you asked me. Something deep in my chest let out a protective rumble, the sudden need to care for him making my fingers itch. "Do you need me to grab you some bits?"

"Would you mind? Just some cold and flu tablets and maybe some Lucozade. And some orange juice."

"No worries, we'll be finishing up here soon. I'll be back in a bit."

"Cheers," Evan said with a sniff and a cough. I grimaced and resisted the temptation to say anything like "I told you so." "See you soon."

"See you soon. And go the fuck to bed."

I hung up and sighed. I loved that man but he was going to fucking kill himself if he didn't slow down. And I doubted a cold would stop him unless it was serious.

I turned my phone over in my hand and smiled. Fuck, I loved him. Every ridiculous, stubborn, grumpy, gorgeous inch of him.

The feeling didn't scare me; it only made me more determined to make Evan realise just how unsustainable his life was. Because I wasn't going anywhere, and I hadn't done all that introspection about myself and fallen in love to give up that easily.

Evan might be stubborn.

But he was about to find out that I was worse.

CHAPTER TWENTY-SIX

Eva Nessence

I WAS BEGINNING to think that, maybe, there was something wrong with me.

Having pushed through my shift with no small amount of Lucozade, stubbornness, and complete and utter denial, I'd arrived home feeling beyond exhausted and fallen asleep on the sofa as soon as I'd shut the door. I'd woken up several hours later feeling like dog shit, which was when I'd finally given in and called Rhys.

I didn't need him to take care of me. All I needed was a few supplies and an early night, and then I'd be fine by the morning.

When Rhys arrived, I was still lying on the sofa staring into space while white noise played in my brain.

"I thought I told you to go to bed," Rhys said with a raised eyebrow as he put his backpack on the floor and toed off his shoes. "You look bloody awful."

"I'm fine."

"No, you're fucking not."

"It's just a cold," I said, taking the bottle of Lucozade he handed me.

"Like hell it is. Can you please just admit you're not feeling well and go to fucking bed?"

I sighed and pinched the bridge of my nose. "Fine, I feel like shit. Happy now?"

"Not really, no." He leant over the back of the sofa and kissed the top of my head. "Come on, upstairs. When was the last time you took any pills? And when did you last eat?"

"I'm not hungry," I said as my stomach roiled at the idea of food. "But pills… about two. I meant to take some when I got home but I fell asleep."

"You can take some upstairs."

"You're very determined to get me into bed."

"And you're very determined to ignore me. I swear it wasn't this difficult to get you to fuck me the first time."

I snorted, then sneezed so hard it made my sternum pop. I let out a pathetic mewl of pain and Rhys made a soft, hushing sound as he petted the top of my head. "I can't get ill," I said quietly. "I've got too much on. I'm supposed to be performing all weekend, and Eli wants an answer about the panto too. Plus, I'm supposed to have the monsters all day Saturday. And then I've got two night shifts Sunday and Monday."

"At this rate you won't be doing any of that. You need rest." Rhys walked around the sofa and took my hands in his, pulling me to my feet. I didn't bother to resist. I knew it was futile.

Rhys led me upstairs and helped me strip down before digging out a pair of old pyjama bottoms and a baggy T-shirt. Once I was dressed, he pulled back the duvet and guided me into bed, tucking me in like I was five. I couldn't remember the last time I'd let anyone take care of me like this, and the feeling burned in my chest like an open flame.

Although knowing my luck, I could also have been developing a fever.

He made me take some pills and left the bottle of Lucozade on my bedside table before disappearing briefly and returning with a large glass of water. Then he unplugged my alarm clock, ignoring my vague noises of protest, and told me to get some sleep.

I wanted to be stubborn and stay up, but all my resistance had drained away and it wasn't long until I fell into a deep, dreamless sleep.

When I woke, bleary-eyed, snotty, and still fucking exhausted, I heard voices downstairs. There was a little bit of light outside the curtains, but I had no clue what time it was because Rhys had unplugged my damn clock and I didn't know where my phone had ended up. My watch wasn't on my bedside table either, even though I was sure I'd taken it off.

I sat up slowly, ignoring the way my head spun, and swung my legs out of bed, letting them rest on the cold floor for a few minutes before I tried to stand. The floorboards creaked loudly as I put my weight on them, and I shuffled forward a few steps to the door. A shiver ran through me but when I touched my face, the skin burned hot under my fingers and I felt sweat beading on my forehead.

I'd been planning on going downstairs and finding out who else was here, but I desperately needed a pee and when I came out of the bathroom, Rhys was waiting on the landing.

"How're you feeling?" he asked, taking my hand and scrutinizing my face. "You still don't look well."

"Honestly? I still feel like shit." I tried to smile but that made my face ache, so I stopped. "What time is it?"

"About half ten. Morning, though, not evening."

"Seriously? I slept through?"

"Yeah, since about nine last night." He smiled softly. "You need to go back to bed. And you can't argue with me because you just said you feel rubbish."

"How dare you take care of me," I said, my rasping voice dripping with sarcasm. At least I could still manage that.

"I know, I'm a proper bastard." He leant in and kissed my cheek. "Go and lie down. I'll bring you a drink and some toast."

I shook my head. "I'm not hungry."

"Sorry, but you need to eat something."

"Who's downstairs?" I hoped the question would divert him enough that he'd stop fixating on feeding me.

Rhys grinned sheepishly. "You've got visitors."

"Visitors? Why?"

"I may have messaged Bitch Fit to tell her you weren't feeling well and were going to have to take a few days off," he said.

"And Sparkles and I may have decided to drop in and bring you some goodies." Eli's face appeared at the bottom of the stairs, a wry smile on his face. "I figured you had to be seriously in the shit if you were going to call in sick, and I wanted to make sure you weren't dead."

"How generous of you."

"I know," Eli said. "You should listen to your boyfriend and go back to bed. You look like shit, babe."

"Thanks," I said. "You're so sweet."

"I'm not telling you you're fine when you look like that." He gestured to all of me. "You look two seconds away from collapse."

I did feel a bit wobbly but instead of admitting it, I huffed and shuffled back towards my room. It was only when I'd sat down I realised Eli had said Rory was here too, and I groaned. I didn't want either of them seeing me like this, but I apparently didn't get a choice because two seconds later there was a knock on the door and it swung open to reveal the pair of them carrying all manner of stuff.

"Hey, babe," Rory said as he set a glass of orange juice on my bedside table before putting a bag down on the floor and plonking himself on the end of the bed. "How're you feeling?"

"Not great."

He tutted softly. "You don't look well."

"You're nicer about it than he is at least," I said, tilting my head to Eli, who'd walked around to the other side of the bed. He was holding a tray with a steaming mug on it and a plate of thick-cut toast that was oozing butter and smelt heavenly. My stomach rumbled loudly as Eli put the tray on the bed and sat down carefully beside it, pushing it towards me so I could reach the toast. "Why are you here?"

"I told you, we were worried about you." Eli patted my shin softly. "Silly goose."

"Silly goose?" I raised my eyebrow and picked up a piece of toast. The bread looked like one of those loaves you got from a supermarket bakery counter, and that meant someone had gone out of their way to get it. The gesture was oddly touching. I took a small bite, chewing it slowly and allowing myself to savour the taste. Then I took another, larger this time. Suddenly, I was ravenous, even with my stomach bubbling horribly.

"Yeah, because you are. Why didn't you tell us you had so much going on?"

"What did Rhys tell you?"

"Don't get mad at him," Rory said, poking my thigh. "Or us for asking. Anyway, it's not like he spilled all your worldly secrets. He just said you've been really busy with work, with your sister and your niblings, who I can't believe you didn't tell us about, and all your drag stuff, and that it seemed like it'd finally all caught up with you."

"It's not… I've just got a cold."

"Maybe," Rory said gently. "But I think you're burning out."

"I agree with Sparkles," Eli said. "You're doing too much, babe."

"I'm not. Plenty of people do more than me! Sparkles has a full-time job too."

"Yeah, but mine's different to yours," Rory said. "I work for my dad for one and we've made it fit around my drag career. Anyway, this isn't a fucking competition, babe. There's no winning or losing or the 'right' amount of suffering. You can't compare yourself to anyone else."

"Exactly! You can't work yourself to death by constantly comparing your life to other people's," Eli said, nudging the plate of toast closer so I picked up another slice. "Look, you might think you've got a handle on everything, but it won't last forever. I'm sure you love your job and your family, and I know you love being Eva, but something has to give. And it can't be you."

"I think this might be a sign something has given," Rory said. He was giving me the same gentle smile I always tried to give the people I treated, the one that said everything was going to be okay.

"I don't want it to give, though," I said, nibbling on the edge of my piece of toast.

"You don't have a choice, babe."

"But I don't… I don't know how to change. Or what to change. Where do I even start? I don't want to stop doing drag, even if it's started to feel like hard work, and I can't stop working if I'm not performing. And as for my family… Kirsty needs me. The kids need me. They have to come first."

"And what about you?" Eli asked pointedly.

"What about me?"

"What about your needs? Your dreams? Your damn

health." He gestured towards the door, which was still half-open, and I wondered if Rhys could hear us. "Look, I get wanting to take care of the people you love, and unfortunately we live in a capitalist hellscape where money makes the world go round, but please, Evan, open your fucking eyes and realise something needs to change." He jabbed my shin sharply, then lowered his voice and leant in conspiratorially. "Also, there is a very gorgeous Welshman downstairs who's worried sick about you and *this* close to smothering you with love until you feel better."

Guilt tightened my chest and twisted my stomach. It was a low blow of Eli's to bring Rhys into this, but I had to admit it'd worked. Because even if I couldn't put myself first, maybe I could put *him* first. "I thought you just said I need to put myself first?" I asked. "Isn't using Rhys as your pawn counterproductive?"

"Maybe, but who the fuck knows. Maybe you'll start realising things have to change if you have someone to change for."

"Especially one who clearly adores you," said Rory, whose expression had morphed into one of sickening sweetness. "You two are so freaking cute, honestly it's—" He made a little squeaking sound of delight and I glared at him. "Don't pull that face! You obviously like him too! Like, you asked him for help. And you were so shocked when he turned up at The Court, but in the best way."

"You two are dicks and I love you," I said, trying hard not to laugh because it hurt.

"We love you too, but we're going to be keeping a very

close eye on you," Eli said. "You can't shut us out. We know where you live *and* we know your boyfriend."

"No more secrets," Rory said. "You're our friend, Evan, so please let us in."

"I'll try."

"Nope, not good enough." Rory grinned, sticking out his hand and extending his little finger. "Pinky swear."

"What are we, twelve?"

"I don't care. Pinky swear that you will let us in."

"Fine," I said as I locked my little finger with his and shook. Rory was as demanding as Rhys, but at least he was sweeter about it. I couldn't be upset, though, because the three of them all cared so much more than I deserved. They wanted the best for me, and the least I could do was let them in and be a better friend.

And boyfriend.

Rhys was always there when I needed him, whether I asked or not, and I realised how much I wanted him in my life. How much I *needed* him. All I had to do was show him I could be the man he deserved, and suddenly that didn't seem so hard.

"Good. Now"—Rory pulled out his phone—"when are you supposed to be performing? We'll find some cover for you. I already talked to Moxxie, Legs, and Peaches, and they're happy to pitch in. You need some time off."

"Do I get a say in this?" I asked, already knowing the answer was no. I looked around for my phone and realised Rhys had put it back by the bed. The simple gesture made affection burst in my chest.

Rory grinned. "No. And if you argue, I'll get Rhys to

come and tie you to the bed. I bet you've got some cuffs around here. You seem like the type."

Eli snickered and a burst of laughter bubbled out through my throat, and soon the three of us had collapsed in a heap on the bed, giggling uncontrollably like a bunch of teenagers at a sleepover.

CHAPTER TWENTY-SEVEN

Rhys

I LEFT Evan with his friends while I nipped back to mine to shower, grab more clothes, and then call Ianto with a shopping list. He'd already promised to cover my classes at the gym today and said he'd drop everything round at some point in the afternoon after he'd had time to run to Tesco.

I'd felt horribly guilty for telling Eli and Rory what was going on, but I couldn't let Evan try and drag himself up to Lincoln in his current state, and if I was going to convince him to make changes, then I needed help. I was pretty sure he was burned out and running on fumes, but I couldn't nag him into listening to me.

I was cute, but not that cute.

And nagging him when he didn't want to hear it was only going to tank our relationship.

When I got back, Rory and Eli were still chatting with Evan, so I headed into the kitchen to see about prepping a few simple meals to stick in the freezer. If I could ease Evan's stress a little by giving him plenty to eat whenever he got back late, or early, then I'd feel better. I stuck my headphones in and bounced around the kitchen, lost in my own little world until someone tapped me on the shoulder and made me scream. "Fucking Christ!"

"Sorry!" It was Rory, who looked both startled and embarrassed. I hadn't been expecting him to arrive alongside Eli, but I'd gotten the feeling he hadn't given Eli a choice about bringing him. It seemed like the pair of them were determined to make Evan open up to them by hook or by crook. "I didn't mean to make you jump."

"It's fine," I said as I clutched my chest, my heart pounding so loudly I could practically feel it in my ears.

"I just wanted to let you know that we're off," Rory said. "And I think Evan's *this* close to falling asleep again."

"He needs it. I'll be here when he wakes up." I'd deliberately cleared my diary of all plans, even my regular training. Our next Ironman wasn't for another couple of months, so a few days off wasn't going to hurt, especially compared to the weeks I'd had to go lightly because of my nose. "Thanks for coming. I really appreciate it. I'm sure grumble bum upstairs does too, although I'm sorry if he chewed your ear off."

"Nonsense, don't apologise," Eli said, appearing with the breakfast tray. I noticed with satisfaction that all the toast had been eaten. "He'll get over it. He's just so used to hoarding all his secrets and his problems like a little dragon, and he can't imagine sharing any of them."

Rory giggled. "Evan would make a cute dragon. All gothic and dramatic with plenty of shiny things."

"And spikes," Eli said. "Plenty of those too."

"We've covered all of Eva's performances at The Court for two weeks," Rory said with a smile which didn't quite reach his eyes. "We wanted it to be longer, but that's all he'd give us."

"That'll do for a start," I said as I took the tray from Eli and slid it onto the kitchen counter. "I'll come up to his first show back so he doesn't have to drive. Some of my pole class really want to go to a show, so I'll get them to come too so it doesn't look like I'm wrapping him in cotton wool." A thought popped into my head and I quickly added, "This is weird but… one of the people in my advanced class, if he wanted to get into drag, do you know how he'd go about it?"

Colin hadn't outright said he wanted to be a performer and maybe I was meddling where I didn't need to, but it never hurt to put some feelers out just in case.

"Get them to message me or Bitch," Rory said, his eyes lighting up. "We'll be able to give them some pointers. I'd start with me, though, because Bitch is *mean*. And badly dressed."

"You cheeky cow," Eli said, playfully smacking Rory's ass.

"It could've been a lot worse," Rory said with a grin. "I could've mentioned your make-up too. Not your wigs, though, because at least Orlando makes you look good and not like you've been dragged through a hedge backwards."

"Shady bitch, there's nothing wrong with my make-up.

Unlike yours, where you seem to think rhinestones are a substitute for style. Honestly, I've seen five-year-olds with more controlled glitter use than you."

"I will take too much glitter over neon green eye shadow and trying-too-hard bangs any day."

I bit my lip and tried to suppress my laughter but it was too much. "Are all drag queens like this? Or just the two of you?"

"Oh honey, this is nothing," Eli said. "Shade is a core part of any drag performer's DNA. It's what we live for, and reading each other for filth is just what we do." He put his arm around Rory's waist and kissed his cheek loudly. "But it's all meant with love. Well, most of it."

"With you, none of it's love," Rory said, laughing. "You're just a demon of chaos."

"I'm a chaos goblin, darling. There's a difference."

I chuckled. I could see why Evan was friends with the pair of them. They'd be good for him, but the amount of shade being thrown would probably be enough to keep him cool in the desert.

They continued their playful bickering all the way to the door before promising to keep in touch and come and visit again soon.

After they'd left, I went back upstairs to check on Evan, expecting to find him asleep after all the excitement, but he was sitting up in bed and scrolling through his phone. He still looked exhausted, but for once it didn't seem like he was being crushed by the weight of the world.

"I like your friends," I said from the doorway, watching Evan smile fondly.

"Yeah, they're… sweet. Overbearing and loud as fuck, but sweet."

"I think that means they care about you."

"Poor sods."

"Hey," I said, walking over to sit on the bed and prodding his thigh through the duvet. "That's my boyfriend you're talking about. I won't let you be rude to him."

"What if I said he's a poor sod for having such ridiculous friends?" he asked with a grin, reaching out to take my hand and interlace our fingers, letting them rest on his thigh. "And putting up with them for so long? Even though they are interfering, dramatic, and leave their shit all over our dressing room?"

"I'd say he's actually a pretty lucky sod for having friends who love him so much they dropped everything to come all the way here, want to be a part of your life, and encourage you to be happy," I said in a gently pointed tone.

"I suppose you're right," he said, squeezing my hand and smiling at me in a way that made my stomach flip. "I'm very lucky. Not just because I have them but because I have you." He paused for a moment, his eyes flicking to the curtain-covered window and down to the duvet, which had a pastel teal, grey, and lavender tartan pattern on it.

"I owe you an apology," he continued. "I've been a dick lately, trying to insist I'm fine, that I don't need help, that everything is… fine. It's not, though, and I still don't really want to admit it."

"You're admitting it now," I said, scooting closer to him along the edge of the bed. "That's a good first step. And you asked for help last night."

"I did the bare fucking minimum," he said dryly. "Yay me."

I snorted and prodded him with my other hand. "Hey, what did I say about being rude to my boyfriend?"

He smirked. "You can't be mean to me. I'm sick."

"Oh, so you're actually sick now?"

"Yes, fine, I'm sick. I'm tired. I'm…" He let out a long sigh accompanied by a frustrated groan. "I fucking hate this."

"I know." I moved closer so I could lean in and kiss his forehead. "You hate relying on other people."

"I do but…" His eyes met mine, a plaintive look shining out from them. "Maybe I could rely on you? Just a little bit, until I feel better. Then you can go and I'll do whatever it takes to—"

"If you're about to end that sentence by saying you'll make it up to me, then don't you bloody dare," I said firmly. "You don't have to make anything up to me." The words to tell him exactly how I felt were there, ready and waiting to be unleashed, but now wasn't the right time.

As much as I wanted Evan to know I loved him, I didn't want him to feel burdened by any kind of obligation to me. Especially not when we were trying to break him of the habit. All he needed was for me to be here while he figured things out, both about himself and his life.

And I couldn't deny how nice it felt to have someone to take care of again.

"Fine," he said, obviously unimpressed. "I'll… I don't know. What am I supposed to do?"

"Say thank you," I said, pressing a tiny kiss to his lips.

"And when you're better you can fuck my brains out. How does that sound?"

He laughed, and it sounded like music. "I can definitely do that."

"Good, but between now and then, you have to focus on yourself."

"God, that sounds like torture."

"Tough, that's the way it's going to be. You're going to rest and figure out what's going to change so this doesn't happen again."

He opened his mouth to argue, but instead he yawned and I felt mildly satisfied that he'd be forced to shelve his objections for another day. "You should get some more sleep," I said, preparing myself to get up and leave him in peace, but Evan tugged my hand, holding me in place.

"Will you stay for a bit?" he asked.

"Sure. Budge over."

"But this is my side," he said, laughing as I tried to push him across the bed. "Go round."

He kept laughing as I climbed over his thighs and into bed next to him, pulling him into my arms as we snuggled down under the duvet. I ran my fingers through his hair, stroking it softly as we lay quietly for a moment. I thought Evan might have drifted off until he said, "How was pole? I forgot to ask."

"Good, but I'm covered in bruises this morning. It's like someone's thrown purple paint all down the inside of my thighs and under my arms."

Evan snorted. "Want me to kiss them better?"

"Later. When you feel better."

"Done." He yawned again. "I remember the first pole class I ever went to. It was the university taster and I was the only guy there. I only went because one of my housemates wanted to go but didn't want to go by herself."

I smiled as I listened, my heart glowing as Evan slowly began to open up. "The first time Ianto and I went, I tripped over my own feet twice just trying to walk around the pole. Never thought I'd end up being able to hang off it upside down."

"I never got that far, but I'd like to have another go one day. It was always fun, and the couple of heels workshops I did really helped with drag."

"Oh, Connor does those. You should come and give it a go one day."

"I think I will," he said. He sighed happily and snuggled deeper into my arms. "What other sports have you and your brother tried? I've never really been good at anything sporty."

The glow in my heart pulsed, and if I could have physically shone, I would have.

As I held Evan in my arms, I told him about Ianto's and my sporting adventures and how we wanted to try a little of everything. I told him about the things we'd loved, the things we'd failed spectacularly at—neither of us could surf to save our lives—and the things we did regularly.

Evan sleepily told me about Rory's boyfriend, West, playing rugby and going to watch him play for England—which was where I'd seen his face when he'd lined up to play Wales. God, could the poor man not be Welsh instead?

He told me about learning to walk in heels and the time

he'd fallen off the front of the stage in the middle of a gig, got up, and kept going.

His voice stretched out as he told me about being Eva, about The Court and his friends there, about doing a drag story hour last Christmas and wanting to do more. And he told me about how he desperately wanted to get Milo into ballet and Grace into football but didn't know how to tell Kirsty to just let him pay.

Eventually he fell asleep, head on my chest, halfway through telling me about the first time he'd done drag at a university bar. I kissed the top of his head and held him tightly as he slept, my heart about ready to explode with adoration.

CHAPTER TWENTY-EIGHT

Eva Nessence

After a week of doing nothing, I was bored out of my fucking skull.

I'd been forced to call in sick to work for the last of my shifts before my ten-day break since that cold had hit me heavy and hard. Rhys said it was burnout flu, and I'd begrudgingly started to concede he was right when I'd tried to get up to do some housework and nearly passed out.

Rhys had caught me and I'd never seen him so close to apoplectic. There'd been a vein pulsing in his forehead, which would've been funny if I hadn't been spending so much energy trying to pretend I was fine.

He'd grabbed the hoover out of my hand and banished me to the sofa to lie down. I'd never heard anyone hoover with such righteous anger before. The addition of a string of Welsh cursing was a nice touch too, and although I couldn't understand a word of it, nothing spoken with that much venom could be sweet. Maybe I needed to see if Duolingo did a Welsh course and sign up for it. I was sure I'd be able to find five or ten minutes a day to practice.

It would give me something to do for the rest of this ten-day break too because despite the fact I was feeling human again, I didn't have any shows, Rhys refused to let me lift more than a cushion, and Kirsty had been strangely cagey about sorting out babysitting. She'd gotten the shift leader job, which came with new hours, and I knew she'd need me to look after Milo and Grace because some of her shifts started at five and six in the morning and some went on until midnight, but all she'd said was we'd sort it out when I was feeling better.

I was going to have to give her a call and work it out because if it wasn't me, then who was going to look after them? As far as I knew she didn't have a boyfriend, we didn't have any family, and I didn't think any childminders or breakfast clubs started that early.

The not knowing was making me anxious and while Kirsty was probably trying to protect me and give me some peace, it wasn't working.

I made a mental note to call her in the next day or two because if I messaged her, she'd avoid me until some vague time she felt I was ready.

A sharp knock on the door distracted me from my thoughts and I grinned to myself as I paused the old episode of *Murder, She Wrote* I'd been watching. I knew it wasn't Rhys because he'd given up knocking and just walked in whenever he fancied it. He was also at the gym, so there was no chance of him interrupting me.

Now all I had to hope was I could carry my new arrival upstairs and get it built before he got home.

Once the DPD delivery driver had handed the large unmarked box to me, I kicked the door shut and made my way to the stairs. It wasn't as heavy as I'd expected, which was a good start, although my chest was still tight by the time I'd reached my room. That could have been from my general lack of fitness, though, since the only exercise I got was strutting around on stage and even then I didn't do fully choreographed routines like Bubblegum or Moxxie.

Putting the box on the bed, I grabbed the pair of scissors I'd brought down from my drag room earlier and sliced the box open, my heart racing with anticipation. A smirk blossomed across my face as I pulled out the instructions for the sex machine I'd treated Rhys and me to, flicking through them quickly. It didn't look like it would take me too long to put together.

And it looked like it was going to be a lot of fucking fun.

I couldn't wait to watch Rhys split open and begging on its robotic cock.

It was going to be worth every penny I'd spent on it.

I took everything out of the box and laid all the pieces on the bed along with the little tools that came with it. The instructions were easy to follow and within a couple of hours I had a working fuck machine, complete with an eight-inch dildo and a remote control, ready and waiting to go.

The front door slammed and Rhys called, "Hey, I'm home! Where are you?"

"Just coming down," I said, throwing the remote quickly onto the bed and kicking the box under it. I closed the bedroom door behind me and tried to walk down the stairs as nonchalantly as possible, like I hadn't been thinking about all the deliciously filthy things we could do this evening. "How was work?"

"Busy as fuck today! I've got a couple of new personal training clients who've just started, and then I had two circuits classes and spin to teach," Rhys said. He was standing in the kitchen putting his lunchbox on the side. I wasn't quite sure *when* Rhys had virtually moved into my house, but at some point in the last week he'd started staying here and it was only now I realised he hadn't left.

I wasn't quite sure how I felt about that, but since I had plans for him, I wasn't going to ask him to leave. Not tonight at least. And tomorrow we'd already agreed to go food shopping for the week since it would be easier to go together. We'd talked about watching a couple of films together too, maybe even going to the cinema or going out to grab something to eat, and at that point it would be silly of him to go home.

But if he really wanted to spend one night in his own bed, maybe I could go with him. I was getting quite used to waking up with Rhys sprawled across my chest like a giant drooling weighted blanket.

"Sounds painful," I said, opening the fridge to see what our options for dinner were and wondering if I could convince Rhys to make more of the incredible chicken curry.

"Eh, not too bad. Spin's the only one where I end up doing the whole class. I'll demonstrate for circuits and do the warm-up, but most of the time I'm wandering around checking on people and watching the timer. The worst part was having to sit and do paperwork this afternoon—writing up plans, nutrition guides, that sort of stuff. That's the necessary but less interesting part of my job." He closed the gap between us and kissed me softly. "How was your day? Are you still bored?"

"Out of my mind," I said sourly. "I rearranged all my shoes, cleaned all my make-up brushes, took a nap, and watched like, three episodes of *Murder, She Wrote*. I want to do more but I'm so fucking tired too." I sighed and rested my head on his shoulder. "Why am I so tired?"

"Because you're burned out." His voice was like a warm hug as he slid his fingers into mine. "And you need rest."

"I feel like I've slept for weeks."

"It's barely been one."

"It's been more than that. I'm almost looking forward to going back to work."

"Have you thought about what you want to do?"

I shook my head slightly, still leaning on his shoulder. "No. Every time I sit down to think about it and do the maths, I find something to distract me. It's like I can't wrap my head around the idea of changing anything."

"Do you want help?" Rhys asked.

"You've done enough. I can't keep leaning on you." Rhys chuckled and I felt his body shake under me. I straightened up and smiled. "Okay, that was a poor choice of words but you know what I mean."

He shot me an unimpressed look. "How is me helping you make a list you leaning on me?"

"I should be able to figure this out myself... shouldn't I?" For the first time I wavered, doubt wriggling in my stomach like something fetid and disgusting. It wasn't an emotion I liked, and I'd always tried to experience it as little as possible. I'd always pushed forward, trying never to doubt myself or my decisions because I hated the idea that I'd find a mistake or something I couldn't fix.

"You can, but you don't have to," Rhys said softly. "It's not a bad thing to want help, and help doesn't have to be a huge thing where I ride to your rescue and drag you from a burning building. It can just be me listening to you while you bounce ideas around. And I'll remind you it doesn't mean you owe me either. My help isn't conditional. It doesn't have a price tag."

"I know."

"Do you?"

I stared at him. There was a determined look in his eyes as he held my gaze, a gentle challenge to my assumptions. "You might say it, but I'm not sure you believe it," he said. "It's why you think you owe Kirsty, even though I know she's told you otherwise. It's why you do everything for those you love and never ask for anything in return. It's like you think your time... your love... is worthless somehow. That you're only worth something if you can do something for people and ask nothing in return. I think you don't want to take up space in people's lives unless you can do something for them because you don't think you matter outside of what you can offer someone." He reached up and brushed my face. "But you matter, Evan. What you want matters. Your value as a person isn't tied to your productivity or your usefulness. You're allowed to be messy and imperfect and to need things. You're allowed to be human."

"I don't… I don't think I know how to be," I said in a hushed, hoarse voice accompanied by rattled breaths. Rhys's words hurt but only because I knew he was right, and admitting I felt that way felt like exposing a raw nerve. "I don't know how to stop. I do things for myself but—"

"Only if they don't inconvenience other people."

"Something like that. Eva is… fuck, she's everything I wish I was every day."

"Be more Eva then," Rhys said. "Be a fucking queen."

"It feels like work, though." My voice shook at that admission. "I don't want it to, but even being Eva feels like work."

"One step at a time. You can't change everything overnight. You just have to be willing to try."

"How?" My emotions felt like an open wound, like the back of my ankle when I'd worn badly fitting shoes all night—wet and bloody and raw. Never in my life had I allowed myself to be this open or vulnerable, to admit, even to myself, that I didn't know where to begin when it came to changing direction. I'd been walking this road for so long it felt like the only option, and I'd refused to look for another. But if I continued down this path, one day I'd hit my destination and I doubted that would be at the end of a rainbow with a pot of gold.

"What do you want?" Rhys asked, smiling at me. "It's not a trick question. What do you want to do with your life? What are your hopes? Dreams? Where do you want to be in five years? You don't have to know the answers, and if you did they don't have to be fixed forever. But knowing is half the battle."

"I don't think I know that either."

"Okay then, that's where we can start." He kissed me softly. "Want me to make dinner while you think?"

"Maybe…" I frowned. "I'm not sure I want to think about it tonight, though."

It was Rhys's turn to frown. "Why?"

"I kinda had other plans."

"Fun plans?"

"Yeah," I said, relaxing slightly as I let my fantasies from earlier sweep away my doubts. "I might have bought you something."

"Oh?"

"Technically it's for both of us, but… if I say any more, I'll spoil the surprise."

"Is this your way of getting out of this conversation that you obviously don't want to have?"

"Maybe," I said with a wry chuckle. "But the present arrived before you started calling me out. I wasn't expecting any of this."

Rhys grinned. "I'll make you a deal. We can put all the talking about you and your internal dilemmas on hold until tomorrow, *but* in the morning we're going to make a list and a plan. Deal?"

"Deal." I kissed him firmly, all thoughts of dinner and

introspection and the horrifying prospect of change put to one side for at least a few hours. I was well aware I was using the idea of watching Rhys come apart as a distraction, but I could live with that. As Rhys said, it was all about baby steps, and admitting I had no idea what I wanted was the first one. The rest could wait until later.

"Want to go and see your present?"

CHAPTER TWENTY-NINE

Rhys

A SEX MACHINE.

He'd bought us a fucking sex machine.

Never in my wildest dreams would I have imagined that was what Evan had meant when he said he'd got us a present, but I wasn't going to question it. Seeing it ready and waiting was a dream come true, and I was going to do my best to ignore the fact it'd cost him a bloody fortune and just be grateful he shared my fantasies.

He'd also given me some backless black lace panties that stretched over my dripping cock and left my hole waiting and exposed, and some black knee-high socks with two white bands around the top with the words Good Boy printed on the soles of the feet, one word on each foot, which he was able to read now I was on all fours. Just knowing those words were there, a blatant marker of my desires, sent a shiver down my spine.

"Fuck, you look so hot like this," Evan said in a smooth, silken voice that made my cock pulse. I groaned as the lace rubbed over the sensitive skin, making more precum drip into the thin fabric. God, I was going to make such a mess of them by the time we were done.

Evan ran a hand down my back and squeezed one of my ass cheeks firmly, spanking it playfully and sending heat blossoming across my skin. He was still fully dressed, and there was something about being on display for him that made everything a thousand times more intense. "You're so desperate for it, aren't you?"

"Y-yes," I said, gasping as he spanked my other cheek. My fingers clutched the sheet tightly in their grip, and all I wanted was to bury my head in the mattress and push my ass into the air to be used. But Evan wanted to see my face.

"Good." I heard the click of the bottle of lube and groaned as the thick, cool liquid ran down my crack. Evan's fingers followed, circling my hole before he began to work me open. His movements weren't slow or teasing tonight because he knew both of us wanted to get to the main event. I was already on edge and the briefest brush of his fingers across my prostate was enough to have me moaning and pushing back onto his hand. There was so much I wanted but I couldn't even think about how to ask. It was like my mind was blank, all my thoughts replaced by pure need.

"Are you ready?" Evan asked as he gently pulled his fingers out of me.

"God yes," I said, looking over my shoulder at him. I

hoped my desperation was obvious because I really fucking needed him to get on with it.

"Good." He smirked and picked the remote control up off the mattress. "We'll start slowly and see how you get on. Let me know if it's uncomfortable, too much, or you need to stop."

I wanted to tell him it wasn't going to be a problem, but I knew not to joke about stuff like that. And I wasn't exactly going to ease Evan's stress if I hurt myself. "I will."

"I know you will," he said, putting one knee on the bed and leaning forward to kiss me. "Because you love being good for me."

My heart melted along with the rest of my body. I didn't know how I'd gotten so lucky in finding a man as filthy as he was charming, but I wasn't going to question it.

There was a soft mechanical whir as Evan switched the machine on. My blood pounded in my ears as I waited for the press of the dildo against my hole, and every second seemed to take fucking forever. But when it breached me... fucking hell!

The dildo's motion was smooth and slow as it pushed past my rim, barely easing half of itself inside before it pulled most of the way out and began again. The thick shaft stretched me open, making pleasure radiate through me.

Somewhere in the back of my mind, I knew Evan had it on the lowest settings for speed and depth of thrust, but all I could focus on was how fucking good it felt. It was totally different to using a dildo on myself or being fucked by Evan because the machine kept up a constant momentum, but I didn't want to compare them. I just wanted to lose myself in the way my body felt.

"Fuck, darling," Evan said, moving around the bed to stand in front of me. He tilted my head up with his fingers, drawing my gaze to his, which burned with white-hot intensity. There was a dark possessive edge to his expression too, like he was revelling in the fact that he and only he got to see me this way. "You look so damn perfect like this. Does it feel good?"

I groaned and tried to nod, even though he was holding my jaw. "So fucking good."

"Shall we try more?"

"Yes, please."

He smirked. "So polite for me." He leant down and captured my mouth in a filthy kiss, claiming me with his tongue and pulling my bottom lip between his teeth. "Make some noise for me. I want to hear you scream."

I gasped as he pushed a button on the remote, causing the machine to thrust the dildo deeper inside me. He'd increased the speed too, only fractionally but it was enough to make stars burst behind my eyes as the dildo rubbed across my prostate over and over again. I groaned and whined as pleasure pulsed through my muscles, setting every inch of me on fire. I didn't even attempt to keep my voice down as Evan turned it up again, wailing loudly as the machine fucked me with mechanically precise intensity.

"Is it good?" Evan asked, his low voice almost teasing. He knew exactly what this machine was doing to me but he wanted to hear me say it. "Is it everything you wanted, my darling little slut? Does it feel like you're being used?"

"Y-yes," I said, barely able to get the word out amongst all my whimpering moans. "I... shit... Evan..." I didn't know if I wanted more. All I knew was I didn't want it to stop.

My cock throbbed in my lace panties, precum dripping into the material and making it cling to my skin. I tried to hump the air as the mechanical cock fucked me, desperately searching for friction I knew wasn't there.

Evan turned the machine up again, making me howl as it thrust deeper and harder inside me. The dildo slammed into my prostate, shredding my nerve endings and making my muscles shake. If this was being fucked within an inch of my life, then death had never looked so glorious.

I looked up at Evan and saw pure possessive want shining in his eyes. My stomach twisted, knowing he loved seeing me like this, and it made my torment sweeter. He pressed his thumb to my lips and I eagerly sucked it between them. Evan let out a rumbling groan that went straight to my dick and I sucked his thumb harder, wanting him to make that sound again and wishing I could find the words to ask for more.

"That's enough," Evan said, pulling his thumb out of my mouth with a wet pop. I whined at the loss. "Do you want something else? Do you want to suck me while our toy fucks you? Want to be spit-roasted and split open with two cocks?"

"P-please... fuck, Evan... please."

He tugged his grey joggers down and pulled out his hard cock, holding the shaft with one hand as he guided the soft mushroom head towards my waiting mouth. "That's it," he said, his voice like molten pleasure as it trickled down my spine. "Open your mouth for me. Take my cock."

I groaned as his dick filled my mouth, hot and heavy on my tongue. His precum dripped down my throat leaving a ghost of its taste behind. I tried to bob my head and suck him, but Evan stopped me. "Please, darling. Let me use you."

Fuck me. How could I say no to that? All my fantasies were coming true at once.

I hummed and nodded, hoping it was clear what I meant. I knew he'd got the message when he began to rock his hips slowly, pushing his cock deeper into my mouth with every thrust. He wasn't going as fast or hard as the machine, which probably wasn't even halfway through its settings, but he didn't need to. I'd never felt so fucking full and it was pure fucking bliss.

My muscles turned to marshmallow and my mind floated away, lost to pleasure. Everything felt like too much and not enough at the same time. I wanted to come, but I didn't want this feeling to end. But it was going to because that dildo had been torturing my prostate and there was a searing heat building under my skin. The lace panties rubbed against my cock and my trapped, aching balls as Evan fucked deeper into my mouth.

Tears prickled my eyes as I gazed up at him and he wiped the corner of one with his thumb as he thrust deep inside me, letting his cock fill my throat. "Are you going to come for me? I know you can. You look so fucking amazing like this, so beautiful." He lowered his voice until it was a sweet caress. "You're such a good boy, Rhys. You take such good care of me. Now it's my turn… come for me."

He flicked the remote one final time and I let out a silent scream as I came, my body wrecked by the force of the pleasure overtaking me. My cock pulsed over and over, shooting thick wads of cum into the black lace clinging to it, and my knuckles gripped the sheets so hard I doubted they had any colour left in them. Evan's dick still filled my mouth, fucking my throat as he chased his release. I knew he was close from the deep growls and groans he made, but at least he had the forethought to slow the machine down before I fucking exploded from raw sensitivity.

"So. Fucking. Good. For. Me," Evan said as he gripped my jaw. "So. Fucking. Perfect."

I groaned, too overstimulated to do anything else, but that was all it took to send him crashing over the edge. His cock swelled on my tongue as his cum spilled down my throat, flooding my senses with the scent and sound of his release. I swallowed every drop before he gently let me go and leant down to taste himself on my lips.

"You're amazing," he said quietly, his kisses laden with gentleness. "I hope you know that."

"Uh-huh." That was all I could manage as I slowly wiggled myself off the dildo and flopped onto the bed, all the strength gone from my muscles. I hoped Evan wasn't planning on me moving any time soon. "You too."

He chuckled softly, running his hand through my hair before he walked around the bed. I heard him moving the machine and then disappearing out of the room. The hot tap creaked in the bathroom and a few moments later, Evan returned with a warm flannel. He gently rolled me over and eased the sodden lingerie over my thighs, wiping away the last of my cum that had soaked into the lace.

He threw the panties and the flannel off the bed, then leant over me and gently brushed hair off my forehead. "Thank you."

"For what? If anything, I should be thanking you."

"For just… being you." He kissed me softly. "I promise tomorrow I'll make the list. And I'd love your help, please."

I smiled up at him, my heart feeling altogether too big for my chest. I really did love him. One day soon I'd have to tell him. But if I did it now, it'd probably sound disingenuous, like I only loved him for melting my brains with cock. "Of course," I said, returning his kiss with all the energy I could muster.

Evan lay down next to me and pulled me into his arms, running his fingers up and down my spine as I lay with my head on his chest, thinking about just how fucking lucky I was.

CHAPTER THIRTY

Eva Nessence

LOOKING down the list I'd made with Rhys, I was pleased to see the progress I'd managed to make over the past two weeks. It hadn't been easy, but there'd definitely been steps forward.

The first item on the list, which I'd printed in large red letters, was Day Job. And underneath I'd written a couple of options that I'd decided on after scouring the NHS jobs website, which included part-time hours, a practice-based paramedic position, and working events.

When we'd sat down to make the list, I'd been reluctant to even consider changing my day job until it had finally sunk in that making an adjustment now didn't mean I couldn't go back if things didn't work out. My paramedic career wasn't this fixed, immovable thing I was stuck with until I retired, and thinking about it that way helped to loosen some of the panic clawing at my skin.

I'd thought bringing up part-time hours to Pete, the clinical operations manager and the man who'd been my boss since I'd first joined the service after university, would be a nightmare. I'd been fully expecting him to tell me it wasn't something they could accommodate, despite the fact I'd seen them advertising it in the past, and if I wanted to do that, I'd have to find another job elsewhere.

But instead, he'd just nodded and smiled and started asking me about how I was feeling. It'd thrown me for a second and the shock had made me admit to my burnout and trying to do too much. I'd even told him about my drag career, which Pete had sort of known about in a vague way since I'd mentioned performing at various Pride events and being unable to work them because of that.

Pete had nodded, listened, offered me some chocolate biscuits from the pack in his desk drawer, and then said, "So, part-time hours would be twenty hours a week and your salary would obviously have to be adjusted to match—just making sure you're aware of that. I'd have to put the request through senior leadership and we'd have to sort it all out with HR, but in principle we could make it work. Assuming you're happy with that and it gets signed off, when would you want to start?"

I genuinely hadn't expected it to be that easy, and I still wasn't convinced it would be since I hadn't had formal confirmation, but with any luck on the first of August I'd be starting a new shift pattern of only twenty hours a week. It would mean taking a chunk out of my budget, but it would give me more room to breathe and the opportunity to take on more drag gigs once I got my feet underneath me. I'd promised Rhys I wouldn't immediately rush into more work unless I had to, but it did mean I could do one of the other things on my list.

Audition for the drag panto.

I'd be able to tell Eli in a couple of hours since tonight would be my first show since I'd crashed and burned, and I was anticipating his reaction going one of two ways. Both of them involved tight hugs and a mild dose of screaming.

There were still details to work out, like fitting it around our regular shows at The Court, my part-time hours, and babysitting Milo and Grace, although that wasn't quite as much of an issue as I'd assumed it would be.

I'd finally gotten hold of Kirsty to talk about childcare and her new job, and after dancing around it for a while, she'd admitted she'd found an extra pair of hands—if necessary—in Jade, her neighbour's seventeen-year-old daughter.

Jade was studying childcare at college and was more than happy to babysit for a few hours after school or drop in first thing to be with Milo and Grace when Kirsty started early. I wasn't super happy about Kirsty forking out for babysitting, which had led to a small argument, but as a compromise she'd agreed to let me pay for some after-school activities.

There was a football team at school Grace could join for the summer term, and Milo was going to be starting one of Connor's junior ballet classes at Above The Barre. Both had nearly exploded with excitement when we'd told them, and that'd been enough for me to finally accept I wasn't always going to be around to babysit whenever Kirsty needed me.

That and the absolute bollocking she'd given me about burning out.

I felt like I was fifteen and being told off for ditching PE to make out with boys behind the bike sheds all over again.

Footsteps sounded on the creaking stairs and two seconds later Rhys's head appeared around the door of my drag den. "How're you getting on? Nearly ready to go?"

"Sort of," I said, looking up from my list and around at the veritable array of wigs and dresses I'd laid out around me on the craft table. "I thought I knew what I wanted to wear but then I kept seeing more options. It doesn't help I got so bored over the last few weeks I went through Eva's entire wardrobe and found a ton of shit I'd forgotten about."

Rhys chuckled. "Is this your way of saying we need to cart half your bloody wardrobe to Lincoln then?"

"No, I need to make a decision. I'm not going to be like the others and clog up the damn dressing room with useless shit."

"You need to ask Phil about getting some proper hanging racks installed."

"Yeah, we've talked about it but having moving rails is also really useful when we do variety nights or special events and there's more of us." I shook my head. The dressing rooms at The Court were not my problem to fix. I was grateful we had some to start with. "Not my circus. Not my monkeys."

Rhys snorted and walked over to the table, casting his eyes over everything. I watched his gaze linger on a deep green velvet dress with a plunging neckline, thigh-high slit, and an embroidered golden snake on the waist. It was one of those dresses that looked nice on the hanger but putting it on made it just *serve*. The first time I'd worn it, Sparkles had squealed in delight and yelled, "Oh my god, it's serving pussy!"

"That one?" I asked with a wry smile, pointing to it.

"Yeah, what do you think?"

"Absolutely."

If there was ever a time for Eva to serve cunt, it was tonight.

"Oh my fucking god, bitch, look at you! It's giving Morticia, Queen of the Damned, ultimate slay, don't fuck with me honey, and I love it," Bubblegum cried as soon as she walked into the dressing room and saw me half-dressed and ready to work. She threw her arms around my shoulders and squeezed me tight. "I missed you so much."

"I've been gone for two weeks," I said, patting her hand and leaning into her touch. The truth was I'd missed her too, but I wasn't going to admit that. Not yet. "Are you really that lonely and friendless?"

"Er, you left me with the scheming trash goblin, the murder twins—who I swear are *this* close to fucking—and Moxxie… okay, Moxxie is fine, but the other three?"

"Fine? What do you mean fine?" Moxxie asked with a laugh as they strolled through the door, rhinestoned cowboy hat in hand. "That makes me sound like a cockroach you found in the shower."

"No, that's Bitch," I said as I reached for my eyelashes,

shooting Moxxie a smile through the mirror. "Howdy, cowboy. Did you rob Swarovski or did you fall into Sparkles's make-up bag?"

"If anything, Swarovski robbed me. Do you know how much this shit costs?"

"Can't you buy them in bulk?" Bubblegum asked, putting her bag down and starting to strip off. "Wouldn't that be easier?"

"Probably, but I haven't looked." Moxxie shrugged and dumped their stuff on the chair in the corner. "How're you doing, Eva? Feeling any better?"

"Yeah, not bad," I said, half focused on pressing one of my lashes into place. "I've felt worse."

"Hun, don't play off how shit you felt," Bubblegum said. "Are you still tired?"

"Fucking exhausted. But I had a nap this afternoon, and I'm not working tomorrow, so I can sleep. And I… I'm actually going to be dropping down to part-time hours at work soon."

Bubblegum squealed with delight and clapped her hands. "That's amazing! I'm so proud of you."

"Fucking hell, seriously?" Moxxie asked, staring at me with wide eyes. "Did I miss something? Did you get abducted by fucking aliens?"

"No, she burned the hell out by thinking she had to do everything," Bubblegum said, jabbing me playfully on the cheek with one finger. "And then refused to admit it until she literally couldn't stand up without passing out."

"I wasn't *that* bad!"

"Er, excuse me, I was there when you were denying it. I almost hit you with a pillow."

"Your restraint is noted," I said dryly but unable to stop myself from smiling. What would I have done without this ridiculous lot?

"Thank you." Bubblegum blew a kiss at me.

"Shit, burnout is no joke," Moxxie said. "You're taking it easy, right?"

"Trying to. My body isn't really giving me a choice."

Moxxie nodded. "I burned out a few years ago, just with life shit, and it was hard. I think it took nearly a year for me to feel like myself again, but by the sound of it, you actually listened to yourself and stopped. I just kept going until I ended up in hospital being treated for exhaustion and pneumonia."

"Shit," I said, because there wasn't much else I could say. Despite my medical training, I'd never considered things could get that bad. But I supposed people never thought things would affect them in the same way they affected others. There was a good chance I'd have ended up in Moxxie's position if Rhys hadn't forced me to stop. "I'm glad you're okay now."

"Thanks." They smiled at me warmly. "Baby steps, okay?"

"Baby steps." And I meant it. Two weeks without Eva had made me start to miss her and the thought of having to take a break from drag had made my stomach twist. I didn't ever want to stop being Eva, and it had given me the chance to start thinking about my long-term goals as a performer.

Tonight was my first opportunity to dip my toes back into the water, and Phil had rearranged the routines so I could go first with a shorter set because I'd been forced to admit doing my normal thirty or forty minutes would exhaust me.

The three of us continued chatting while we got ready, and I was just starting to wonder where the hell Bitch had gotten to when she suddenly burst through the door with the rabid energy of a sugar-high squirrel.

"Fuck me sideways with a pineapple, sluts. You will never fucking guess who's agreed to star in the drag panto!" She laughed maniacally, like some sort of nefarious cartoon villain, clapping her hands while she stomped up and down on the spot. "Gah, it's so fucking brilliant!"

"Who?" I asked. The only other times I'd seen Bitch this excited was when she'd won *It's A Drag!* A couple of years ago, and when Tristan had proposed onstage in February. Although the second had been accompanied by shocked, silent awe rather than cackling laughter.

"Oh my God, did you get someone famous?" Bubblegum asked with wide, eager eyes. "Like from *Drag Stars*?"

"Not just *someone*. I've got *Drag Stars* royalty. Barbie fucking Summers."

"Bloody hell," Moxxie said with a low whistle while Bubblegum dissolved into gleeful squeaks of, "Oh my God, oh my God, oh my God!"

"That is impressive," I said. "How did you manage that?"

I wasn't a die-hard *Drag Stars* fan, but I knew Barbie Summers had won last year's UK crown, headlined the countrywide *Drag Stars* tour, done a solo sold-out tour, and had even been rumoured to be appearing on a couple of other TV shows. The fact she'd even consider coming to do a small drag panto in the East Midlands made no sense, but if she was, then Bitch had to have pulled some serious strings.

Bitch's smile was wild, her eyes gleaming with pure elation. "Apparently she's moving back this way and wants to get involved with the local scene. She's from Newark originally. Mercy knows her and put us in touch. I think you'll love her! She'll be back in Newark from the end of May, so hopefully she'll come by and say hi around then."

"Do you think she'd want to perform here regularly?" Bubblegum asked with wonder. "That would be so cool."

"Maybe," Bitch said. "Anyway, the panto is now full steam ahead." She turned to me, expression softening. "Think you'd be up for it? My little gothic nightmare."

"Yeah," I said. "I wouldn't miss it."

"That's my girl." Bitch winked and then threw her arms around my shoulders, kissing the air next to my cheek. "I missed you, bitch."

"I missed you too," I said with a petite air kiss. "I missed all of you, actually."

"Good, because we'd be really fucking sad if you didn't," Bubblegum said, dragging Moxxie over to join in the group hug. I let out a deep breath and relaxed into their touch.

I was still exhausted, still struggling to let go of my need to do everything, but I was here and that was a start.

Baby steps.

CHAPTER THIRTY-ONE

Rhys

Sitting in the audience at The Court waiting for Eva to come on stage was making my emotional state oscillate between nervous, excited, and wildly horny.

"I can't believe I didn't know about this place," Connor said from beside me, sipping a large strawberry daiquiri from a wide glass dusted with pink sugar. It was the perfect encapsulation of him in drink form. As promised, this was a pole night out and I was grateful to have them all here, even if only Ianto knew the real reason why I'd suggested tonight. "It's so cool! I'm definitely coming here again. I wonder if they hire the space out… It would be the perfect venue for our next showcase. Or even a small pole competition."

"That'd be fun," Ianto said from my other side. He'd deliberately chosen an outfit that was very different from mine so it was easier to tell us apart because we both knew that from a distance we were virtually impossible to distinguish. Even Ben struggled, which was saying something. "We could do a doubles routine."

"Oh my God, yes! Yes! You have to," Connor said, a bright smile on his perfectly painted mouth. His make-up always slayed, but tonight it was a gorgeously extravagant celebration of pink. "What about you, Colin? Would you compete?"

"Maybe," Colin said thoughtfully, twirling the straw in his glass around with a long, slim finger. He'd let his hair down and it shimmered down to his waist like a fiery curtain. He was wearing skin-tight leather trousers, a ruffled white shirt, and a black and gold embroidered corset belt that shimmered faintly in the low light. "I haven't for a while, but it might be fun."

Connor patted his hand. "I'd make it fun, I promise."

I let them chat as I sipped my own drink, which was just a Diet Coke to keep my head clear, too lost in my own thoughts to contribute. I felt a hand on my leg and glanced around with a start to see Ianto looking at me pensively. "You okay?"

"Yeah, I'm fine," I said. "Just want it to go well. Also… I'm not really sure what to expect. The last time I tried to come to one of these I got dragged away before the show started and missed most of it."

Ianto chuckled fondly as the lights dimmed, the music swelled, and a rousing cheer went up from around us. "Well, you're doing better than last time then."

"Hello, my darlings! It's me, Violet *Bouquet*. Have you missed me?" asked the drag queen, a vision in extravagantly bright florals, who was strolling onto the stage. Her dress looked like a more over-the-top version of something my aunty Gladys had worn to a friend of the family's wedding in the late nineties when Ianto and I had been about seven or eight. That dress had been so bright Tadcu had asked if she planned on standing in for Mumbles Lighthouse.

"God, look at you lot," the queen continued as she surveyed the audience. She exuded confidence from every curve and had that air of one of those older aunties you gave plenty of gin to at Christmas because she knew all the secrets, both your family's and everyone else's. Very much like aunty Gladys to be honest. "I keep expecting you to get better looking but I should probably stop putting my contacts in. Then you'd all improve a great deal."

Everyone laughed and she smiled benevolently. "At least you'll admit you all need improvement," she said. "Now we have a wonderful show for you this evening, packed full of delights… and Bitch Fit is here too, unfortunately, but there's nothing I can do to stop her getting in. She keeps coming up from the sewers."

My shoulders shook with laughter, releasing some of the tension knotted in my chest.

"First up tonight, we have our absolutely gorgeous gothic goddess, Miss Eva Nessence. We've stolen her away from the clutches of the evil Sheriff of Nottingham and dragged her all the way to Lincoln, and I can't wait to see what she has in store for us. Please go absolutely wild for our beloved queen of the night… Eva Nessence."

I cheered so hard it felt like someone had run a cheese

grater over my vocal cords as the iconic first notes of Evanescence's 'Bring Me to Life' echoed through the speakers and Eva, my Eva, stepped onto the stage.

She moved effortlessly with an ethereal grace that very few people would ever be able to match. Dark green velvet clung to her body, long legs accentuated by the dress's thigh-high slit and her enormous shoes with spiked metallic heels that resembled vertebrae—a new purchase she'd treated herself to during a bad burnout day after seeing Carmilla's Mayday wearing some. Her dark hair fell in glamourous waves that reminded me of Morticia Addams from the sixties, and her lipstick was almost blood red.

Eva truly was a goddess given form, and I would tear out my own heart if it meant she'd kiss me.

She'd been incredible the first time I'd watched her perform, but tonight I couldn't take my eyes off her. I was vaguely aware of Ianto speaking to me as the song smoothly transitioned to 'Spellbound' by Siouxsie and the Banshees, and as Eva looked out into the audience, her body moving to the beat of the music, our eyes locked. My heart stopped, captivated by the beauty before me.

I'd never imagined falling in love, not really, not like this. But now I couldn't imagine not being in love. Living without Evan, or Eva, would be like never seeing the sun rise or a full moon glowing with unearthly light. It would be like missing something foundational to reality.

When Ianto had talked about what being in love with Ben felt like, I'd been convinced he was exaggerating because those sorts of emotions had never seemed physically possible. Now I wasn't sure if my brother had gone far enough.

The song came to an end and the music faded away to rapturous applause. Eva smiled out at us as someone handed her a microphone, and it felt like the sort of smile an empress might give peasants.

"Good evening, my beautiful little nightmares," she said in a soft voice that made my hair stand on end. "How are you tonight?" There was a lot of cheering and a few shouts from the audience, and I realised I hadn't even made a sound. "I'm so glad. I've missed you terribly. Now, I haven't done this in a while, but I thought tonight it might be fun to change things up a little. If it sounds terrible, then you can all pretend you didn't hear it and I won't do it again."

Scattered laughter and a few whistles of encouragement greeted this statement, and it took me a moment to realise what Eva was going to do. And then the opening bars of Carmilla's metal cover of 'Paint It Black' struck up, and Eva began to sing.

All that beauty, all that talent, and now a voice like a fucking god? Fucking Christ, I was ready to drop to one knee and propose marriage.

Eva's voice was rich and velvety, pouring into my ears like liquid silk. There was a haunting quality to it too, which could only have come from practice, and I wondered why she'd never mentioned this talent before. If she seriously thought she wasn't any good, then we were going to have fucking words because in my opinion she'd put half the Welsh choirs to fucking shame.

"You didn't say she could sing," Ianto said, leaning in close. It was the first thing I'd heard from him since Eva came on stage, and he sounded as awed as I felt.

"I didn't know she could."

"If you don't tell Evan you love him after this, I'm going to think you're a bloody idiot."

"Don't worry, I'll think the same," I said. "Do you think…"

"Yeah, I do." Ianto patted my thigh. "The feeling is mutual. Anyone who stares at you that much either wants to kiss you, kill you, or fuck you."

"I'll take the first and last, but maybe avoid the second."

Ianto chuckled then said with a deep sincerity which almost felt out of place in this moment, "You know, I was never able to picture the person you might end up with, but now I realise it's because I didn't think big enough."

"Big enough?" I asked as the music reached its crescendo.

"Yeah, someone extraordinary."

I looked at Eva, who looked and sounded like she should be fronting a goth-rock band at Download Festival, and gave a single nod.

Someone extraordinary indeed.

After the show, I found myself being dragged backstage by Bubblegum Galaxy, who was living up to her name as a vision in deep sparkling blue. She was still fizzing with energy, which seemed impossible after the set I'd just witnessed, but I was going to put it down to adrenaline and youth since Bubblegum was still such a baby.

"I found him!" she announced loudly as she pulled me into the dressing room, which was full of people in various stages of undress. "He looks very cute today too."

"You do know I'm standing right here, don't you?" I asked with a rough chuckle. My voice was still destroyed from all the cheering.

"Hush," Bubblegum said, waving a hand roughly in my direction. She turned to Evan, who was sitting in an armchair in the corner wearing an old pair of joggers and my Carmilla hoodie. I'd have protested about the bloody cheek of him stealing it if I hadn't liked how good he looked in it. "How're you feeling, babe?"

"Tired but good. Really good," Evan said. "That was fun." He looked exhausted, even with half his make-up still on, although the dark eye shadow probably wasn't helping. I was glad we'd come up together so I could drive home because he looked about two seconds from falling asleep. He flicked his gaze across to me and smiled. "Did you enjoy it?"

"You were amazing," I said. "Utterly fabulous." I picked my way across the dressing room, aware that Bubblegum, Bitch, and Moxxie were watching but not really caring, and crouched down beside the chair. "I didn't know you could sing."

"Hidden talent," he said quietly. "That and I did musicals in high school. It was my first proper taste of being on stage, and I was the one guy happy to try being the dame when they did panto at Christmas. I got bored while you were at work and I wasn't allowed to do anything, so I thought I'd practice because technically I can do that sitting on the sofa."

I grinned and leant in to kiss him. "Pretty sure that's still doing something but I'll allow it."

"Too late, I've already done it now." His lips were soft, still stained with remnants of dark lipstick, and tasted vaguely like something fruity. "I love you," he said softly. "Did you know that? You're irritating as fuck but I love you so much it hurts."

"I love you too," I said, ignoring the little gasp and aww that went up from the peanut gallery behind us. Evan loved me and those words, which I'd never expected to hear him say, were going to be branded into my brain for a lifetime and beyond.

Tadcu had told me once he'd known what the true meaning of love was when he'd fallen for my grandmother, and I'd always thought it was a meaningless platitude. But now I knew he was wrong. Evan made love real, tangible, and something I wanted to treasure for all time, despite the highs and lows. If we were starting here, where else could we go? The future looked bright and endless, like the sea in the middle of summer. It felt like home.

I grinned and kissed him again. "And I don't think I'm *that* annoying."

"Really?"

"Well, maybe a bit. But it doesn't seem to have put you off."

"Surprisingly, it hasn't." He kissed me again. "I don't

think I've ever had anyone care about me as much as you do."

"I did tell you I need someone to take care of," I said. "And I think that person is you."

"Only if you let me take care of you too sometimes."

"I suppose."

"And don't play your terrible music at nine in the morning."

I chuckled. "No promises on that one." I glanced around and bit back my laughter when the others suddenly pretended to look very busy, jumping into life like kids who'd been caught listening in. "Want to get out of here? Get McDonald's and go home?"

"Sounds perfect," Evan said, sitting up slowly and giving me one final kiss. "Let me grab my stuff and we can go." He glanced around at his friends and raised an eyebrow. Then he sighed. "All right, you lot, get it out of your system now and then I never want to hear it again."

The screech that went up from all three of them could've been heard from fucking Cardiff as they descended upon us with enough hugs and kisses to power a bloody Care Bear.

CHAPTER THIRTY-TWO

Eva Nessence

Rhys drove us home while I dozed in the front seat despite every effort on my part to stay awake. But for the first time in months, the sleep didn't feel like a frantic, snatched five minutes that left me feeling worse off than before and I didn't wake up in a panic that I'd missed something either. There was no deep-seated anxiety that I should be doing something else, that I was wasting precious time I could be putting to better use.

Performing tonight had drained me, but in a strangely satisfying way. It'd felt like the old days when I'd first gotten into drag and being Eva hadn't felt like a chore. It'd been a rebirth of sorts, if I wanted to get all metaphysical about it.

Something like that anyway.

Whatever way I looked at it, tonight had felt like taking a step towards the place I wanted to be. It wasn't backwards, because I couldn't go that way without a lot of pain, but it wasn't quite forwards either. It was more like sideways, a new path I'd found and forged with the help of those around me. The one they'd pointed out when I couldn't see the wood for the trees.

But taking my first steps as a new Eva had been nothing compared to what had happened afterwards.

I hadn't been expecting to tell Rhys I loved him. The words had simply materialised on my lips, but as soon as I'd said them I'd known, without any doubt, I'd meant them. There'd been very few people I'd loved over the years, and even fewer if we took friends and family out of the equation.

Rhys might have been the first man I'd really, truly loved.

There was a bone-deep certainty to the feeling which felt strangely heavy but not in an unpleasant way, like the weight of expectation or duty I'd come to associate with the emotion. Love had always felt like obligation before, like I had to give and give until there was nothing left. Love had never made me whole.

But with Rhys... love felt like laughter. It felt like sunshine and frosty mornings and cloudless starry nights. It felt like dancing in the rain and falling asleep just before sunrise and long nights full of desperate moans. It felt like music and spotlights and new lipstick and that perfect moment before thunderous applause.

And every time I looked at him, I knew I'd never be alone. That he'd be there, always, with his hand in mine as we wandered down the path of life, seeing where it took us.

There would be good days and bad days and really fucking ugly ones where the whole world felt like it was going to crash down around us.

But if we had each other, we'd be okay.

Besides, it wasn't as if we could have picked much of a worse place to start. If we could fall in love while I burned to a crisp, then who knew what the future would be like. It would be ours for the taking.

"What happens now?" I asked as we pulled up outside our houses, both dark in the empty street.

"Now? We go inside and go to bed because you look bloody shattered."

"No, I mean with us. What happens now?" I looked across at him and watched a soft smile blossom across his face, lighting it up in the most beautiful way.

"I don't know, but that's not a bad thing. We don't have to figure it out right this second."

"This is when I find out you're not a planner," I said with a dry, tired laugh.

"I am, but only when it's important. And flexible. We don't need to plan the rest of our lives out tonight."

He had a point, I had to give him that. "True."

"I do know I want to be with you," he said, leaning across the console to kiss me softly. "For a long time."

"Good, but I want that too. You might have steamrollered your way into my life but I'm not letting you leave so easily."

He scoffed. "Like I'm going anywhere. I'm right where I want to be." He kissed me again, deeper this time, and I sighed into his mouth. Rhys was right—there was no rush.

Now everything was out in the open, I felt more at peace than ever. My life finally felt like mine, and I was going to live it the way I wanted.

"Let's go in," I said, gently pulling away. "I want you."

"Are you sure you're not too tired?" he asked and I was sweetly touched by his concern.

"No, I want to show you all the ways I love you."

He grinned mischievously. "All?"

"Probably not all. I doubt we'll have time for that."

Rhys laughed, darting in for another kiss before he reached for his door and by the time I'd climbed out of the passenger seat, he'd already grabbed my bags from the boot and was pulling my house keys out of his pocket. "You're so slow," he hissed. "Hurry up."

"Desperate, are we?" I asked as I reached the front door, stepping in behind him. He locked the car over my shoulder then slammed the door shut.

"And you're not?"

"Perhaps," I said slowly, backing him against the door and shoving my knee between his thighs. "But it's fun to tease you." I kissed him deeply, sliding my tongue into his mouth and drinking in his moans.

"I thought I was the annoying one?" he asked breathlessly, his fingers fisting in the front of my hoodie. Which was technically his but I'd stolen it because it was comfortable and smelt like him.

"Mostly, but I can be too."

He chuckled and I kissed him again.

One kiss became two, became five, became more than I could be bothered to count as I pulled him through the house, up the stairs, and into my room. Our room. Because it would never be just mine again if I had my way.

I pushed the door shut with my foot, unwilling to take my hands off Rhys for even a second. Our clothes hit the floor in a matter of moments, his body hot and firm against mine. The feel of his fingers on my chest… around my neck… burying into my hair as he dragged me onto the bed, spreading his legs so I could land between them, our bodies pressed so tightly together it was hard to know where mine ended and his began.

Rhys groaned as I ground my erection against his, sending shuddering waves of pleasure through us. He bucked up against me, his nails digging into my scalp as he kissed me fiercely. "Fuck, I love you," he murmured, the words engulfing me and warming me from the inside out, like I'd sunk into a hot bath or taken a shot of the most perfect whiskey. "I love you. Mmm, I… I fucking love you, Evan."

"I love you too," I said, my voice a low, possessive growl. "More than anything."

Rhys hooked his ankle around the back of my thigh, drawing me closer than I'd thought possible as we rutted against each other, lost in the pure pleasure we drew from each other. I'd thought about more, about taking him apart and making love to him slowly, but I didn't need more. I just needed him.

Wherever Rhys was, that was where I needed to be.

We kissed and frotted and murmured endless words of love and possession until it built into a pure crescendo of bliss, the final note the breathless gasp from Rhys's lips as he came, bucking up against me and painting our skin with his release. I gasped, my own orgasm pulsing through me and making my head spin.

My cum mixed with his between us and when I could breathe and bear to be parted from my love for more than a moment, I slid down his body and licked our release from his beautiful, illustrated skin. I collected our cum on my tongue and brought my mouth back to his, and we kissed over and over, sharing the taste between us.

Afterwards, we lay stretched out in each other's arms, limbs still intertwined as we exchanged lazy kisses and soft words.

"We should probably shower," Rhys said eventually. "Or we'll be crusty and sticky tomorrow."

"That's a charming picture," I said with a wry smile.

"Which is why we should do it now before we lose the will to move."

"Who said I haven't already?"

Rhys snorted and shook his head. He pulled himself half up until he was looking down at me. "What's your plan for tomorrow?"

"I don't know. I'm not working."

"Good, I'll make breakfast. Then we can plan."

"Plan what?"

"I don't know, things." He shrugged. "We need to make a shopping list. We're nearly out of food. And we should do something, maybe go out for dinner."

"Where do you want to go?"

"There's a good Vietnamese place in town," Rhys said. "Ianto and Ben have been there before."

"Sounds good," I said. "Want to see if they want to come with us? I haven't really spent much time with your brother, and I want to."

Rhys grinned. "I'd like that." He kissed me again, then pulled me into a sitting position. "Come on, let's go and shower. Then we can sleep, because you still look bloody knackered."

I laughed as he dragged me out of bed and into the bathroom, the pair of us trying to figure out how to both fit in the bath and stand under the spray. Afterwards, we curled up in bed together naked, kissing until Rhys drifted off with his head on my chest.

"I love you," I said, kissing the top of his head and letting out a deep breath.

Once upon a time, I'd never have dreamt I could have this. That I could have someone who loved me the way Rhys did.

All it had taken was some terrible music, a broken nose, breakfast burritos, burnout, and two men willing to cause a scene.

With any other person, it could have been a disaster. It probably should have been.

But in the middle of it all, we'd found each other.

And that was all that mattered.

"I love you too," Rhys muttered, his face pressed into my chest. "Now go the fuck to sleep."

I chuckled and kissed his head again, pulling my beautiful Welsh bastard against me.

And I was never going to let him go.

EPILOGUE
SEVEN MONTHS LATER

Rhys

"I'M REALLY EXCITED about this. I can't remember the last time we went to see a panto," Ianto said as we waited for the curtain to rise on the opening night of *Cinderella*, the East Midland's latest drag pantomime.

Apparently the original plan had been to do *Sleeping Beauty* or *Dick Whittington* but according to Evan, when Eli and Madam Mercy had gotten Barbie Summers on board, there'd been a quick pivot based on them making the most of her. I didn't quite understand all the ins and outs, but Evan had been pleased with the final script and the cast, even if Peachy Keen and Ginger Biscuits, Peaches supposed arch-nemesis from London, who'd been cast as the ugly sisters, had apparently come *this* close to either murdering each other or shagging in a cupboard.

Evan was putting money on both happening by the end of the run.

"Oh, it's been a while," said Tadcu, who was sitting on the other side of Ben, who was on Ianto's other side. I hadn't been sure about bringing my eighty-odd-year-old grandfather to watch, but he'd insisted and I wasn't about to tell him no. There was no way I was explaining any of the jokes to him, though. Ben and Ianto could do that later if he had questions. "We used to go all the time when you were kids, though. Do you remember the time we went to see *Jack and the Beanstalk* with aunty Linda and Gavin? I think William must have only been about four or five, but he screamed bloody murder when that cow came on stage."

"To be fair, that cow was terrifying," I said, remembering exactly how horrifying the cow costume in question had been. If Ianto and I had been William's age, we'd have had nightmares for weeks.

"I think my first experience with panto was when school took us," Kirsty said. She was sat next to me, having gotten Jade to babysit Milo and Grace for the evening. "All I remember was someone's wig fell off halfway through their number. We all thought it was hysterical."

"Praying that doesn't happen now," I said with a laugh. "Although with the amount of tape, pins, hair spray, and wig glue this lot are using, then none of them should fucking move."

I'd learnt a hell of a lot about drag in the past seven months, including what the fuck contour was, how to score the soles of shoes so they didn't slip on stage, and, most importantly, how to give Eva a blow job in full drag and get her on stage ten minutes later looking put-together as fuck.

That was probably my proudest accomplishment.

"It's all going to be fine," Ianto said, nudging me gently with his shoulder and offering me an encouraging smile. As much as I tried to pretend I wasn't nervous, there was no fooling my twin. "More than that, it's going to be amazing."

"I know… I just…" I sighed. "Do you think this is how they all feel watching us doing Ironman?" My nerves fizzed in my stomach and my tongue felt fuzzy, like I'd eaten too many sour sweets and thrown them all back up again.

"Maybe, although maybe it's more waiting for us to finish? Like knowing we should be coming up to the finish line and waiting to see us, since the whole thing takes so long in the first place."

"True. It does kind of feel like that anyway, since this is the end of all the rehearsals. It all feels very real now, and I'm not even getting up on the sodding stage."

After three months of rehearsals, reaching the fourteen shows over two weeks should have felt like a relief, but now was the agonising waiting period to see if the work had paid off. I'd heard little bits when Evan had been practising at home and thought it was brilliant, but then again, I was a little biased.

"I promise," Ianto said. "It'll be fine. None of us know what's supposed to happen, and they're all seasoned performers, so if there's any mistakes, they can roll with it."

I nodded because he made a fair point.

Our relationship had shifted over the past few months, and eventually we'd forced ourselves to sit down and talk about it. It hadn't been easy and there'd been a few tears, some hugs, and some very loving brotherly smacks around the head, but we'd finally gotten all our feelings out in the open.

I'd told Ianto about my realisation that I'd held off relationships because I never wanted to leave him behind, and he'd confessed how worried he'd been that Ben would come between us. We'd talked about how much we still needed each other, but that it was okay if it was less than it used to be, especially since Ben had proposed in September and he and Ianto were firmly on their way to creating a whole new life together.

We still messaged every day and saw each other at least once a week outside of work, but now it felt like we were very much two separate people with our own lives.

We'd mourned that realisation together, and Evan had understood when I'd randomly broken down in tears on our sofa one afternoon not long after I'd formally moved into his. It'd felt like the final nail in the coffin because there was no way things would ever go back now. And while I was unbelievably happy with my life, and happy for Ianto, there was a part of me which would always miss what we'd once had.

Evan had understood and let me ramble for bloody hours about my brother and our escapades, and after that I'd felt better.

I glanced around the small theatre again and checked my watch. There was two minutes until curtain up. My eyes wandered across the audience and caught on a random figure dressed in pastel blue sitting a couple of rows in front of us.

"Ianto," I hissed, gripping my twin's thigh with white knuckles. "Two rows down, three to the left. Is that…"

"Fuck. Is that Theo Foxx?" Ianto asked, his voice hushed and full of awe. "It can't be. What would he be doing here?"

"I don't know but… fuck, that's West with him. Bubblegum's boyfriend." I stared at the two men and the dark-haired gothic man sat beside them, doing some quick mental puzzling. Rory had mentioned West's brother was coming down to watch. And there was a vague resemblance between West and Theo, whose face I knew very well from following him on every platform possible. There was something about the way they were talking too, like they knew each other well. "I think West might be his brother."

"Seriously? Do you think we could get a picture?"

"I don't know, maybe?" I was sure Bubblegum could introduce us. "Can't hurt to ask."

Was it weird that my twin brother and I were both fans of the same porn star? Maybe.

Was it also weird that we both knew the other was a massive fan? Probably.

Did I give a fuck? Absolutely not. Especially not if we got to meet Theo Foxx.

I smiled to myself. Maybe Ianto and I weren't drifting as far apart as we'd thought.

The lights dimmed and an excited hush settled over the crowd as music filled the air. The curtain drew back, revealing a brightly coloured set of a classic fairy-tale town square with various drag performers as members of the townsfolk. They all looked fabulously camp and over the top, and I snorted when I realised some of the shops on the set had bad puns or sex jokes as their business names.

When Barbie Summers, looking picture-perfect as Cinderella, strolled onto the set, there was a huge round of applause from the audience, and while I joined in, I was waiting for a different face. And a couple of moments later, I got my wish.

Ginger and Peaches had been doing a ridiculously funny bit about wigs that seemed to simmer with both lust and loathing when a familiar figure swept onto the back of the stage looking utterly stunning in dark red and dripping in jewels. There was only one queen who could have played Cinderella's wicked stepmother with the perfect blend of elegance and contempt while being so fucking gorgeous she demanded everyone's attention.

It had to be Eva Nessence.

And I couldn't take my eyes off her.

"Where are my girls?" Eva asked in a voice that was so deliciously menacing and full of disdain it made the back of my neck prickle as she swept downstage. She gestured to the crowd. "They can't be any of you. My girls are far too beautiful to be mistaken for anyone here." The crowd booed and hissed playfully while Eva toyed with them, and it was fun watching my boyfriend turn his acerbic take-down skills onto the general public.

I knew Evan had been worried about taking on the role, because although it didn't involve hours of stage time, being a good villain required an actor to have a commanding stage presence and to make the audience hate them in only a few minutes. But I didn't know why he'd been worried because Eva was fucking magnificent.

Watching her reminded me how much I loved both her and Evan. I loved the freedom and escape Eva gave him, and I was so glad Evan had been able to find his way forward as Eva. Drag might still have been work, but after the rehearsals had started, Evan had told me how much fun it had felt again. The joy had returned with full force, and I'd never been happier.

The past seven months might not have always been easy, but I'd hoped the only place to go from where we'd started was up and luckily I'd gotten my wish.

We'd clicked in a way I'd never experienced with anyone before, and suddenly things that'd always seemed so silly or overrated made sense. There was the joy in waking up late together, in cooking dinner and talking about our days, being excited about random things because the other person loved it, and a hundred other things and more.

Life might have been complicated at times but being together at least meant we had someone to go through things with.

And I couldn't ever see that changing.

I loved Evan more than I'd ever thought it possible to love anyone. He was my whole world, and Eva was the night sky, brilliant and beautiful.

Nothing could have been better.

. . .

After the show was over and most of the audience had finally drained away, I found myself waiting in the front of the theatre with Kirsty, Ianto, Ben, Tadcu, West, his brother —who *had* turned out to be Theo Foxx and who'd been more than happy to take a picture with Ianto and me before kissing our cheeks and telling us how cute we were—and the gothic man, who was Theo's fiancé. There were a few other people around too, including a group who sounded like they might be here for Eli.

I had a bunch of black and red paper roses in hand that I'd bought as a surprise, which Ianto had brought with him because I'd known if I'd kept them in the house, Evan would have found them. Our house wasn't exactly huge and our storage space was limited, but it was perfect for us right now, so moving wasn't in our current plan, especially with the way house prices were looking. We'd be dead before we'd be able to afford a deposit at this rate.

A door opened somewhere with a loud creak, and a moment later a couple of the performers appeared, all out of drag and looking happy but utterly exhausted. Evan was walking out next to Rory, who broke away to fling himself into West's arms, and I sighed internally because we really needed a good hooker on the Welsh rugby team and it was a bloody shame he was English.

"Evan! You were amazing," Kirsty said, leaping in to pull her brother into a hug and squeezing him tight. "So good! Okay, I have to dash because I promised I'd be home by half ten. We'll catch up tomorrow. Love you!" She kissed his cheek before hugging him again and speeding off towards the exit. Evan chuckled as he watched her go, then turned to me, and I knew he'd spotted the roses because his eyes went wide.

"She's right," I said as I walked over to him and held out the flowers. "You were fucking spectacular."

"Thank you. Paper roses?" he asked, running his fingers over the petals.

"Then you can keep them forever. Plus I thought they'd match your aesthetic."

He smiled and grabbed the front of my shirt to pull me in for a kiss. "I fucking love you, you know that?"

"I love you too," I said as I threw my arms around him, a giddy joy filling me. "Want to say hi to the others and then get some food? You must be fucking starving!"

"Sounds perfect," he said, kissing me again. "McDonald's?"

"Man after my own heart."

"After it? I already own it."

"Does that mean I own yours?"

He grinned against my lips. "It's yours. Has been from the moment we met."

"I can't have been that annoying then," I said, my smile matching his.

"You were but that didn't stop me from falling."

I laughed. "Good, because I'm keeping your heart and never letting you go."

Our kiss was fire and sweetness and the promise of forever.

And I couldn't fucking wait.

WELCOME HOME
BONUS SHORT

Rhys

My body shivered in anticipation as I heard the front door slam, my aching cock dripping into the brand-new lace panties that were stretched over it. It felt like I'd been waiting on all fours for hours, and now I was finally going to get what I'd wanted all afternoon.

"I'm home," Evan called, his voice slightly muffled by the floor. "Babe? Where are you?"

"Upstairs," I said, trying to keep my voice casual and not give away what I was doing. "In our room."

I wanted to tell him to come up here right fucking now, but that would definitely arouse his suspicions. Although if he started pottering around downstairs, sorting his lunchbox and shit, I'd have to say something.

Evan had been on one of his two shifts this week, and he'd messaged me just before he'd left to say it'd been a bit stressful—mostly because students were morons and several had decided to celebrate freshers week by getting drunk and trying to go swimming in the Trent.

After dealing with that, I'd decided my poor boyfriend needed some stress relief.

And my horny, desperate ass was very happy to provide.

I heard Evan downstairs and the sound of the understairs cupboard door opening and shutting as he put his boots away. Another shiver ran down my spine and I stretched backwards, dropping my shoulders into the mattress, pushing my ass into the air, and wiggling it. The large plug in my ass nudged my prostate and I had to bite my lip to hold back the moan rising in my throat as my cock throbbed against the lace confining it.

I needed Evan to get his ass upstairs right the fuck now.

And a few moments later I heard his footsteps on the stairs and I rolled back onto all fours. "Rhys? Are you still in our room?"

"Yeah."

"What are you..." Evan's voice trailed off as he pushed the door open and I heard it squeaking on its hinges. I kept my eyes ahead, arching my back and pushing my butt out so he could get the full picture. "Holy fuck."

"What do you think?" I asked, finally glancing over my shoulder and smirking at him.

His expression was priceless, and I watched his eyes roam over me, drinking in the backless, deep red, lace panties with a little bow resting just above my ass crack, the flared base of the plug which was set with a red, heart-shaped gem that I knew he could see when I pushed my butt into the air, and the crop top I'd made from one of my ragged, old band T-shirts, cutting it across the chest so it just about covered my pecs.

I'd also added a matching deep red garter belt and black, lace topped stockings that stretched around my thighs. They'd been a pain in the ass to get up and attached to the straps of the garter belt, and it was a good thing I'd bought a multi-pack of cheap stockings because I'd put my fingers through two pairs trying to get the bloody things on.

The struggle had been worth it though because I looked sexy as fuck.

"I think… Jesus fucking Christ, what did I do to deserve this?" Evan asked, stepping into the room, and running his hand across one of my butt cheeks. "You look incredible, darling."

"I know," I said, winking at him and then groaning as he playfully spanked my cheek. "Mmm, yes… more."

Evan chuckled. "I'm guessing this isn't just a present for me?"

"I mean it is… but I'm really fucking horny and I'd quite like it if you got your dick inside me right now."

"So impatient," Evan said, caressing my ass before smacking my cheeks, one after another. His touch was harder and heat blossomed across my skin, making me gasp and push back into his hand. "Do you like that? Like me spanking this perfect ass?"

"Yes." I groaned as he smacked me again, distributing them perfectly across my heated skin. I wondered if my ass was turning red yet. I was betting it looked really good, especially with the lace framing my bare skin. "More."

"Are you sure?" Evan asked softly, rubbing his fingers across my cheeks, and skimming them across the top of the plug. "I thought you wanted me to fuck you?"

"I… I…" Fuck, why did he have to give me options? Wait, couldn't I have both? "I want both."

Evan chuckled again, that dark, rich sound that made my hole twitch around the plug. "I thought you were desperate, though? I thought you wanted fucking right now?"

"I, fuck, I can wait," I said, gasping the words out as Evan teased the base of the plug, nudging it against my prostate. "P-Please, Evan. You can have whatever you want. Just… fuck, just fucking use me."

"Mmm, you spoil me." He leant down and pressed kisses to the exposed skin of my ass, his lips so hot it felt like they were branding me. "You're such a good boy for me."

"Y-Yes. Want to be your good boy."

"So good," Evan repeated, kissing me again. "I can't wait to use this gorgeous ass and fill it with my cum. And I want to watch you make a mess of those pretty panties too."

I groaned, pushing back against his mouth, desperately hoping it would get me more of what I wanted. Suddenly his touch was gone and I almost cried out because I needed more, but when I glanced over my shoulder again, I realised he was stripping off his uniform and my stomach flipped in delight.

Evan's cock was already filling as he tugged his boxers down and I licked my lips because, fuck, I'd been dreaming about getting it inside me for *hours* and now he was so close I could practically taste him.

I opened my mouth to ask… something, but my words were stolen from my tongue as he smirked at me and spanked my ass again. My skin had cooled and the sudden application of his hand sent sharp heat coursing through me, a delicious sting of pain bursting under the skin.

All I could do was moan like the needy slut I was as he spanked me over and over, moving his hand between my cheeks and giving me just enough time between each blow so I felt every single one with perfect clarity.

My fingers gripped the sheets tightly as I sank my forehead into the bed, trying desperately to resist grasping my cock and jacking myself off. I knew Evan would make it good for me, but I'd never been a patient man and I needed to come so much it hurt.

All of a sudden, just as the spanking was starting to reach the wrong side of painful, he stopped, leaving my head spinning and my body aching with need.

"Fuck, darling," Evan said in a low voice that was practically a fucking purr. "You look so gorgeous like this." He ran his fingers gently over the burning skin. "Red is definitely your colour. And I love seeing my handprints on your ass… mmm, reminds me that you're mine. Would you like to see? Shall I take a photo so you can see how pretty you look like this? My beautiful slut."

"Fuck yes," I said, arching back. "I want to see."

"Stay there then. Let me grab my phone."

I froze in place and listened to him rummaging around in the pockets of his discarded trousers. The seconds stretched out and then he said, "That's it. Good boy. Let me take a couple more... perfect. Fuck, I can't wait for you to see these."

"Can I see them now?" I asked, twisting my head to gaze at him but Evan shook his head and put his phone on the bedside table, next to the bottle of lube I'd left out.

"No, not yet. I have other plans for you first." He reached down and started stroking his cock as his other hand reached for the base of my plug, gently starting to tease it in and out of my hole. "I like this," he added casually, like he wasn't tormenting me with every stroke. "You look good wearing a plug."

"T-Thanks," I said. Fuck, why was forming words suddenly so bloody hard? I couldn't even think of anything else to say. All my vocabulary had been replaced with a litany of sounds instead.

Another long, loud groan slipped from my lips as Evan finally tugged the plug free, leaving my hole clenching desperately around nothing but air.

"Lie down for me," Evan said as he tossed the plug onto the bed next to me. "I want to see your face when I fuck you."

I dropped onto the bed and flipped onto my back, spreading my legs wide so he could slot between them. He was still stood over me and I loved looking up at him like this. There was a reverent expression on his face that filled my chest with fireworks.

"I love you, Rhys," he said softly, bending down to kiss me with a gentleness that made me melt. "So much."

"I love you too."

He kissed me again and as he pulled away he reached for my thighs, grasping them in his hands and lifting my legs and hips up. I knew where he was going with this and moved my ankles to rest on his shoulders as he reached underneath me to line his cock up with my waiting hole.

My own, aching cock was still trapped inside soaking, red lace and every tiny move made the material scrape against the slick, sensitive skin of the exposed head. Evan had said he wanted to watch me make a mess of them, and that wasn't going to take long. I was already so on edge that a stiff breeze would have made me shoot.

Our groans echoed in my ears as Evan pushed his cock inside me, stretching and filling me so perfectly that I almost forgot to breathe. His hands were on my thighs, holding and lifting me, and it pushed his dick so fucking deep that I could feel his balls brushing against the hot skin of my ass.

He started to rock his hips, slowly at first but the minute movements were enough to make me gasp and claw at the sheets as his dick slid over my prostate.

"Evan," I said, looking up at him and praying to every fucking force in the universe that he could see the need on my face. "M-more, please."

"I've got you, darling," he said as he gripped me tighter and slid his cock almost all the way out of me before slamming back inside and making me howl with delight. "Is that what you need?"

"Yes… fucking… use me."

"Fuck, you feel so good," Evan said, growling as he stepped slightly closer, folding my legs over me as he began to pound me deep and hard, filling me to the hilt with every thrust. His face was flushed and his gaze was fixed on me, adoration burning deep into my soul. "I love you so much."

"I love you too." Pleasure rose inside me and it felt like I was cresting a wave, ready to crash into the shore and break apart. I tried to push my orgasm down, but it was no use. I was going to shatter under Evan's touch, whether he was ready for it or not. "Evan," I said, his name a broken moan on my tongue. "I'm… fuck, I'm gonna…"

"Yeah? Are you going to come for me?" He growled as he thrust deep inside me, his cock hammering my prostate. "Be a good boy for me, Rhys. Come."

I didn't even need to touch my cock. All it took was Evan's filthy words and the feeling of his cock filling me up and I broke, my body tensing in his arms as I cried out, my cock flooding my lacy underwear with cum as blissful pleasure swept through me and carried me away.

My eyes stung with over-sensitive tears and my thighs started to shake as the last vestiges of my orgasm died away, leaving my muscles feeling wrung out and my mind drained of all thoughts except how fucking good I felt.

Evan was still fucking me, chasing his release, and I watched him with reverence as he used me. "Rhys," he said.

"Yes," I said. "Please, fill me up baby."

Evan growled, gripping my hips tighter and thrust deep

inside me again, growling out his release as his cock pulsed inside me, filling me with his cum and giving me everything I wanted.

I groaned happily as he gently released me, lowering my legs to the bed. He staggered slightly and I patted the mattress, laughing breathlessly as he flopped down next to me. Our legs were still hanging over the edge of the bed, and I could feel his cum trickling out of me and my own gluing my panties to my skin, but I didn't care. Those were things to deal with in a minute.

For now, I wanted a moment with the man I loved.

I rolled to my side and into Evan's arms, looking down at him with love and smirking as I kissed him softly. "Welcome home."

WHEN WE'RE TOGETHER
BONUS SHORT

Three Years Later

Eva Nessence

I LET OUT A LONG, contented breath as my toes sunk into the sand and I gazed across the empty beach, grey-blue waves rolling gently against the shore as thick, fluffy clouds floated lazily across the plush summer sky.

We'd started coming to Wales to visit Tadcu every couple of months since Rhys and I had moved in together three years ago, spending the weekend by the sea and doing nothing but eating, reading, and walking along the beach, and now as soon as we crossed the border I felt the knots of any stress lingering in my chest start to untie themselves.

"Think I might get you into the water again this weekend?" Rhys asked, strolling beside me, shoes in one hand and smiling at me fondly. "You did well last time."

"Maybe, depends how brave I feel. Or whether I feel like spending half my time getting drenched." I grinned and shrugged. Rhys was determined to teach me the basics of surfing, but despite his patience my balance had proved to be nothing short of appalling.

I could dance in six-inch heels with no issue whatsoever, but attempting to remain upright for more than five seconds on a surfboard was like asking me to scale Everest.

It probably didn't help that I only got a chance to practice every three or four months, and whenever I tried, I usually got the giggles and that fucked my centre of gravity over instantly. Plus, I refused to even try in the winter, because the water was far too fucking cold to consider dipping more than a toe in.

So, while I enjoyed giving surfing a go, I was also more than happy to sit on the beach with my toes in the sand, watching my boyfriend stride out of the waves in a skintight wetsuit, his hair plastered to his face, and a bright smile lighting up his expression.

It was obvious Rhys loved the sea, and coming back was more akin to coming home than going away. I sometimes wondered if we should look at moving here, especially with Tadcu starting to get on in years, but I didn't know if Rhys would cope with living so far away from Ianto. And there wasn't exactly much of a local drag scene, which would mean I'd have to travel frequently, even if it was just hauling my ass into Cardiff or Swansea several times a week.

Perhaps it would be better for us to just visit often, especially because it gave us a well-deserved break from the stress of our daily lives. Tadcu was always happy to have us, and he'd welcomed me into his little family from the day we'd first been introduced. He was very happy to help me practice my Welsh whenever I could, which was now getting to the point I could hold full conversations, although if Rhys and Tadcu were speaking quickly I still only caught about one in five words.

"If you're going to get wet anyway, you might as well try surfing," Rhys said as he slipped his free hand in to mine, the pair of us meandering slowly down towards the water.

"Who said I want to get wet? Maybe I'll just sit on the beach with a picnic and a glass of wine and watch you."

"At nine in the morning?"

"In which case I'll swap the wine for coffee," I said with a laugh, nudging him gently with my shoulder. "You weren't seriously planning to get down here for nine tomorrow though, were you?"

"Depends on the weather. And the tide. Also, I do want to try and get at least one swim in this weekend because it'll be good practice for September."

"That makes sense," I said with a nod. The swimming leg of the Pembrokeshire Ironman took place in the sea off of Tenby, and while Rhys could easily practice the distance in our local pool, it was very different to swimming in the ocean. "I'll happily come and watch you swim. I can time you if you want."

"While you sit on the beach with you coffee and breakfast picnic and build sandcastles?"

"Exactly." I grinned and squeezed his hand as we

reached the water, paddling in the shallows and letting the waves wash over our feet.

We walked along the shore hand in hand, talking about everything from work, to the upcoming auditions for the next drag panto, to what Tadcu might be cooking to dinner, and what we should get Grace for her birthday. And once we'd reached the end of the beach we started to walk back again, still hand in hand.

"You know," Rhys said, after a few minutes of comfortable silence. "I've been thinking."

"About what?"

"This and that. Us mostly."

"Yeah?" I asked as my heart flipped and started to speed up. "What are you thinking?"

"About how much I love you," he said, glancing up at me with the sweetest smile on his face. "And how proud I am of you."

I swallowed, the skin across the bridge of my nose prickling with heat. "W-Why?"

"Because I am. You're fucking incredible, Evan. Look at everything you've done since we met—drag pantos, regular shows in three different cities, that Halloween variety show in London, and you haven't come close to burning out again."

"Er, if we're talking about me then we're definitely talking about you, Mr 'invited to the Ironman World Championship'," I said, stopping him in his tracks and pulling him in for a kiss. "And you've put up with my shit for three years now."

"True." He kissed me softly and I heard a thump as he

dropped his shoes onto the sand. "It's not hard though, you're perfect."

"I'm—"

"No, you don't get to disagree with me," he said. "You're fucking everything to me, Evan. And three years isn't enough, I want forever."

"What are…" My question trailed away as Rhys broke away from me, lowering himself down one knee and reaching into the pocket of his shorts to pull out a black velvet box.

"I should have done this ages ago," he said, looking up at me with pure adoration. "But I couldn't find the perfect moment, and then I realised I was searching for the impossible, because with you, every moment is perfect. Even on the bad days, when one of us is being a stroppy bastard, it's perfect. Because we're together."

He flicked the box open, revealing a silver ring with three glittering rubies set into the band. "Evan, will you marry me, please? Will you give me forever?"

"Shit… fuck, yes! Fuck yes!" I grabbed his face and pulled him onto his feet and into my arms, kissing him fiercely with all the love that I possessed. "I love you, Rhys. More than anything. You are… always have been… the most wonderful, annoying, beautiful, stubborn bastard I've ever known. And I can't imagine life without you. So, yeah, I'll marry you. Because then you'll be mine forever too."

Rhys let out a half-cheer, half-sob, his eyes shining with tears. "Fuck, why am I crying?" He reached for the ring and nearly dropped it. "Shit, my bloody hands are shaking."

We both fumbled for it, laughing as we did, and I dove

to catch it just before it hit the sand. "Do you want to put it on me?" I asked, looking up at Rhys from where I'd landed. My knees were soaked and covered in sand, and I was glad Rhys had convinced me to put shorts on before we'd come down to the beach.

"Of course, you can't put it on yourself," Rhys said. He didn't pull me up but instead knelt in front of me, quickly rescuing his shoes from being carried away by the tide, which was slowly starting to come in around us, the waves lapping at our legs.

But I didn't care about getting a little wet. Not at that moment.

Rhys took the ring from me with trembling fingers and I held out my hand, letting him slide it onto my finger. "Okay, I really hope it fits," he said. "I guessed based on some of your other jewellery."

I chuckled and winced as the ring hit my knuckle, the skin pinching under it. "This probably isn't the best time to tell you my knuckle is still a bit swollen from when I broke it."

I'd broken two of the fingers on my left hand back in April playing football with Grace, when I'd tried to catch the ball and failed spectacularly, and while they'd healed, maybe I should have gone to A&E and gotten them strapped up properly. Or at least let one of the people at work look at it. But at the time I'd insisted it wasn't that bad, and now it was a bit fucking late to do anything about it.

"Fuck… I don't think it's going to fit," Rhys said, his expression filling with panic as he looked between my face and the ring that refused to go past my slightly crooked, swollen knuckle. "I'm sorry! Shit, I'm sorry. I should've checked. This wasn't how it was supposed to go."

"Hey, don't panic." I caressed his jaw and kissed him softly. "I'm sure we can get it resized."

"Or I can return it and get you a bigger size. I, er, I didn't get it custom made."

"That doesn't matter to me," I said. "You chose it, and it's beautiful."

We gently eased the ring off my finger and Rhys put it back in the box, slipping it into his pocket for safe keeping. "I'm still saying yes," I said, sliding my hand into Rhys's as we stood. "You don't need to ask me again. That was perfect, and my answer isn't changing because the ring doesn't fit. This can just be some funny anecdote we add to the story, emphasis on the fact I broke my fucking fingers and didn't bother to get them looked at."

Rhys laughed, picking up his shoes before we resumed our stroll back down the beach. "You remember how cross you got with me when I broke my nose? Should I get as pissed with you now?"

"Bit late to be honest. The damage is already done. But if Grace breaks them again, then I promise you can absolutely take the piss out of me."

"Oh I won't be taking the piss, I'll be driving you to A&E and then reminding you of it every time I do something stupid."

"I'll probably deserve it," I said with a laugh. I squeezed his hand tightly and leant over to kiss his cheek. "I love you, you know that?"

"I know," Rhys said. "I love you too. And I promise, as soon as we get home I'll get the ring changed."

"No rush. And we don't have to rush to plan the wedding either." The idea of planning a wedding already sounded stressful, and I remembered how hectic the run up to Ianto and Ben's had been. I was in no hurry to repeat that.

"As long as you're there, I don't care when or where it is," Rhys said. "And as long as we get a honeymoon afterwards too." He smirked at me, hunger burning in his eyes. "You. Me. And two weeks of being alone and naked together."

"Two weeks?"

"Definitely. One week where I never let you get out of bed, and one week where we go out and do a few things and *then* fuck."

I grinned and pulled him in another kiss, sliding my tongue between the seam of his lips. "Sounds perfect. Fuck it, maybe we'll just pick the honeymoon destination and get married while we're there. We can always have a party when we get back."

"Done!" Rhys kissed me again. "I love you, Evan."

"*Dw i'n dy garu di,*" I said, the Welsh rolling off my tongue and Rhys melted in my arms with a happy sigh.

"Say it again," he murmured. "Welsh sounds good on your tongue."

"*Dw i'n dy garu di.*"

I love you.

ACKNOWLEDGMENTS

Rhys is another of my men who's been waiting a long time for his happily ever after, but it's taken me a while to find him the perfect match. As Ianto said, Rhys needed someone extraordinary, and Evan truly is that.

I didn't set out to write a book about loneliness, burnout, losing your passion for the things you love, learning to ask for help, and finding someone to share the burden, but life, and writing, has a funny way of digging into things you'd sometimes rather avoid.

Burnout is something that all creatives are familiar with and as someone who's struggled with burnout before, writing Evan's story has been very cathartic

My thanks go out to Charity and Noah for all their insight and encouragement as I wrote, and for convincing Evan's journey was the right one.

To all my incredible writer friends; Carly, Toby, Jodi, Lark, Willow, Kat and more, I owe you so much and I'm so grateful to all of you.

To my fabulous D&DVania crew; Rosie, Stuart, Blair, James, Beth, Mia, and Jess. Thank you for letting me share my author life with you, and for always supporting me. I love you so much. Here's to all the adventures; past, present, and future.

To Jennifer, for catching all the tiny details I forget, for polishing and shining my stories, and being very patient with my use of commas. And to Lori, for finding all the stray typos that are determined to slip through.

To Wander and Andrey for finding me the perfect Evan, and to Natasha for creating the most beautiful covers for him.

To Linda, and her wonderful team, who's enthusiasm is infectious and who writes wonderful lists. Thank you for helping me bring Rhys and Evan to life.

To Dan, for bringing The Court to our ears and making it all the more real.

To my husband, for naming Evan in the first place by saying that any drag queen named Eva Nessence had to be called Evan.

And last, but never least, to you, my fabulous readers. Whether I'm new to you or you've been here since the start, I am grateful for you love and support.

If you enjoyed *Scene Queen*, please consider leaving a review. Reviews are invaluable for indie authors, and may help other readers find this book.

Until next time.

ALSO BY CHARLIE NOVAK

The Court
Drama Queen

Scene Queen

Baby Queen *(May 2024)*

Heather Bay
Like I Pictured

Like I Promised

Like I Wished

Like I Needed

Like I Pretended

Like I Wanted

Roll for Love
Natural Twenty

Charisma Check

Proficiency Bonus

Bonus Action: The Roll for Love Short Story Collection

Roll for Love: The Complete Collection (Boxset)

Forever Love
Always Eli

Finding Finn

Oh So Oscar

Kiss Me

Strawberry Kisses

Summer Kisses

Spiced Kisses

The Kiss Me Short Collection

Kiss Me: The Complete Collection (Boxset)

Off the Pitch

Breakaway

Extra Time

Final Score

The Off the Pitch Short Collection

Off the Pitch: The Complete Collection (Boxset)

Standalones

Screens Apart

Couture Crush

Up To Snow Good

Pole Position

Short Stories

One More Night

Twenty-Two Years (Newsletter Exclusive)

Snow Way In Hell

Audiobooks

Buy audiobooks directly from Charlie at charlienovakshop.com

Drama Queen

Like I Promised

Like I Wished

Like I Needed

Like I Pretended

Like I Wanted

Natural Twenty

Charisma Check

Proficiency Bonus

Always Eli

Finding Finn

Oh So Oscar

Strawberry Kisses

Summer Kisses

Spiced Kisses

Up To Snow Good

Translations

ITALIAN

Qui Neve Ci Cova

For a regularly updated list, please visit:
charlienovak.com/books
charlienovak.com/audiobooks

CHARLIE NOVAK

Charlie lives in England with her husband and two cheeky dogs. She spends most of her days wrangling other people's words in her day job and then trying to force her own onto the page in the evening.

She loves cute stories with a healthy dollop of fluff, plenty of delicious sex, and happily ever afters — because the world needs more of them.

Charlie has very little spare time, but what she does have she fills with baking, Dungeons and Dragons, reading and many other nerdy pursuits. She also thinks that everyone should have at least one favourite dinosaur…

Website charlienovak.com
Shop charlienovakshop.com
Facebook Group Charlie's Angels
Sign up for her newsletter for bonus scenes, new releases and extras.
Or Patreon for early access chapters, flash fiction, first looks, and serial stories.

- facebook.com/charlienovakauthor
- instagram.com/charlienwrites
- bookbub.com/profile/charlie-novak
- amazon.com/author/charlienovak
- patreon.com/charlienovak

Printed in Great Britain
by Amazon